THE GUARDIAN

The Taskforce Series

Book Two

Marliss Melton

Cover and Book design by eBook Prep
www.ebookprep.com

June, 2014
ISBN: 978-1-61417-613-8

ePublishing Works!
www.epublishingworks.com

DEDICATION

This book is dedicated to the brave men and women of the United States Marine Corps, in gratitude for the sacrifice and commitment you have given to the American people throughout our turbid history. May God bless you all for your extreme dedication.

ACKNOWLEDGMENTS

I could not have completed this ambitious work of fiction without the help of several very devoted people who deserve to be acknowledged. Heartfelt thanks goes to Rachel Fontana, my beta reader extraordinaire, who devoted untold hours editing and re-editing chapters. I am grateful to Jeff, a counselor for prisoners, for answering my many questions about legal processes. And I owe so much thanks to my best friend and editor, Sydney Baily-Gould, who knows how to make a manuscript sparkle. There are others, too, who helped—Janie Hawkins, Trish Dechant, Wendie Grogan, Don Klein, and Marilyn Rowe. Thank you, all, from the bottom of my heart!

FOREWORD

An article in the newspaper caught my eye: the body of an unidentified African American male had been found on fire just up the road from where I lived. An autopsy later showed that he had been burned alive. The tattoo on his arm, that of a crescent moon, a star and the number seven, all circumscribed by a sun, labeled the victim as a member of a gang called the Five Percent Nation. He had probably tried to leave the gang, and for that offense, he was beaten, drugged, dumped on the side of the road and set on fire. His fate prompted a story idea, resulting in this book.

There are elements in THE GUARDIAN that made me uncomfortable to touch upon—both racial and religious elements. Readers, please be assured that I consider all people of every race and religion to be my brothers and sisters. We are all children of the one true God. I also respect everyone's right to choose whatever pathway brings them closer to peace and enlightenment. But extremism and fanaticism of any kind is dangerous, in my opinion. Gangs are dangerous. And labeling anyone on the basis of race is dangerous. And that is the statement I wish for this story to make.

In addition, THE GUARDIAN has political elements that do not necessarily reflect my personal beliefs. I am in no way qualified to say whether the government is overly suspicious of certain sectors of the American population. I only know that threats exist. And I am grateful to the men and women who safeguard the majority by watching over us as they do.

PROLOGUE

Officer Rupert Davis glanced in the rearview mirror at the teenage girl in his back seat. A young one. Not even scared yet—thinking he was taking her home. He smirked, and she glanced up, saw his smile, and smiled timidly back. Then she rapped on the glass. *Left here, please.*

He ignored her. Sorry, little mama. Not on my scheduled stop tonight.

Accelerating, he continued on to the southeast side of Washington D.C., where folks turned a blind eye to things they didn't want to hear or see. Minutes later, he turned into a dark alley between two abandoned buildings. She had started to panic. He could see that in his rearview mirror. Coming to a sudden stop, he hit the unlock button, and she scrambled to escape, but he was quicker. Clamping a hand over her mouth, he dragged her to the nearest building, down three steps into his basement hideaway.

"I don't understand!" she wailed, as he tossed her down on a pile of blankets like a rag doll.

Ignoring her, feeding off of her rising panic, he threw himself down on her, counting on his burly frame to knock the wind out of her so she couldn't scream. By the time she dragged enough air into her lungs to shriek in protest, he had torn her clothes to shreds. She bucked beneath him, screaming. Her helplessness made him feel all-powerful, like a god.

"Quiet, bitch!" He slapped her face with an open palm. There was just enough light in the gloomy space to see her eyes flare with horror. He almost pitied her—almost. After all, she was just an innocent-looking girl, still dressed in her school uniform, allegedly walking home from a special church service. It had been pure bad luck that made her run into the coke-sniffing hoodlum, Curtis, who tried to make time with her.

Good thing Officer Davis had shown up when he did.

Good thing she'd gotten into the back of his cop car quickly, with no one but Curtis to see.

"No more screaming," he warned her as he slipped on a condom.

He groped her breasts with one hand, her crotch with the other. She tried to twist away but kept quiet. When he entered her, she screamed again, on a note so piercing that he flinched and cuffed her hard, without thinking.

The scream broke off abruptly as her head snapped to one side. With a muttered curse, he pushed deeper into her untried flesh then stilled when he realized she wasn't fighting him anymore. *Son of a bitch*. Had he knocked her out? He liked it when they struggled.

"Wake up, girl."

He gave her cheek another slap, and her head lolled lifelessly the other way. *Shit!*

He jerked away from her rapidly cooling flesh. What the hell? She had gone and died on him, the little bitch. Hell if he was into fucking dead girls.

Luckily, he was well-prepared to erase the evidence. Bundling her body in the blankets, he strafed the chamber with an ultraviolet light to make sure no trace of DNA remained, then carried her back into the alley and tossed her in the dumpster, blanket and all. Her body hit the refuse inside with a soft *thump*.

Locating the gasoline can he kept tucked away for emergencies, Rupert Davis sloshed gas into the dumpster. Then he stood back, lit a match, and tossed it in.

The contents exploded with a *whoosh*. Flames crackled and writhed, licking the dark alley with amber tongues.

Whistling a casual tune, he retreated to his cruiser, backed it into the street, and drove away.

By the time the girl's body was found, there'd be no evidence left to indict him. He was an eight-year veteran of the Metropolitan Police Department. He knew how to frustrate forensics. He also knew everything and everyone in D.C.'s teeming underworld. Hell, he orchestrated most of what went on. And he owned thugs like Curtis. The boy wouldn't dare betray him. This would be just one more unsolved case for the detectives to gnaw on.

CHAPTER 1

Journalist Lena Alexandra jeopardized her surveillance by lowering the windows of the Jeep Wrangler several inches. A brisk breeze wafted in, alleviating the sauna-like temperature within the vehicle. Climbing onto her knees in the passenger seat, she put her flushed face to the vent she'd created, inhaled the pungent scent of the nearby Patuxent River, and aimed her camera through the crack, hoping no one would see her.

She knew she'd be a lot cooler standing out in the open, but she needed the long-range scope on her camera to help her identify her sister's killer, and she couldn't risk the ex-cons across the street guessing she was a reporter, specifically the prolific crime journalist Lena Alexandra. That would ruin all her plans.

The ex-cons were fresh out of prison. Their reintegration program, aptly named Gateway, was situated near the rural town of Mechanicville, Maryland on a campus consisting of a roadside motel, a lovely gold-domed mosque with a minaret, and a modest home for the leaders. Every parolee at

Gateway had converted to Islam, adopting new names and identities while serving time in jail.

TIME magazine called Gateway "a triumph for moderate Muslims." With ninety percent of its graduates living crime-free, socially responsible lives, it had become a national model for effective reintegration.

But every positive statistic had a downside didn't it?

Of the twelve parolees she had counted, one or two would revert to criminal behavior. Picking out the subject of her investigation, Lena had no doubt Rupert D. Davis would return to his former ways, which meant that he would kill again.

But not if she could help it.

Nausea roiled through her as the face of her sister's killer came into focus. To think he'd gotten away with such a monstrous crime. A charred skeleton and a tiny scrap of a school uniform were all that had remained of Alexa. And when the only witness to Alexa's abduction disappeared, the case against Davis had been dropped.

Six months later, he'd gone to jail for drug-trafficking. Eight years into his fifteen-year sentence, Davis convinced the parole board he was a changed man because he'd found Allah in prison.

"*Malakas*," Lena hissed in her parents' native Greek as she depressed the shutter.

To her disgust, Davis didn't look a day older than when her family had faced him in the pre-trial hearing. If anything, he was trimmer and more muscular than ever, and not a single silver hair glimmered in the dark whorls of his closely-cropped hair.

So unfair, she thought, having plucked occasional silver threads from her own dark curls since the bastard got away with murder.

Unable to stomach the sight of him a moment longer, she panned her camera over the remaining parolees. The majority of them were African American. One appeared Asian, another Hispanic. *These are the ninety percent who will turn their lives around,* she assured herself, determined not to judge them for what they'd done. They might have committed felonies and petty larceny, but their crimes were probably not like Davis's. Their conversions might have been sincere. She felt vaguely sorry for them laboring to construct a shed under the blazing August sun.

A man of commanding stature caught her eye as he hauled on the pulley rope to raise the rafter beams. Rivulets of sweat trekked from his neatly shaved hairline, past thick lashes that obscured eyes of a light hue, over his square jaw. The effort he put in to his work aroused her respect.

Handsome devil, she mused, snapping off several shots. His dusky-colored skin made her think of mocha-flavored coffee, her favorite.

Look this way, Mocha Man, she willed, but his feet remained planted. With each tug of the rope, his long, powerful limbs flexed. Lena switched to the sport's setting on her camera and caught the fluid motion in a series of rapid-fire shots.

Then she sat back on her heels to admire them. *Very nice.*

He was honed from shoulder to calf. The damp cotton of his sleeveless T-shirt outlined a muscular chest and taut abs. Basketball shorts hung so low on his round butt they looked in danger of falling off. He could make a fortune modeling underwear, she considered with a cynical smile. What a shame he'd gone to jail, instead.

Rising onto her knees again, she forced her attention

back on Davis, only to swivel it toward Mocha Man as he turned suddenly in her direction.

The vision in her lens made her gasp with appreciation. Handsome was an understatement. Gray-green eyes, so unexpectedly light against his tan complexion, narrowed as he scanned the side of the street where her Jeep was parked. In the next instant, he looked straight into her camera.

Lena jerked away from the window. Dropping onto her bottom, she slid to the end of the seat so that her head barely cleared the door panel. Her heart thumped as she sneaked a peak out the window to see if he was still looking.

And he was.

He can't see me through the tinted window.

But apparently he could. Either that or those freaky-deaky eyes gave him X-ray vision.

With her mouth desert dry, she threw a leg over the gear shift and clambered awkwardly into the driver's seat. Keeping her head low, she disassembled her camera, placed the components back inside the carrying case, and stuffed the case under the seat out of sight.

She had just one thing left to do.

Who the hell? Special Agent Jackson Maddox stewed, shading his eyes from the sun's harsh glare. Above the cracked passenger window of the black Jeep Wrangler parked across the old highway, he had glimpsed the unmistakable glare of a camera lens. Behind it, the face of the woman holding it had reflected guilt before she ducked out of sight.

He'd known it. The prickling of his scalp had warned him that he was being watched. He'd just assumed it was the clergy at Gateway secretly spying on the men, looking out for slackers feigning their exertion and leaving the labor-intensive work up to the others. Only the creeping sensation had continued, prompting him to take a good look around.

The truth turned out to be far worse. A stranger had just taken his picture with a camera typically used by professional journalists. *Well, God damn.*

Gateway had been the object of media attention since *TIME* Magazine published an article about its success rate. But journalist or not, Jackson couldn't risk his likeness appearing in any public forum. Curiously, the woman didn't appear to be in any great hurry to leave. He could just make out the top of her head as she stepped out of the far side of her vehicle.

"You can take a break right after you seat this rafter," promised the engineer overseeing the project.

Jackson put all his weight into hauling on the rope. With any luck, he could dart across the highway and confront the journalist before she left.

Lena stepped out of the driver's side door, shielded from the parolees' view by the Jeep's tall frame. It had to be twenty degrees cooler outside the vehicle than in it, not that Maryland was cool in August.

Checking her reflection in the tinted window, she combed fingers through her jet-black ringlets and realized her pink bra could be seen through the damp silk of her ivory blouse. The narrow black skirt she wore was sticking to her thighs. She looked like she'd been sitting in a sauna fully clothed. Not the best look for a job interview.

With a shrug of resignation, she turned and hastened into the convenience store on strappy high-heeled sandals. Her gaze snared briefly on the horse and buggy that had pulled up to the lot minutes before. It wasn't every day you saw an Amish man pop into a convenience store, but Mechanicsville, she recalled, was home to a small Amish community.

Hauling open the heavy door, Lena set off a chime that prompted the only two occupants turning their heads to gawk at her. One was the clerk, the other the Amish man, dressed in black suspenders and clutching his broad-brimmed hat. He appeared to be purchasing a Lotto ticket, of all things.

"Hello," she said as they continued to stare. Accustomed to her effect on the opposite sex, Lena closed her eyes a moment, gathering up her hair to cool her neck under the blasting A/C. Then she headed toward the drinks at the back of the store, aware that the place was dead silent but for the classical music coming from the overhead speakers. Commuters likely thronged the place on their way in and out of D.C., the closest city, but during the day, it was just a quaint country store off an old highway.

By the time she approached the register with her bottle of grape Gatorade, the gambling Amish man had taken off. She could hear his buggy rumbling away with the clip-clop of horse hooves, leaving just her and the clerk alone, just as she'd hoped.

"Dollar seventy four," said the clerk, trying not to ogle at her as he took her money and fished change from the register. He was middle-aged and balding with a friendly face.

"How are you today?" she asked him.

"Oh, can't complain." He colored faintly as he glanced up, his gray eyes straying toward her bosom.

"Are you still looking for help?" She had spotted the HELP WANTED poster while suffering miserably in the hot SUV, and it had seemed like serendipity. Before seeing it, she had wondered how she was going to befriend the parolees while appearing to be a part of the community. A job at Artie's One Stop Shop offered the perfect cover from which to incriminate her sister's killer.

The clerk stared at her for a stunned moment. Then he bent over to feel beneath the counter. "Sure. Here's an application," he said sliding it toward her.

"Great." She couldn't have hoped for a more prodigious start.

"You from the area?" the clerk asked her as she hunted down a pen.

"No, I'm from D.C, but I just moved here." She had found a cottage with a short-term lease.

He handed her the pen from the cash register. "Name's Bill," he said, holding out his hand.

"Nice to meet you, Bill. I'm Maggie Alexandra." As with other undercover jobs, she used a variant of her first name, Magdalena. Her seven silver bracelets, worn for luck, tinkled as she raised her hand to his.

"Moving here for good?" Bill asked.

"Well, I'm going to write a book, and I thought this rural town would be conducive to my writing."

"A book, huh? What about?"

"The long-term effect of religious conversion on prisoners."

Bill's eyes widened. Another customer ambled in, and Lena stepped aside to fill out the application, using her boss, who knew of her scheme, as a character reference.

When the customer moved off, she handed Bill her application and held her breath while he skimmed through it.

"Looks good to me," he declared. "You know, we only pay ten bucks an hour." He sent her an apologetic look.

"That's all I need," she assured him.

He still looked skeptical. "Can you work seven days a week until I find another part-timer?"

"What are the hours?"

"Six P.M. till close, which is midnight every night, except for Sunday when we close at ten."

The thought of locking up at midnight with parolees prowling the area made Lena's blood thin. "That's fine," she said. "Do the men across the street ever come over here often?"

"Pretty much every day," he acknowledged. "But if you're worried about your safety, we do have security cameras." He pointed up at the black domes on the ceiling.

"Oh, I'm not worried." Their visits would make her undertaking that much easier. "When can I start?"

"Show up tomorrow morning at nine, and I'll train you for a full day. Starting Friday evening, you can work by yourself. How's that sound?"

"Terrific. Thank you, Bill. I'll see you at nine tomorrow." Unscrewing the cap to her Gatorade, she backed toward the door, beaming.

"Bye, now." He waved in a way that suggested he couldn't believe his good fortune.

It never ceased to amaze Lena how susceptible men were to her charms. At least she channeled her power to good use, using it to pry information out of criminals.

Whirling at the door, she pushed it open with her hip as she tipped the liquid she craved to her lips. The last thing she expected was for the door to give way suddenly causing her to stumble into an unyielding, sun-warmed body.

Gatorade showered her blouse. "Hey!" she cried, her protest trailing off with a gasp as she found herself face-to-face with the subject of her voyeuristic impulse.

Oh, my God. He was even more striking up-close. Staring aghast into his gray-green gaze, she found she couldn't breathe. "Sorry," she muttered, trying to squeeze past him. But he stepped into her path again, and her wet bosom bounced off his rock-hard chest like rubber balls bouncing off of concrete. A whiff of sweat, soap, and man made her head spin.

"Excuse me!" She managed to sound indignant when, in fact, she was hoping the sidewalk would just swallow her.

"Personal or public?" he inquired, coiling a large, surprisingly gentle hand around her elbow and drawing her farther outside. The door bumped shut behind them.

"I'm sorry?" She could hardly hear him for the blood rushing past her eardrums. An ex-con was holding onto her!

"Your reason for taking pictures." His deep voice held a cadence that brought to mind steel drums and fruity rum beverages, suggesting some Caribbean heritage.

"I don't know what you're talking about." She tried diving past him a third time, but his grip, however gentle, proved unbreakable.

"You don't have my consent to publish those photos," he stated. Both his warning and his educated-sounding speech astonished her. As Lena gaped at him, his gaze dipped appraisingly toward her soaked blouse. Her nipples responded to his gaze as if he'd stroked them, springing to attention like diligent soldiers.

"What photos?" Ignoring her body's response, she sent him a blank look. "I think you've mistaken me for someone else."

Her denial wrested his gaze upward. His thick lashes came together as he narrowed his eyes, stepped closer, and enfolded her in his cool shadow. "I know what I saw," he insisted, his breath warm across her cheek. "Come. We're going to go delete them." His grip on her elbow tightened as he drew her in the direction of her vehicle.

Digging her heels into the sidewalk, Lena resisted. The realization that he could easily overpower her both frightened and enthralled her. If any man was going to have his way with her, she'd want it to be him, but the issue with the pictures was unsettling.

Suddenly, the door behind her opened. Mocha Man glanced over her shoulder and reluctantly released her.

"Everything okay here?" Bill asked, dividing an anxious look between them.

"Fine," Lena assured him with a bright smile. Taking advantage of the ex-con's slackened grasp, she broke free. Without a backward glance, she fled for her Jeep, slamming the door shut and locking it. Then she peeled out of the gas station, racing a yellow light at the intersection to distance herself from the man's blistering regard.

A glance into her rearview mirror showed him standing at the corner of the building with his arms crossed, his eyes potent and intense, transmuting his will.

Cristemou! Lena kept a lead foot on the accelerator until Highway 235 curved, blocking the convenience store and Mocha Man from view.

Two miles later, she turned off the four-lane highway onto the rural route that took her to her rental cottage. Her racing heart slowly subsided. A parolee had seen her taking pictures. So what? He couldn't prove she'd had a camera, could he? And now that she'd gotten away, he couldn't stop her from uploading her pictures, either.

But he might tell Davis what he'd seen and point her out to him. If Davis had any reason to be suspicious of her, she would never gain his confidence and trust. *Damn it!*

Who did Mocha Man think he was, telling her about the law? There was nothing remotely illegal about photographing people in a public setting, not unless she used the pictures for commercial gain, which wasn't her plan at all. She would probably have deleted the man's pictures if he hadn't jumped down her throat. But not now. Oh, no, there had to be a reason why the ex-con had treated her like paparazzi.

Maybe he was a celebrity.

Nah, if he were famous, she'd have recognized him. More likely he had testified against powerful men, and he was worried about their retribution.

Whatever his reason and whoever he was, she was likely to run into him again. The prospect turned her mouth dry. As long as she kept her camera out of sight, using her hidden camera, she would be alright, she assured herself.

She lifted a hand to finger the pendant hanging between her collarbones. Above the interchangeable gemstones, the filigreed bail disguised the tiny camera's lens. No one looking at it would ever suspect its filming functionality.

Not even Davis would know, she assured herself, when she befriended him—when she conned the ex-con, luring him into friendship by teasing him with the possibility of getting to know her better.

The thought alone made her break into a clammy sweat. But what choice did she have? The detectives she had hired over the years had failed to find evidence that would implicate Davis in her sister's murder. The only witness, a boy named Curtis, could not be found. Davis would never pay for his heinous crime unless he confessed to it.

If Mocha Man ruined Lena's golden opportunity to

outsmart her sister's killer, by God, he would regret it. She would take those sexy pictures of him and plaster them on the front cover of *Crime and Liberty*.

Lena Alexandra was after justice. And no mere mortal was going to stand in her way.

CHAPTER 2

The bombshell had gotten away, taking her snapshots with her.

Special Agent Jackson Maddox stalked to the corner of the building to watch her speed away. She appeared to be heading straight toward Washington D.C., where her tags told him she was from. No doubt she intended to publish her photos in some magazine or newspaper headquartered in the capital. *Damn it straight to hell.*

Cutting a glance at Gateway, he realized construction was once more underway. Break time was over, and he'd be missed if he didn't hurry, but he had to make a call first.

Slipping into the loading area at the back of the store, Jackson wedged himself between the dumpster and a chain link fence. His colleague, Toby, had sabotaged the security camera aimed in his direction. Taking an ear bud equipped with a mike from the hidden pocket in his shorts, Jackson pushed it into his right ear. Feeling inside the same pocket for his sleek, multipurpose cell phone, he speed-dialed headquarters.

Isaac Calhoun, team lead for the Inter-Agency

Counterterrorism Taskforce, answered on the third ring. "What's up, son?" Communications over an unsecure line, like a cell phone, required both men to encrypt their speech.

"Not much, Pops, but I just met a hot chick in a Jeep with D.C. plates," Jackson answered, talking like a college-aged son.

"Oh, yeah?"

"Yeah, I think she digs me 'cause she just took my picture."

"That right?" Ike's tone turned dour.

"Maybe you could find out who she is for me." Jackson rattled off the numbers and letters on the tags he'd committed to memory.

"I'll see what I can do."

"Thanks, Dad. Gotta go." The parolees had been taught from day one to look out for one another. If "Abdul" didn't return soon, a couple of his brothers would come looking for him. That was one thing you could count on at Gateway; someone always had your back.

Returning the ear bud to his pocket, he headed back across the highway. As he paused on the grassy median between the double lanes, waiting for a vehicle to pass, an awful thought occurred to him.

He'd been so distracted by the bombshell's allure that he'd forgotten to speak and act like Abdul Ibn Wasi, the ex-con he was impersonating. *Double damn.* All he could do was wait to see what she would do with her pictures. One click of a shutter could thwart an investigation that was three months in the making.

Was Gateway a breeding ground for terrorists?

The Taskforce had reason to suspect so. Twice, money had been wired from the reintegration program to Islamic insurgency groups overseas, in Algeria and in South Africa. While the donations themselves were too modest to propagate the overthrow of democratic governments, they raised a legitimate concern: Were the leaders of Gateway, both vetted chaplains of the National Islamic Prison Foundation, brainwashing parolees to believe in the preeminence of Islamic law over Democracy?

Jackson, the FBI's contribution to the Taskforce, had been at Gateway for less than a week of the four-week program. In that short time, he had seen nothing but good work being done. The parolees were challenged on a daily basis to see themselves and others as Allah saw them, precious and irreplaceable. Projects like the building of the shed built team cohesion and cooperation. During the second half of the program, each man would be trained in truck driver safety and issued a commercial driver's license, giving him a means to earn an honest living.

Choose Allah, and the road will rise up to meet you.

That was Gateway's motto and, by every outward sign, the program seemed to live up to it. If the leadership wanted to back insurgents overseas, that was their prerogative. But if they were also secretly advocating the overthrow of the government to whom they pledged their allegiance, then the Taskforce needed to know about it.

On the other hand, civil libertarians and the Maryland Probation and Parole Association would throw a hissy fit if they caught wind of the investigation. The Taskforce had tried limiting their investigation to just wiretaps but, aside from their televised Friday service, the clergy didn't appear to communicate with anybody in the outside world.

The only way to tell what was going on inside the program was to send in an undercover agent to act as a parolee. Jackson, the only dark-skinned agent in the

Taskforce was the obvious choice for replacing a black man named Abdul Ibn Wasi. Only, now his cover had been threatened by one hot-as-hell journalist who'd just run off with his photo.

Not to worry, he assured himself, as he rejoined the others on the job site. Former Navy SEAL Ike Calhoun would do whatever lay within his powers to prevent Jackson's picture from appearing in the press. Problem solved.

"Get me a hammer, Abdul," Jackson's roommate, Corey requested, pointing him toward two buckets, one full of hammers, the other full of nails.

As he scooped up two hammers and some nails, Jackson slipped back into the role of a man convicted of animal cruelty for fighting pit bulls.

Intent on banishing all thoughts of the bombshell, he channeled his energy into securing the framing of the new shed. The memory of the woman's sherry-colored eyes and her stunning breasts danced before his eyes. He swung the hammer, missed the head of the nail by a mile, and clobbered his thumb.

Lena cut the engine and stared in dismay at her new rental home. Hidden in the shade of towering pine trees, the clapboard cottage looked diminutive and neglected. In the online advertisement, it had resembled a doll house, complete with a rocking chair on the front porch and ornamental lattice work. She had jumped at the offer of a month-by-month lease and made arrangements over the phone, signing paperwork via fax.

What she ought to have done was to drive out to the country to see the place for herself. The porch was covered in cobwebs; weeds ran rampant in the flowerbed; and there were shingles missing on the dormered roof.

Maybe it's a sign, she considered, worrying her
lower lip. Coming on the heels of her encounter with
Mocha Man, no one would blame her if she started up
the Jeep, pulled a U-turn in the nonexistent driveway,
and headed straight for home.

But with characteristic tenacity, Lena plucked the
key from the ignition and stepped out of the car.
Moving to the rear hatch, she dragged out her suitcase
and rolled it over the carpet of pine needles to the
covered porch.

The landlord had said he would leave the key under
a flower vase. She found it under a pot of withered
marigolds, inserted the key into the single lock, and
pushed the door open.

A gloomy interior, a deep hush, and the smell of
furniture polish greeted her. A flick of the light switch
revealed a diminutive living area, table for two, and a
kitchen built into a nook at the rear. To her right, a
door led to the only bedroom and attached bath.

Bumping her suitcase across the braided rug, Lena
paused at the bedroom door to take in the four-poster
bed covered by a patchwork quilt. There was an
armoire in lieu of a closet and a vanity with a faded
mirror. "Home sweet home," she murmured, propping
her suitcase against the wall.

A sense of isolation had her reaching for her
disposable cell phone. She'd developed a habit of
using phones that couldn't be traced while working
undercover. Before she realized what she was doing,
she had dialed her boss and long-time friend, Peter.
"Hi," she said, immediately cursing her impulse.

"Is that you, babe? I didn't recognize the number."

She'd forgotten Peter's recent habit of calling her
babe. Having enjoyed a professional friendship for
years; imagining him as anything more repelled her.

"Yeah, it's me," she said, with less warmth.

"So, you made it. How's it going?"

"Good. I found Gateway; took some pictures already." She considered telling him about her run-in with Mocha Man then changed her mind. "As a matter of fact, I even got a cover job that'll put me in direct contact with the parolees," she informed him.

"Get out! Where?"

"At the convenience store across the street."

"They let the parolees shop there?"

"They've already served their time, Peter. I'm sure they have a curfew, but they have some freedom, too."

"So, you're going to go through with your book story?"

"That's the plan."

"Well, I hope you know what you're doing, babe. I know you've interviewed a lot of sick people over the years, but this time you're emotionally involved."

His words tossed salt on an open wound, but he was just looking out for her. "I'll be okay," she assured him. "So, why are you taking time off work?"

"Heading to Rehoboth to visit my cousins, remember?"

"That's right." He'd invited her to join him at his family's beach house in Delaware, only Lena hadn't wanted to cross that line from friendship into to something more.

"It's not too late to join me."

"That's okay. But thanks for loaning me your Jeep. The tinted windows came in handy." *Not as much as she'd hoped, though.* "I hope you're not planning to drive my Jaguar out on the beach." She winced at the idea.

"Of course not. I'll take good care of it."

"You'd better."

"Listen, I gotta run, babe. Call me if anything comes up."

Not if he was going to keep calling her babe. "I will. Bye, Peter." With isolation creeping over her again, Lena thumbed the call to a close.

Dragging her suitcase closer, she pulled out the framed photo of her sister that she habitually kept beside her bed. As she propped it on the bedside table, she thought of Rupert Davis and how dauntingly powerful he had looked today. Goose bumps sprouted on her arms and prickled down her back. "It doesn't matter," she whispered to her sister. "We'll get him this time."

Jackson repositioned his dinner of *halal* chicken and rice on the white, ceramic plate. The possibility of his cover being exposed by a journalist had stripped him of an appetite. Until the bombshell was apprehended, her photos deleted, he'd be walking on eggshells, expecting the worst.

Part of being a Marine was learning to expect the worst so you weren't taken off guard. Having served twelve years in the Corps before leaving to work for the FBI and subsequently the Taskforce, it was second nature to Jackson to expect a shit-storm.

As he toyed with his food in the mosque's dining hall, he recalled the secretive look on the woman's face, not to mention his powerful, visceral attraction when he saw her up close.

I think you've mistaken me for someone else. Her sexy voice could not disguise the lie. What bullshit. She'd known exactly what she was up to. If he hadn't been so distracted by his response to her sex appeal, he'd have gotten her to surrender her camera before the store owner interrupted their tête-à-tête.

Instead, he'd been so wrapped up in how

unbelievably silky her skin felt within his grasp and wishing he could kiss her wide, succulent-looking lips.

As he lifted his fork to his mouth, Jackson's thumb, with blood caught under the nail, gave a painful throb. *That's what happens when you lose your focus,* he reminded himself.

But his mind was obviously acting of its own accord because it still swam with thoughts of her, which was unusual in itself. Since his wife's death three years ago, he hadn't given much thought to sex, with one slight exception, but that woman had already been claimed by Ike. The fact that he could envision himself taking slow possession of this black-haired beauty without really knowing her was therefore extraordinary. And he could picture it perfectly—her head thrown back, breasts bobbing just below his lips like ripe cherry-topped delights, her hips undulating, as he drove himself between her thighs. He wallowed in the fantasy, until a booming voice jarred him back to reality.

"Abdul Ibn Wasi!"

Imam Ibrahim, one of Gateway's two leaders, stood in the doorway. With a slight smile, the mahogany-skinned leader with the salt-and-pepper beard gestured for Abdul to follow. Jackson jumped up. With a heaviness still in his groin, he carried his tray to the rubber container by the exit and followed the man's flowing robes down the hallway to join him in his office.

Twice a week, the ex-cons touched base with their parole officers. Under the tolerant eye of Ibrahim, Jackson dialed the number that would put him in touch with another of his colleagues, Tobias Burke.

"This is Abdul Ibn Wasi," he announced, careful to speak in the appropriate dialect when Toby answered.

Out of the corner of his eye, he saw Ibrahim open his file and rifle through it.

One of Jackson's priorities was to search both imams' offices for information casting light on Gateway's affiliation with Islamic militants. But in the short time he'd been here, he had yet to find an opportunity. By day, the hallways bustled with activity. At night, the mosque was secured by an alarm system that required consultation with experts before the Taskforce could confidently override it. It was only during this brief time in Ibrahim's office that Jackson had the chance to look around.

This evening, while supplying rote answers to Toby's usual questions, he scrutinized the titles in Ibrahim's bookcase, hunting for the book that had caught his eye the last time. His gaze finally snagged on it and he tipped his head slightly, straining his eyes to read the title on the spine.

Supreme 120 Lessons: for the Nation of Gods
& Earths.

The strange title strummed a chord of recognition, as did the logo under the title: a crescent moon, a star and the number seven, all circumscribed by a sun. He'd seen that somewhere else, but where?

"We'll talk," Toby said, hindering Jackson's memory as he recalled that *We'll talk* was code for *Call Headquarters*. Ike must have tracked down the bombshell. *Hot damn!*

"A'right. Night, sir," he answered, conveying that he would call HQ that very night.

As he lowered the receiver into the handset, he saw Ibrahim jot himself a note. Concern clamped down on Jackson's shoulders. Had the cleric caught him staring at the book? "Thank you, Imam." He started backing toward the door.

"Just a minute, Abdul." Ibrahim waved him closer to the desk, where he sat beneath matching tribal tapestries.

Jackson's pulse spiked as he retraced his footsteps.

"Your file says you are from Baltimore," the imam noted, "yet I hear something peculiar in your speech. What is your heritage?" He looked up, his dark eyes bright with interest.

"My mother was from Grand Cayman Island," Jackson answered, relieved that Ike had layered that detail into the original Abdul Ibn Wasi's file.

"I see. And you never knew your father," the imam added with a grimace of compassion.

That detail was true of the real Abdul Ibn Wasi, but not of Jackson, whose father was a judge in Rockville. "Allah is my father now," he answered simply.

The imam's expression turned thoughtful. "It gladdens my heart to hear so, Abdul." He switched topics abruptly. "I noticed you have memorized the recitations already. You obviously have a strong mind."

"Thank you." Jackson looked down at the desk. Maybe he should have pretended to struggle with the Arabic like the others, but having served three tours in Iraq, the passages flowed from him without effort. He shifted on his feet.

"I can use a man of your intelligence," Ibrahim admitted, snatching Jackson's gaze upward.

Pretending to be pleased, Jackson grinned. "Okay. How?" Wouldn't it be nice if the imam dumped incriminating information in his lap, sparing him from having to endure all four weeks of the program?

Ibrahim winked. "In good time," he answered, disappointing Jackson. "You may return to the dining hall." He looked down at his paperwork. "Kindly send in Yusuf Ibn Ismail."

Heaving an inward sigh, Jackson ducked into the hall and went in search of his roommate, Corey, who rarely went by his conversion name, Yusuf. He found him in the dining hall finishing his dessert. "Imam Ibrahim is waitin' for you," he conveyed.

Scraping back his chair, Corey sent him a hopeful look through his glasses. "You gonna play ball with us tonight?" When it wasn't raining, the parolees had taken to shooting hoops on the blacktop during their free evenings.

"No, man. I gotta run." Jackson patted his stomach. "I'm gettin' fat."

Shaking his head at the exaggeration, Corey scooped up his tray and went to report to the imam. In the same instance, Imam Zakariya, who was small and spry and reminded Jackson of an African witch doctor with his eternally youthful face, dismissed them for their free time.

"Peace and blessings," he called as all the men but Corey bolted for the exit.

Jackson pushed out of the sandstone mosque into a sultry August evening. It was not yet dark but the lights over the basketball cage blinked on in anticipation of nightfall. Turning his back on his peers, he darted to his dorm to don his running shoes.

The parolees had been granted freedom to roam within a two mile radius of the campus from six to nine in the evening, starting from their first night here. Given their isolation in the country, the two-mile limit restricted them from visiting Mechanicsville proper. Jackson had made a habit of going running during that time, in a circuit that put him a mile up Highway 235 and another mile down an access road that ran deep into a deciduous forest. There, beneath the power lines, he touched base with Ike Calhoun via his tiny cell phone. Toby, who stayed in a motel in town, had met him deep in the woods once, so Jackson could describe the imams' patterns in a more detailed way than texting permitted.

Leaving the campus at an easy lope, he arrived at the lush, isolated spot where he usually placed his calls. Slowing to a walk, he swept the shadowed undergrowth before sticking in his ear bud and dialing his team lead. "Hey, Pops. You got news for me?" he huffed.

"The girl you asked about, was she driving a 2010 Jeep Wrangler?" Ike sounded as dour as he had that afternoon.

"Yeah, that's her." Jackson's heart pumped with confidence. The Taskforce would send out some discreet soul to bargain for the release of those photos. His cover would be safe again.

"The vehicle belongs to a Peter Schlesser," the Taskforce lead added, "forty-eight-year-old single male living in Columbia Heights."

At the unexpected news, Jackson listened more intently. So, maybe the bombshell had borrowed the car, only Ike's terse tone assured him that her connection to Peter Schlesser wasn't good news.

"He's the Editor-in-Chief of *Crime and Liberty*, which is a fairly reputable tabloid," Ike bit out.

Oh, hell, no. Jackson was well acquainted with *Crime and Liberty.* The tabloid took a strong civil rights stance, putting it in the same category as *Libertarian News.* While it enjoyed national circulation, most of its readers lived in Northern Virginia.

He pinched the ridge of his nose. The bombshell had looked him right in the eye and *lied* to him! And now his photo might show up in a publication read by college professors and human rights activists nationwide, but most especially in the capital where he lived and worked. Hundreds of people would recognize him—his neighbors, folks from church, members of the PTA…

"We have to find her," he grated.

"We're working on it. I need a physical description."

"Late twenties, with dark, wavy hair, and kind of exotic-looking. Greek, I think," he guessed.

"There are a couple women on his payroll who fit that description."

"Why don't we just ask Schlesser?"

Their encrypted speech was slipping, but here in the woods that wasn't too critical.

"Schlesser's on vacation. Office is closed. And he's not answering the cell number I tracked down."

Jackson turned full circle under a darkening sky. "There has to be a way."

"There is. We track down the couple of women who fit your description. I should be able to reclaim those pictures by tomorrow."

Tomorrow wasn't soon enough. "What if she uploads them to their website tonight?"

"She can't. We crashed their server. Nothing can get in or out."

Jackson's temples throbbed. It looked like a waiting game no matter what they did. "Text me when you have more news," he requested.

"Will do." The call ended abruptly.

Jackson realized he hadn't even mentioned the book in Ibrahim's office, the one with the familiar logo on the spine. It was probably nothing, even though his gut told him it might be something.

Putting away his ear bud, he eyed the dark track ahead of him. Twelve miles away, in a riverside rental on the Patuxent River, his daughter Naomi and her grandmother awaited his first visit "home." Rather than waste time driving back to Northern Virginia, he'd installed them at a nearby waterfront rental. He couldn't wait to see them this weekend.

But, hell, by then the Taskforce's efforts could be blown out of the water by one slippery, hot-as-hell tabloid journalist. They needed to find her fast. Jackson couldn't risk his cover being blown, not before he learned whether Gateway had ties to terrorism.

CHAPTER 3

With a gasp of horror, Lena lurched awake and found herself in the four-poster bed in her rental cottage. Her heart still raced. Plumbing the unfamiliar shadows, she was relieved to find herself alone. Rupert Davis, who had been choking her to death in her dream, was nowhere to be seen.

Just a dream, she assured herself, though her sweat-soaked nightshirt suggested it was actually a full-blown nightmare. Snatching up her cell phone, she checked the time—3 A.M.—before swinging out of bed and crossing to the door to flip the light switch.

As the lamp blinked on, her gaze went to the curtains fluttering at the open window. No wonder she hadn't slept well. Open windows left a city girl feeling exposed. But, as it turned out, the cottage didn't come with central air. She should have checked that out, too, before signing the lease.

Slipping into the adjacent bathroom, Lena tried emptying her mind with a cool, cleansing shower. But it didn't work. Had the dream been a warning? she wondered as she soaped herself. Like most Greeks, she believed in signs and portents. This one suggested she should throw her clothes back in her suitcase and head straight for home tonight.

Only, she'd gone too far to turn back now. Everything she had done for the past ten years from majoring in journalism, to monitoring Davis's incarceration, to hiring detectives in the hopes of finding the missing Curtis—it would all be for nothing if she gave up now.

Wrapped in a towel, she returned to her room, snapping off the light so she could dress with no one outside watching. When daylight came, she would toss her line into the water and see if Davis took the bait.

If his ego was bigger than his brain, she'd have him right where she wanted him.

Jackson spotted the black Jeep out the corner of his eye, barreling up the 235 toward Gateway. *Hot damn, the bombshell was back!*

Ducking back inside his dorm room in the converted motel, he tabbed the blinds to verify that the woman he'd confronted yesterday was behind the wheel. Indeed, she was. There was no mistaking her shoulder-length curls as she slowed at the intersection and turned right into the gas station.

Thankful for his roommate's absence, Jackson pulled out his cell phone while she parked near the store's entrance. Why the hell had she returned?

He accessed the camera application and snapped off several shots as she stepped out of the car, glancing over the hood in his direction. The sensible clothes she wore today didn't come close to disguising her shapely curves. Even with fifty or so yards between them, she made his temperature rise, but the distance would compromise the quality of the photos.

Nonetheless, he sent them with a message apprising

Ike and Toby of the circumstances. Hopefully the Taskforce analysts could enlarge the image and use their state-of-the-art facial-recognition software to ID the woman. Once they knew who she was, they would put a swift end to her cat and mouse game.

With her feet already aching from just five hours on the job, Lena pushed out of the store into the afternoon heat, a bottle of iced tea in one hand and ham-and-cheese sandwich in the other. She'd had no idea being a cashier at a gas station could be so challenging. Bill had shown her all there was to do, from making fresh coffee, to setting the pumps, to restocking the refrigerators in the back room. It was two o'clock, and the midday rush had waned, affording her a break, at last.

As she crossed the quiet parking lot, she glanced toward Gateway, surprised to see construction once more underway. Hunting automatically for Mocha Man, she realized with a leaping of her pulse that he was watching her from the height of a ladder.

With a defiant smile, Lena showed him her sandwich. *See, no camera here.*

He tipped her a nod. *I see that.*

Heading doggedly toward the picnic table positioned under a mammoth pecan tree, she sat down, propped her aching feet on the opposite bench, and watched the parolees work while she ate.

Not that there was all that much work going on anymore. One by one, the men had ceased their hammering and sawing to squint and shade their eyes as they stared across the highway at her, even Davis. She countered her sudden discomfort with a swig of iced tea.

Would he recognize her as his victim's sister after all these years? Surely not. It had been ten years since

Davis had faced the Xenakis family at the pre-trial hearing. Back then, Lena had worn a thick braid down her back, glasses with lenses as thick as soda bottle bottoms, and fifteen pounds of extra weight. Plus, she'd dropped her real last name, Xenakis, for the sake of her professional career since no one knew how to pronounce it. There wasn't any way Davis would make the connection, she assured herself. Eye laser surgery and rigorous Pilates made her look like a whole new woman.

The sound of a bell had her glancing back up to see the men dispersing. Roughly half turned toward the mosque, but the other half, including Davis and Mocha Man were preparing to cross the highway.

Like buzzards, they seemed oblivious to the sparse traffic. A school bus loaded with campers nearly bowled them over—all but Mocha Man who remained as alert as yesterday.

Lena swam in a cold sweat. *Ready or not, here they come.*

Lifting a hand to the gemstone at her neck, she flipped the tiny switch on the bail with her thumbnail. Her intent was to film her developing relationship with Davis, so that when he finally did confess, his words would come across as truthful, not just idle boasting.

Last night's dream flashed through her mind. *Don't think about it.* She'd interviewed dozens of criminals in the course of her career. She could do this.

"Damn, I'd like to get with that bitch," Jamal Ibn Nasser exclaimed as they drew close enough to make out the woman's supple curves.

"Watch your mouth," Jackson snapped, as much annoyed by the lanky man's outburst as he was by the fact that he felt the same way, even now that he'd learned who she was: Lena Alexandra, freelance editor for *Crime and Liberty* tabloid.

He'd received a text from Ike confirming his suspicions just an hour ago.

The woman had trouble written all over her. And he knew he ought to keep his distance, except he was dying to discover her agenda. Given her come-hither smile and the fingers she waggled at them invitingly, it was obvious she was after something—hopefully not him.

"I'm going to talk to her," announced the parolee named Muhammed. Switching course abruptly, he inspired the others to trail after him, including Jackson, who kept a sharp look-out for anything resembling a camera.

If the beauty was alarmed at being swarmed by ex-cons, she didn't show it. "Hello," she called, her lush lips curving into a heart-stopping smile.

Damn if there wasn't something about her that made a man think of sex.

"How you doin'?" Muhammed purred, putting a swagger in his stride.

"Super." She tucked a dark curl behind one ear as she regarded them one by one. "How are you all?"

They lined up on the opposite side of the picnic table feasting their eyes on her. "We good now," Muhammed declared, his gaze wandering toward her cleavage. "Wha's your name, baby?"

A spark of cynicism flared in her eyes, but her smile remained fixed. "Maggie," she said, setting her elbows on the table top and giving them a mouthwatering view of the tops of her coconut sized breasts. "I work here now." She nodded toward Artie's.

Jackson couldn't believe his ears. The woman hadn't wasted any time insinuating herself into the local scene, finding the ideal vantage from which to keep tabs on Gateway and making up a fictitious name. Why? Had the media caught whiff of the Taskforce investigation?

"My name's Muhammed," said their spokesperson. "This here is Nadim, Hasan, Jamal, Sulayman, and Abdul."

"Nice to meet all of you." Her gaze lingered a split second longer on Jackson than on the others.

"Maggie, huh," Muhammed continued, giving his chin a thoughtful rub. "Is that short for somethin'?"

Her sexy shrug shifted the pink gemstone dangling from her neck. "What do you think it's short for?" she asked, batting her eyelashes at him.

"Margaret," guessed Davis, looking smug when she gestured that he was right.

"Smart man," she praised him. "It is Margaret."

She was lying through her pearly white teeth. Jackson battled to hide his growing scowl.

"You live here?" he demanded on a note that made her glance at him sharply.

"As a matter of fact I just moved here from D.C.," she answered.

Another lie, Jackson thought.

"No shit. We all from D.C.," Muhammed exclaimed, "'cept for Abdul. He from Baltimore."

"Small world." She sat a little taller, tantalizing them again as her breasts jutted out. "What neighborhoods are you all from?"

"I'm from Anacostia, baddest 'hood in the city," Jamal replied.

Sulayman Ibn Surad, whose real name was Rupert Davis, spoke up suddenly. "I used to be a cop— Metropolitan police," he boasted.

Maggie shifted her whole body to face him. "Oh,

dear," she said with a sympathetic look.

Jackson eyed her incredulously. Couldn't the men tell that she was reeling them in?

"Yeah, we all got busted for one thing or another," Muhammed corroborated. "But don't you worry, baby," he rushed to assure her. "We all cleaned up our act. We God-fearin' men now," he added with conviction. "Ain't that right, fellas?"

"Tha's right," three others confirmed.

"Well, that's a relief," she stated, "especially since I'm writing a book about prison conversions and I'd love to interview some of you, if you're interested."

"You writin' a book?" Muhammed thumped down onto the bench across from her.

Jackson scowled. What book? She wasn't here to write a goddamn book.

"Absolutely. My goal is to show the positive, long-term effects of prison conversion on parolees."

The men gaped at her in awe.

"I want to be in it," Muhammed declared, slapping his hand on the table.

"Well, okay then!" Maggie flashed him a megawatt smile, her gaze jumping up expectantly. "What about the rest of you? I'd love to interview a former cop," she said to Sulayman.

The tension ebbed slowly out of Jackson. He didn't believe a word about her so-called book, but at least she didn't seem to be sniffing out a government spy.

"Not me," Sulayman declared, taking a backward step.

"Man, why not?" Jamal demanded. "I'll do it. I used to be a bank robber, but now that I found Allah, I'm a saved man."

"We all saved," Muhammed insisted. "You could interview all of us."

Ike wouldn't stand for this, Jackson assured himself. It didn't matter if she was hunting him or not; the woman was a threat to his cover.

Nadim, the only Hispanic man, shattered the moment by announcing that break time was almost over.

"Aw, man." Jamal slid a mournful look over Maggie's outrageous curves.

"Time to go." Grabbing Muhammed by the scruff, Jackson hauled him off the bench.

"Bye, baby," Muhammed sang out as Jackson herded them all toward the building.

"Bye." She fluttered her pink-tipped nails at them. "Come visit me soon. I'll be here every night at six," she called, setting Jackson's teeth on edge.

As the men filed into the store to buy their drinks, Jackson handed Muhammed a dollar and told him to buy an extra water while he waited outside. The surveillance cameras in the store, like Lena's camera yesterday, made him uncomfortable unless he was wearing a billed cap. Standing alone on the curb, he sensed the journalist staring at him.

Reluctantly, he looked over at her. "I trust you deleted those photos," he called across the parking lot.

But a mutt in the back of a pickup truck started barking, muffling his words.

Lena put a hand to her ear and shook her head. "I can't hear you."

He directed his glare at the annoying dog. "Quiet," he said with authority he had learned from K-9 handlers in the military. "I said, I trust you deleted those photos," he called to her again when the dog fell silent.

All she did was cast her eyes heavenward and shake her head.

Just you wait, Jackson thought, stewing at her

stubborn refusal to acknowledge the truth. She'd regret it when the Taskforce lead stepped in to protect him.

Muhammed reemerged and handed him his water. The dog started barking again as the men spilled out in his wake, waved farewell at the journalist, and started back across the highway. Jackson could feel her speculative gaze on his back, keeping him prickly in his skin.

He probably wasn't the reason she was here, he acknowledged, but a woman as accomplished as she was at eliciting information was a danger to his cover. Somehow, some way, Ike needed to get rid of her.

There was already one spy in this town; two was just too many.

With shadows sliding up the trunks of the trees outside, Lena flicked on the light in her bedroom, propped her laptop open on her vanity, and connected her camera to it. The time had come to save backup copies of her photos onto her database at work.

Thumbnail images popped onto her screen, and her gaze went straight to her pictures of Abdul Ibn Wasi. Her pulse automatically quickened.

Abdul. His conversion name had caught her off guard, today. Curious to know the meaning of his name, she Googled "Abdul."

Servant, said a site devoted to Islamic conversion names.

As in sex slave? queried a wistful voice in Lena's head.

Her brow furrowed. Why had he presented himself so differently today than yesterday? From his walk to his speech, which had lapsed into a vernacular similar to that of his peers, he'd struck her as an entirely different person than the articulate man who'd accosted her yesterday. The only thing that hadn't changed about him was his blistering resentment toward her and his insistence that she delete her photos.

Why would her pictures pose such a threat to him anyway? And what about him set him apart from his peers, even when he tried to be like them? It wasn't just his lighter coloration. He'd noticed her when the others had remained oblivious. His hawk-like vigilance was evident in his light-colored eyes. She doubted anything escaped his notice, ever. Having a man like that around when she was working undercover made her nervous.

With a shrug, she typed in *Crime and Liberty*'s URL and waited for the log-in page to load, so she could access her personal records.

Nothing. The DSL service at her rental was a far cry from the high-speed wireless she was accustomed to at home. With a sigh of annoyance, Lena hit the refresh button. Still nothing. Something had to be wrong with *Crime and Liberty*'s servers. She found herself thinking about Abdul again.

Maybe if she knew what he was serving time for, that would shed light on his reluctance to have his picture circulating. Opening a new tab on her browser, she typed in the URL for the National Crime Information Center. A friend at the DA's office had provided her his log in and password information so she could have access. She typed in Abdul's name and pasted his image into the facial recognition pane, hitting the search button. The program would scan all twelve Persons Files on the NCIC, saving her hours of research, and bring up his criminal history.

Her pulse thrummed as she waited. What if Abdul's crime was reprehensible? What would that make her for finding an ex-con so appealing?

After several long minutes, the words NO MATCH flashed onto the screen, baffling her. Lena scratched her head. How could there be no match if he was a convicted felon? He would have to have seriously altered his appearance for the program not to identify him.

Curious to see what results Davis's image yielded, she followed the same procedures with his photo, using his conversion name, Sulayman, and received immediate feedback: Rupert D. Davis (aka Sulayman Ibn Surad). Former D.C. Metropolitan Police officer convicted of trafficking marijuana and cocaine. Sentenced to fifteen years in prison. Served eight years at Arlington County Corrections. Paroled July, 2012.

"That's odd." Why would Davis's face be recognized and not Abdul's?

Curiosity nipped at Lena, prompting her to expand her search outside of the NCIC to include celebrities and professional athletes who'd gone to jail, since he struck her as someone who could have been either. But armed with just his first name, and with no facial recognition program of her own to use, her search proved random and inefficient.

By now, the open window formed a dark rectangle against the white wall. Throwing up her hands in frustration, Lena decided to enlist Peter's help. If anyone could identify an unknown person, it was the founder and CEO of *Crime and Liberty*.

She sent him an email from her Google account, attaching Abdul's photo and a concise request that concealed her underlying fascination with the man.

When the email bounced right back, she sat back, thought for a moment, and sent the picture to Peter's Google mail, which he used for personal correspondence.

Then, rubbing her heavy eyelids, Lena saved the pictures on her laptop. Tomorrow she would offload the contents of her pendant. Since it could hold up to two hours of recorded video, there wasn't any rush. Tonight she needed to catch up on her sleep.

Powering down her laptop, she climbed into bed and covered herself with just a sheet. The photo by her bed caught her eye as light from a passing car briefly illumined Alexa's sweet visage. The air wafting through the open window smelled of the small white berries on the shrubs outside. Odd, Alexa used to own a bottle of perfume that smelled like that.

"No bad dreams tonight," Lena told herself.

CHAPTER 4

―――◆―――

"What's the plan, Pops?" Jackson demanded, speaking directly into his cell phone as a late-afternoon thunderstorm rumbled in the direction of the river and rustled the leaves on the trees overhead. His heart still thudded from his jog into the darkening forest.

Over forty-eight hours had passed since Lena Alexandra had snapped his pictures and twenty-eight hours since she'd invited the men to visit her while she worked. Not only had she insinuated herself locally but word of her had spread among the parolees, so that the majority had made plans to accept her invitation to come visit her, tonight after Friday worship. "We're not letting this chick stay here, are we?"

"It's a wait-and-see situation," Ike replied.

There had to be something more they could do besides sabotage *Crime and Liberty's* servers. "Have you found out her phone number yet?"

"I did, but she's not carrying her regular cell."

Obviously, the woman had done this kind of thing before. They couldn't even monitor her phone calls.

Jackson's agitation mounted. "So we do nothing?"

"Your best friend's going to follow her home tonight to find out where she lives," Ike said. "Then you and he can have a party at her place tomorrow, while she's at work," he added, significantly.

Ah, so there was a method to Ike's madness. Ike had Toby keeping an eye on the journalist. "Cool." And by *party*, Ike meant that Jackson and Toby would raid her place of residence and seize her camera, her laptop, and anything else that could be used to jeopardize his cover.

"You'll want to convince her that your college isn't right for her," Ike continued on a steely note.

In other words, scare the crap out of her so she'd leave.

"Right," Jackson agreed, relieved but also reluctant. He drew the line at intimidating women. Plus, he didn't necessarily want to see the last of her. Having her around offered respite from the otherwise tedious experience of working through a program that redeemed ex-cons when he wasn't one, and looking for evidence for the Taskforce that he doubted even existed.

As far as he could tell, Gateway was everything it was held up to be.

"Anything new?" Ike asked.

Jackson thought about the book he'd glimpsed in Ibrahim's office the other day. Just because the logo on the spine had looked familiar, that didn't make the book suspect. "No, nothing. I can't wait to come home," he inserted, aching to hold his daughter whom he hadn't seen since the start of summer when she'd left for Girl Scout Camp.

"Tomorrow," Ike reminded him.

"Yep. See you, Pops."

"'Night, son."

Tucking his phone back in his pocket, Jackson flinched at the terrific crash of thunder that shook the ground under his feet. For a split second he was back in Iraq, his battalion taking mortar rounds.

Working for the Taskforce was a lot like war, he reflected. Sometimes the line between ally and enemy got blurred.

What was Lena Alexandra, aka Maggie? Friend or foe?

One way to find out was to visit her tonight at the store with the other parolees.

Lena cast another anxious glance through the windows at the front of the store. This was her first night of handling the store on her own. She was relieved when floodlights came on outside at either end of the building, driving the mantle of dusk to the perimeter of the parking lot. The gas pumps stood empty under the illuminated shelter. The store was lit up like Las Vegas, only no one was coming to gamble, not even the Lotto-loving Amish man. She hadn't wanted to be too busy, but the lull that had followed the initial rush made the time creep by.

Nerves frayed by the continual classical music, Lena found the source and turned it off. How long would she have to wait for the parolees to venture over? Surely they would take her up on her invitation. The refrigerators hummed and the percolating coffee hissed. Then above those noises, a sing-song voice permeated the store. Seeking the source of the sound, Lena pushed outside to find Gateway's parking lot crammed with vehicles. The eerie incantation was the *muezzin*, she realized—the Muslim calls to prayers, floating down from a minaret that pricked the cobalt sky. Lights shining out of the mosque's high windows suggested a service was underway. No wonder no one had paid her a visit yet.

But as long as the service didn't last till midnight, she might have visitors yet.

"Go forth with Allah's blessing," Ibrahim called from the *minbar,* the high, tower-shaped podium from which he'd issued his sermon. Sweeping down the long steps he stalked to the back of the room to fling open the heavy doors to the foyer.

Freed to move, at last, Jackson unfurled his numb legs and rose from his prayer rug trying not to bump his neighbors. Dozens of men, visitors and current parolees alike, had been kneeling for two hours straight, facing the *mihrab*, an elaborately tiled niche that dominated the wall of the mosque facing the direction of Mecca.

At the start of the service, the visitors had been introduced as former parolees, graduates of Gateway. Jackson's peers regarded them in awe. Dressed in suits, many appeared affluent; all of them struck Jackson as amazingly well integrated, considering they were former felons. If Gateway was responsible for transforming them into such productive, upstanding individuals, then the Taskforce was barking up the wrong tree.

Ibrahim's sermon about restraint and self-respect had been a fitting one, as this weekend would be the parolees' first taste of freedom since getting out of jail. As with previous sermons, it was filmed by a cameraman who would post the sermon on Ibrahim's website. Jackson kept his face averted whenever the camera swung in his direction.

While Ibrahim's words might be influential in preventing some ex-cons from reverting to previous behaviors, Jackson figured the example set by the graduates was more likely to motivate them. Inviting successful graduates to attend Friday night worship was a stroke of genius on the part of the leadership.

"Go straight to your beds, my brothers," Zakariya cautioned, threading his way through the crowd. "Remember that you *will* be tempted in your freedom," he added, laying a knobby hand on Jackson's shoulder. "You must resist temptation."

A vision of Lena Alexandra sprang to Jackson's mind. Now there was temptation incarnate, he mused, joining the others in heading for the door. He noted that Ibrahim greeted each man by name, forgetting no one's. "For you, Abu," he said, doling out a pamphlet to each and every attendee. Accepting his, Jackson glanced at the title, *Judgment Day,* and slipped it into his rear pocket to review later.

He followed the crowd outside. There, the parolees watched with envious eyes as the graduates departed, driving away in Toyotas, Cadillacs, and Lexuses. Then all twelve men trudged in thoughtful silence to their dormitory. As they neared the entrance to the campus, Artie's One Stop Shop came into view, lit up like a whorehouse in a port of call.

"It's too early to go to bed," Muhammed commented.

"I ain't tired," Jamal agreed.

With that consensus, half the men started wordlessly across the highway. Jackson followed the handful that remained on course to the dormitory, but only to fetch a billed cap so he could hide his features from Artie's security cameras.

So much for Zakariya's caution to resist temptation.

As parolees swarmed into the store, dressed in identical gray slacks and white button-up shirts, Lena barricaded herself behind the register, where the raised floor gave her a better vantage from which to keep an eye on everyone.

Muhammed made the introductions. The men joked and jockeyed for standing room next to the counter, each man vying for her attention. She'd decided not to push the book issue until the men felt more comfortable in her presence.

The last person introduced was Corey, Abdul's roommate.

"Where is Abdul?" she asked, pretending to look for him, though she'd realized right away that he wasn't present. She told herself she was relieved. It might prove awkward if he brought up the business about her taking pictures, though her book story provided an excuse for that, too.

Corey shrugged. "I guess he ain't comin'."

"Why not?"

Corey shrugged again. "I hear you write books," he said, eyeing her earnestly through his lenses. "I like readin' nonfiction." His brown cheeks turned a dusky pink.

"Do you?" They discussed the biography he was currently enjoying, before Lena brought up Abdul again. "You know, your roommate looks familiar. Do you know his full name?" It was driving her crazy that she hadn't yet identified him.

"Abdul Ibn Wasi," Corey replied. "That's his conversion name, anyway. I took the name Yusuf Ibn Ismail back in jail when I converted, but I still like Corey better."

"Corey's more approachable," Lena agreed. "Do you know what Abdul's name was before conversion?" Her skin had begun to crawl from Davis's unwavering stare. Planted on her left side next to the bins of Fireballs and Slim Jims, he seemed to be scheming something devious.

"No, ma'am. We ain't allowed to share our old

names with nobody 'cause our conversion name represents who we is now. I'm the only one who still goes by my old name."

Darn, Lena thought, distracted by movement in her peripheral vision. "Jamal," she exclaimed in astonishment, "did you just stick a breakfast bar in your pocket?"

His face was the picture of innocence. "Not me."

Davis sniggered while the other men turned and frowned at Jamal.

"What's in your left front pocket then?" she persisted.

"Nothin'."

Her chance to forge a bond with Davis presented itself unexpectedly. She turned to appeal to him for help. "Weren't you a police officer?"

He hitched up his slacks with an air of worthiness. "I was. What of it?"

"I would think you'd have a problem with people stealing, especially when they do it right under your nose."

"Hmph." He shot Jamal a considering look.

"Plus, why should I have to call the local sheriff when I have a former Metropolitan Police Officer right here to help me?" It took all of Lena's willpower to bat her lashes at him.

In that same instant, Abdul, wearing a large billed cap that looked ridiculous paired with his dress clothes, set off the chime as he stepped through the door. Lena's pulse picked up to see him. Aside from the hat, he looked even more appealing in formal attire than in casual clothing.

She dragged her attention back to Davis, extending a hand as if to touch him but not quite. "Look, I know I can count on you to keep these guys under control," she said in her sexiest voice.

Jamal looked worried. "Man, I didn't take nothin'," he insisted, backing away.

"I got this," Davis decided, puffing out his chest like a bantam rooster in a barn full of hens. Stalking Jamal, he spun him around, kicked his legs apart, and shoved his face toward the floor.

Jamal howled.

The others tittered nervously.

Davis pulled out a squashed breakfast bar from Jamal's pocket. "Is this what you didn't take, boy?" he growled at his victim, shoving his head even lower.

"Don't hurt him!" Lena exclaimed, biting her tongue when Davis shot her an indignant look. "Thank you, though." She held out a hand for the stolen item so that Davis was forced to release his victim. But first he shoved Jamal face-first onto the linoleum tiles.

Hitching his slacks again, he swaggered back toward Lena, his soulless gaze making her scalp creep. "Any time, lady," he purred, caressing her hand as if he'd just earned the right to.

Repulsed by his touch, she glanced longingly at the antibacterial gel, while several men helped Jamal to his feet, telling him he'd deserved the punishment.

Lena tossed the squashed item into the trash. "Well, that was—" *Barbaric,* she thought. "Impressive," she said, glad that she had filmed it on her mini camcorder. She had no expectation of Davis saying anything incriminating yet, but she liked to leave it on, just in case. She tried sending him a flirtatious smile, failed miserably, and glanced over at Abdul, instead.

With his arms folded over his chest and legs set apart like sturdy tree trunks, he seemed to fill the frame of the closed door. The expression in his eyes was hidden under the bill of his cap, but the firm line of his lips conveyed disapproval.

Lena raised her eyebrows inquiringly. *What's with the hat?* And then it came to her. She glanced up at the surveillance camera over head. *Ah.*

At her derisive smile, he looked away.

This was the second time she'd sensed them communicating without a word between them. It was if they shared a different mentality, one that saw beyond the games being played out. Still, she couldn't understand why Abdul dreaded the cameras when no one else showed the least concern.

"Whatchu doin' after work, lady?"

Davis's unexpected question made her blood freeze over. Bracing herself, she turned to face him. "Honey, I work till midnight. I'm sure that's well after your curfew."

His answering sneer conveyed that a curfew posed no deterrent.

Maybe she was crazy to turn down the opportunity to question him alone, but she had much to do to set the stage for his interview. It was still too early to expect him to confess to anything. "Maybe some other time," she suggested.

"We should not be here," Abdul stated out of the blue. "You heard what Imam Zakariya said about temptation. We should all be in our beds." He ran a commanding look over the men.

Lena notched her hands on her hips. "Oh, for heaven's sake, Abdul. We were just getting to know each other."

"Abdul's right." Corey sent her an apologetic grimace. "We should go back before we break curfew. Besides, you have a customer." He nodded outside at the eighteen-wheeler rumbling into the parking lot.

Shoulders slumped with disappointment, the men headed as a unit toward the door—all but Davis, who stayed right where he was, making Lena's heart race with sudden panic. They weren't going to leave her here alone with him, were they?

"Night, Miz Maggie," Muhammed called, blowing her a kiss.

Lena shook her head. "Good night, Muhammed."

"Sorry 'bout what I done," Jamal mumbled as he shuffled past.

"That's okay. You gave it back." *Sort of.*

"See you Sunday," Nadim said as he filed past.

Wait, Sunday? "Are you going somewhere?" she asked at their retreating backs.

"Weekend liberty," Davis supplied, sliding a hand along the counter as he moved reluctantly toward the door.

"You're all leaving?" Her dismay was genuine.

"Just for one night. I'll be back," Davis assured her, sending her a sly wink that made her stomach pitch.

"You comin' or not?" Abdul bit out as he held open the door.

Davis swiveled toward him. Hostility radiated from his stocky body as he advanced on Abdul. "I don't take orders from you," he growled.

Lena held her breath. A fight between such large, undaunted men could only get ugly. She feared one of them getting hurt; or worse yet, being restricted from coming to visit her at Artie's. But Abdul just stared Davis down, giving him no good reason to take the first swing.

At last, her sister's killer stalked off, his dark form sliding past the windows. Just the whites of his eyes remained visible as he glanced over his shoulder at her.

"You should leave this place." Abdul's deep, musical voice recaptured her attention as he prepared to let the door drop shut.

She tossed her head at him. "Says who?"

"These men are dangerous." Once again, his speech sounded educated.

"And you're not?"

He shrugged, lifting and lowering his powerful shoulders as the door started closing between them.

"What got you thrown into jail?" she called out.

But then the door thumped shut and he was walking away, rejecting her question as blatantly as he rejected her presence here. Adopting a bad-ass stroll, he disappeared into the dark.

"Hey, what's it gonna take to get some service here?"

Lena jumped a foot into the air. She'd forgotten all about the truck driver standing by his rig at the illuminated pumps. She slapped her palm over the reply button.

"Sorry, sir. What can I get you?"

As she set the diesel pump for two hundred dollars, she pondered Abdul's attitude. First he'd wanted her to delete his photos; now he wanted her to leave. Obviously, the man was hiding something.

Well, hell, that just gave her one more reason to stick around.

CHAPTER 5

Jackson glanced sidelong at his colleague as they descended the steps of the mosque to cross the broiling parking lot. The weekend was going to be a scorcher.

Much to Jackson's surprise, Toby had shaved his soul patch, cut his overlong hair, and swapped out his usual T-shirt for a stylish suit, one that actually made him look like a parole officer, so much so that Ibrahim had scarcely glanced his way when Toby signed him out. The imam would never have guessed Tobias Burke was a special agent for the Bureau of Alcohol, Tobacco, Firearms and Explosives.

Jackson waited till he was settled in the back seat of their rented Crown Victoria to say it. "You clean up good, Burke," he remarked as Toby slipped behind the wheel.

Toby slipped on a pair of Versace sunglasses. "Yeah, but you'll never look like a thug, Stonewall," he retorted, starting up the car.

"My name's not Stonewall." This wasn't the first time he'd reminded his colleague of that fact. Jackson figured the reason Toby persisted in harassing him was because he'd once been an Army Ranger, and an enlisted one at that. Hence the constant attempts to belittle the former Marine Corps officer. They were both out of the military now, but the competition between the two branches of service remained, and Toby could call Jackson whatever the hell he felt like. Stonewall Jackson happened to be a Confederate Army General, and Toby was a Civil War Buff from Philadelphia.

Tossing a cocky smile at the rearview mirror, the former Ranger swept them onto Highway 235 while punching on a rock and roll station. They barreled north toward Abdul Ibn Wasi's home in Baltimore. Only, they wouldn't go nearly that far.

"So, tonight?" Jackson queried, eager to get the business of chasing Lena out of town behind him. "You found out where she's staying?"

"Yep," Toby answered. "Thanks for the distraction, man. Beats hanging around some dingy motel while you do all the fun stuff."

Fun stuff, right. Jackson dug out the pamphlet Ibrahim had distributed last night. He handed it wordlessly up front.

"What's this?" Taking it, Toby divided his attention between the highway and the booklet. "Looks like the material my mother's church doles out predicting that I'm going straight to hell."

"It's a reference to the Judgment Day," Jackson explained.

"So, what's with the pictures of the Capitol building?"

"That's what I wondered. Here, I'll read it to you." Jackson held out a hand to take it back. "When the Master of the Age appears, the young among his followers will rouse themselves and reach Mecca that very night. At that time, the Mahdi will call upon the entire world to join his movement."

"Are you shittin' me?" Toby muttered, turning off the highway onto a narrow country road that meandered toward the river.

"Those who have suffered and lost all hope that their situation could improve will rally around him and will pay allegiance to him," Jackson continued. "A vast army made up of courageous, sacrificing, and reform-seeking peoples of the world will be prepared to be led by him. They will occupy the east and the west of the world and will bring everything under his command. They will continue their struggle until Allah's pleasure is acquired. That's it," he said, shutting the booklet.

"And Gateway's leaders want the parolees to believe that stuff," Toby marveled. He directed his attention at a tiny house set back beneath the trees on their right. "By the way, that's the rental where the journalist stays." He directed his gaze at the trees on their right.

Jackson's pulse quickened as he recognized Schlesser's Jeep parked beside a tiny white house. The recollection of what he and Toby had planned for the journalist that night dimmed his pleasure in getting a break from the program. He wished they didn't have to chase Lena Alexandra away so soon. He'd never felt more alive than when he was in her presence.

Sitting back in his seat, he focused his thoughts on a different young lady, one he knew he couldn't live without. So why had he made work such a priority and missed so much of her childhood?

Ten minutes later, that question pegged him in the heart when a stunning young lady burst out of the riverfront rental with a long-legged run. "You're here!"

Jackson barely had time to shut the car door before his daughter launched herself into his arms. Nose buried in her auburn hair, he swung her in a circle. Naomi smelled as she always did, of sunshine and laughter and everything good in this world.

"Dad, you are so going to love this place!" she declared, unaware of his private heartbreak as he took in how much she'd grown since heading off to Girl Scout camp at the start of summer. She was coming to resemble her mother more and more, only Colleen's skin had been fair where Naomi's was a caramel brown.

He cut a critical glance at the cedar-sided contemporary home. "What's so good about it?" The damn place had better be a castle considering what he paid to rent it.

"Wait till you see the inside!" she said, oblivious to his satire. Just then Toby stepped into her line of sight, and she lapsed into shyness.

"Honey, this is a friend I work with, Mr. Burke. Toby, meet my twelve-year-old, Naomi." He watched with amusement as Naomi offered Toby a formal handshake. In the very next instant, she lapsed back into the child he knew and tugged him toward the house.

Leaving Toby to collect their technical equipment, Jackson let himself be dragged inside. "Wow," he breathed, knowing it was expected of him.

The vacation home was everything he'd hoped it would be, with an open floor plan, inventive architecture, and a cathedral ceiling. Soaring windows offered a stunning view of the Patuxent River flowing leisurely along a sandy shore some thirty yards below them, at the end of a long run of steps. The house smelled of freshly cut flowers and Windex.

"Isn't it awesome, Dad?"

"It's awesome," he agreed, glad to have done something right.

"She's been swimming and fishing from sunrise to sunset," reported his mother-in-law coming down the spiral steps from the loft.

Jackson greeted Silvia with a stab of guilt. "What about you?" he asked. She ought to have been enjoying her retirement instead of raising his child.

"Oh, I love it," she assured him. Her once-red hair had lost its luster, fading to a muted auburn, but the former school teacher claimed the face of much younger woman. "How are you making out, Jackson?" she asked with a sympathetic hug. "You certainly look the part." Her gaze flickered with distaste over his attire.

"You hear that, Burke?" he called to Toby, who staggered into the kitchen just then, loaded down with their gear. "She says I look the part." He made quick introductions. "Silvia, this is Special Agent Toby Burke. Toby, this is Naomi's grandmother."

"Take this," Toby grunted, unburdening himself onto Jackson and capturing Silvia's hand. "Pleasure ma'am," he said, with a smile reserved exclusively for members of the opposite sex.

As Silvia's face reddened, Jackson mentally rolled his eyes. Toby's reputation with the ladies hadn't been exaggerated. "Where would you like us to put our stuff?" he asked pointedly.

"I'll show you."

Naomi escorted them through to a hallway at the back of the house where two furnished bedrooms, a luxurious bath, and a small office supplied all the space they needed.

Promising he'd rejoin her in a minute, Jackson ducked into his room to change. Seconds later, feeling much more himself in a mint-green Polo crewneck, khaki shorts, and loafers, he stepped into the hall, running into Toby, who'd donned a pair of ragged jean shorts and an orange T-shirt advertising Dirty Dick's Crab Shack. A silver hoop glinted in Toby's left ear. He had on flip-flops.

Toby gestured to the office where they'd dumped their technical equipment. "I think I'll scan that pamphlet so we can send it to the bossman," he offered. "You want to write him an email?"

Jackson could hear his daughter chatting excitedly with her grandmother. "Go ahead. Family first," he reminded himself.

"Right," Toby agreed, backing toward the office door. "So, whatever happened to your daughter's mother?" he inquired, off-hand.

Jackson stopped and slowly turned back. "Car accident," he said shortly.

Toby sent him a searching look. "Sorry to hear that."

"Thanks." The car accident was only half the story, but Jackson didn't know Toby well enough to tell him the rest.

"Let's look up the journalist," Jackson suggested at 9:45 P.M.

Naomi and Silvia had withdrawn upstairs to retire for the night. He and Toby were cozied into their little office waiting for the scheduled teleconference with Ike. Jackson, who couldn't get Lena Alexandra, aka Maggie, out of his head, figured they could use the ten minutes before their conference started to plan their "party" at her place tonight.

Toby sat forward. "Sure, let me show you what I've found."

Jackson's blood flowed faster as his colleague typed her name into their search engine.

Crime and Liberty's website was the first hit to come up, but with the server hacked, they could only view a cached page, several years old. The bombshell's photo was there, nonetheless, her title listed even then as Freelance Editor, and she'd been every bit as sexy in her mid-twenties as she was now. The figure-hugging crimson sweater made Jackson's mouth water.

Toby gave a low whistle. "I get hard just looking at her."

Jackson stabbed a finger at a link. "Click that," he ordered tersely.

The subsequent page was filled with a list of dozens of articles written by Lena Alexandra. Looking at her long list of accomplishments, he felt suddenly queasy.

"She's been busy," Toby noted in a more subdued tone.

Lena. Maggie. Maggie. Lena. Jackson had a sudden thought. "I bet her real name's Magdalena," he wagered, enjoying the way it rolled off his lips and tongue. *Margaret, my ass.*

"Magdalena Alexandra," Toby said with flare. "That's about as Greek as they get."

From what the old website suggested, Lena Alexandra had been contributing articles to *Crime and Liberty* since her first year out of college. There were titles relating to theft, embezzlement, kidnapping, even murder. Jackson scratched his neck, feeling harried. Not only was she beautiful and crafty, but her accomplishments bespoke of a highly intelligent woman. A pro. She could probably smell an imposter a mile away, which meant he would be in some deep shit if they didn't succeed in getting rid of her.

"You really think she'll leave if we cramp her style?" Jackson was starting to have his doubts.

Toby shrugged. "Only one way to find out. If that

doesn't work, I volunteer to hold her hostage in my hotel room until the investigation's over," he said with a straight face and a twinkle in his eyes.

Like hell, Jackson thought, hiding a scowl. "Maybe we could get her arrested."

"Her?" Toby scoffed. "She probably knows fifteen lawyers off the top of her head."

Given her profession, she probably did. Jackson reminded himself that she would be Ike's problem if she refused to leave.

As if summoned by thought, their conferencing program chimed. Ike's rugged features filled the screen, his thick head of silver hair glinting under the halogen lighting at the National Center for Counterterrorism. "Evening," he bit out, as terse as ever.

Subdued by their lead's grim presence, Jackson and Toby returned the greeting. To Jackson's practiced eye, Ike looked more haggard than usual, which was saying something since his default expression was that of a man predicting world calamity. The only time he ever looked relaxed was when he took off to his mountain hideaway with his lovely bride, Eryn.

Of course, Eryn could make any man feel better, Jackson reflected. There'd been a time about a year ago when he'd hoped she'd be a balm for his own soul. He'd even taken Eryn out on a couple of dates while Ike was in Afghanistan, but with her heart already pledged to Ike, Jackson had never really stood a chance. Especially not when Ike came home early— gravely injured—but alive enough to claim Eryn's hand in marriage.

"Starting with the Judgment Day pamphlet," Ike began, diving right in. "Our analysts came back with this report." He read from a printout. "The passage is a direct quote from the *Qu'ran*. It's the same story that's found in the Bible and the Torah, only with its own particulars. In Islam, the prophesied redeemer is called the *Mahdi*, who is predicted to live on Earth for seven, nine, or nineteen years before Judgment Day, depending on the translation. Then on Judgment Day, he'll rid the world of wrongdoing, injustice and tyranny."

"So the pamphlet is harmless," Jackson concluded, with relief. The report corroborated his gut impression that Gateway's agenda was perfectly benign.

"Except that the illustrations suggest that it's going to go down in our Nation's capital," Ike countered, scowling.

"That's to give modern significance to ancient scripture," Jackson argued. "They have to appeal to the parolees' mindset."

"Possibly," his boss agreed. "But we can't afford to overlook a reference to some planned attack, when Gateway donates funds to Islamist rebel groups that slaughter civilians. Jackson—"

"Sir." Twelve years in the Marine Corps had conditioned the respectful term to come out of his mouth. Ike was the team lead, yes, but they'd had equal rank when they left the military.

"What have you seen and heard this week?"

Jackson shook his head. Because he had nothing else to offer up, he finally mentioned the book that had caught his eye. "In my visual search of Ibrahim's office, I saw a book called *Supreme 120 Lessons: for the Nation of Gods & Earths*. It struck me as...off." He shrugged.

Ike's eyebrows came slowly together. He leaned toward his keyboard and started typing. Then he sat back with a frown. "The Nation of Gods and Earths is another name for the gang called the Five Percenters."

A faint alarm went off in Jackson's head. "Who are

they?"

"Allegedly, they're the number of enlightened people living on the planet who are willing to share their knowledge with less enlightened black men." Ike continued to scan the information on his end. "NGE was founded in the 1960s by a student of Malcolm X. They broke away from the Nation of Islam over a fundamental difference in how they perceived God."

"I've heard of this gang," Toby volunteered.

"The NGE doesn't believe in a traditional God," Ike continued. "For them, the black man is Allah, which stands for arm, leg, leg, arm, head, not a separate and divine entity. Being the original man, Allah is destined to rule other races."

"Plus, most Five Percenters are prison converts," Toby chimed in. "They tattoo a sun, moon, star, and the number seven onto their bodies to identify themselves."

Crap. "That was the logo on the side of the book," Jackson admitted, realizing now why the image had looked familiar. He must have seen it while studying gangs for his Master's in Criminology.

Ike sat back. "Okay, let's assume Ibrahim is a Five Percenter," he proposed. "How does that change things?"

Jackson had trouble envisioning the beneficent leader as a gang member.

"He is from Harlem, remember?" Toby pointed out. "That's where the gang originated."

"I thought we were looking for terrorists, not gang members," Jackson objected.

"What's the difference?" Ike sent him a hard look.

Jackson pondered the question. Gangs and terrorist cells alike emerged out of a sense of social helplessness, its members drawn to the structure and moral order imposed on them, as well as to the sense of belonging. Actually, they had more in common than he'd realized.

Toby broke the silence. "Don't forget Ibrahim spent twenty years as a jail chaplain," he reminded them. "He could've converted hundreds of inmates to the NGE."

Ike continued to scan the information on his end. "A lot of hip hop artists are Five Percenters," he announced.

Jackson remained dubious. "Ibrahim might be a Five Percenter, but aside from this pamphlet all he and Zakariya have ever preached is moderate, mainstream Islam."

"Have they ever mentioned Supreme Mathematics or the Supreme Alphabet?" Ike pressed.

"Not that I've heard."

The leader scraped a hand over the short bristles of his silver hair, thinking. "I want you looking for more about this Five Percent stuff when you search the place," he decided.

"How are you coming with the alarm system?" Jackson asked.

Ike grimaced. "They have a Cinch Security System, one of the trickiest to override, which is a red flag in itself. Why would they need that in a mosque? Plus it has encrypted end-to-end communications, which means that any kind of sabotage alerts the company to a break-in. That means I have to broker a deal with the company." Ike didn't look too thrilled about it. "I'll let you know when it's clear to break in. In the meantime, Toby, start monitoring the imams' sleeping hours, taking note of their rituals. And, Jackson, keep alert to any mention of the Five Percent Nation."

"Yes, sir," Jackson said.

Toby nodded.

"I don't need to remind you both that the eleventh

anniversary of 9/11 is just weeks away." Ike's voice turned as rough as sandpaper. "I don't want any acts of terror happening on my watch. You copy?"

"Copy," Jackson confirmed.

"Yep," Toby said.

"Let's talk about the journalist," Ike said in the same terse voice. "You know how I feel about the media."

Jackson did know. Ever since MSNBC broadcasted the rumor that Eryn had been abducted by a Navy SEAL, Ike had harbored a deep resentment for journalists, especially since he'd been that SEAL, protecting Eryn from a crazed terrorist, and their live coverage had exposed her location, putting her right in harm's way.

"You know *Crime and Liberty* wrote a huge spread about my involvement in the Yaqubi disaster," Ike added, referring to the tragedy that had taken the life of nearly every man in Ike's SEAL squad several years ago. "Do whatever it takes to send her packing," he said meaningfully.

Jackson suffered a pang of compunction. He would miss his adrenaline-racing encounters with Lena, but she had to go.

"I'll check with you tomorrow." Ike tapped a key on his end, and their screen went black.

"In and out like a lightning strike," Toby commented.

"Never seen him quite so irritable." Jackson glanced at his watch. "Let's get this party started."

Toby jumped to his feet. "Hooah," he said, which, in Ranger speech, meant, *hell yeah*.

"I'll meet you by the car," Jackson reluctantly agreed.

Five minutes later, dressed all in black, the two men slipped into the Crown Vic and rolled stealthily out of the driveway. Toby glanced over at Jackson. "Jack, I'm jealous. I can't even see you in the dark."

"My name's not Jack, either," Jackson retorted.

Toby just chuckled.

CHAPTER 6

Lena stepped out of the Jeep into pitch-black darkness and eyed the outline of her rental with sudden foreboding. She was positive she had left the porch light on when she went to work, so either the bulb had burned out or…She didn't want to think about the other possibilities.

The crickets chirping in the fallen pine needles fell mute as she felt her way to the porch. Stubbing her toe on the step, she hobbled for the door. At her touch alone, the door cracked open, and fear shot straight up Lena's spine. She dropped the keys, plunging her hand inside her purse to reach for the Micro Compact .45 caliber pistol she never left home without. The reassuring feel of its stainless steel frame steadied her pulse as she thumbed off the safety and cautiously pushed the door open.

A hush emanated out of the darkness. Sliding her free hand along the wall, she felt for the switch and snapped on the light.

"Diavolos!"

It looked like a tornado had swept through her rental. Cushions littered the floor. The recliner lay on its side. Even the braided rug had been ripped from the hardwood. In the kitchenette, drawers and cupboards stood open, their contents swept onto the counters and floor. Ceramic and glass shards lay broken and gleaming on every surface. And in the midst of the chaos, a steak knife stood straight up out of a cutting board, its point imbedded deep into the wood.

Shock ricocheted through Lena's body.

The silence suggested the intruder was gone, but he might still be here, lying in wait. Holding her gun aloft, she waded deeper into the wreckage. Was there some malicious intent behind this ransacking? What had the intruder been looking for? Hopefully not her.

Oh, crap, my camera! My laptop!

She pushed open her bedroom door with her toe. The room stood dark and still. Braced for the mess, Lena hit the light switch. The house appeared clear, but God in heaven, her laptop was gone and so, it seemed, was her camera.

The wardrobe, where her camera had been hidden, stood gutted, its contents strewn like entrails across the floor. When she failed to spy her camera case, she laid her pistol on the bed and sifted hopefully through the piles of clothing at her feet, to no avail.

Devastated, she crossed to the vanity where she had left her laptop and stared at the table top, where a single sheet of notebook paper lay with the message *GO HOME OR DIE* scrawled on it.

The warning yanked Lena's scalp tight. Her gaze flew to the window. Was someone out there watching, even now? Assailed by vulnerability, she spun toward her bed and snatched up her pistol.

Bang!

It discharged without warning, tearing a startled scream from her throat and ripping a hole into the drywall by the head of her bed.

Cristemou! She'd forgotten the safety was off.

Numb with shock, she reset the safety, whipped the curtains across the window to conceal herself from spying eyes, and sank onto the edge of her bed, shaking. She could have shot herself.

Calm down. Breathe.

She had faced retaliation in the past, but never anything this personal. Who would do this?

Abdul Ibn Wasi.

The name jumped into her head, and her spine stiffened.

Yes, he was the only soul in Mechanicsville who even knew about her camera. Plus, he'd demanded she delete her photos, the ones she'd already offloaded onto her computer, which was now stolen. All those pictures of Davis and Abdul Ibn Wasi, gone!

Violation gave way to chagrin. If he was somehow able to circumvent her password and examine the contents of her hard drive, he might guess her obsession with him. Either that, or he'd wrongly assume that she'd been spying on him all along. A look at her browser history would reveal that she'd researched his arrest history, or tried to. That would be misleading, too.

That bastard!

But wait. How could Abdul have broken into her place when, according to Bill, all the parolees had left Gateway that morning with their parole officers. Her six-hour shift had been endless and uneventful without them.

Leaping off the bed, Lena paced her room, kicking aside the clothes that littered her path.

Could Abdul have discovered where she lived? Why not? He could have had her followed after work by some crony he had contacted. And if he could do that, he could certainly have orchestrated this kind of havoc. "Malakas," she cursed, gnawing on a manicured fingernail.

What now? Calling authorities was out of the question. The last thing she wanted was for the local sheriff to poke his nose into her business. All she could do was ignore the fear that his death threat evoked and confront Abdul upon his return.

How dared he steal her work and threaten her life in such an ugly fashion! The man was nothing but a thug. And going to such extremes suggested he was trying to protect a secret even bigger than she'd imagined.

Unfortunately, if he didn't already suspect she was a journalist, he would know she worked for *Crime and Liberty* by the contents of her hard drive. And if he told Rupert Davis she was an undercover journalist, Davis would never let his guard down long enough to say something incriminating.

She would have to cut a deal with Abdul, promising that she would ignore him from now on if he would keep mum about her occupation. Of course she wouldn't really ignore him. How could she, after what he'd done?

A sudden, consoling thought had her reaching for the smooth green stone at her throat. She still had her pendant; she was still in business.

Abdul might have put a dent in her intentions, but as long as he didn't tell Davis his suspicions, she could complete her objective with the tools she had. If she ran out of storage space in her mini-camcorder, she could offload her files onto the computer in Artie's storeroom.

The note lying on the floor caught her eye, rekindling her outrage.

Like hell she'd go home. Abdul Ibn Wasi was hiding

something big, or he wouldn't be so driven to get rid of her. She might be busy wrangling a murder confession out of Davis, but she knew a good story when she smelled one.

Now, this is the life.

Jackson closed his eyes and sank deeper into the lounge chair. The heat of the morning sun warmed his bare limbs and the backs of his eyelids, but the briny breeze wafting off the Patuxent River kept him cool.

Over the sound of waves lapping at the sand by his feet, he discerned the call of a white heron echoing from the other side of the tree-lined river. Nearer by, Naomi flipped like a fish as she dove with goggles to scan the river bottom for treasures. Silvia had gone inside to whip up lunch. How long had it been since he'd taken a vacation?

Oh, yes. Four years ago, he'd taken Colleen and Naomi to Myrtle Beach, only to rent a car so he could drive back to work early. A vision of Colleen's red face and watering eyes as she watched him pull away shackled him with belated guilt. He'd tried persuading her that he hadn't had a choice. His battalion chief had contracted the flu and he had to stand in for him. Or had he actually volunteered to return? Either way, he'd expected Colleen to understand, to console herself with the satisfaction of having made sacrifices for her country.

Only, she never seemed to get that. In her eyes, Jackson's commitment to the Corps was a direct snub against his family. The days he'd missed with them were days he would never be able to get back. Strange, but with the benefit of hindsight and maturity, Jackson realized she'd been right all along. How could it have taken him years, on top of his wife's senseless death—a death he had contributed to because of his workaholic lifestyle—to come to his senses?

In one summer, his daughter had gone from a child to a woman, and he'd missed it, right along with all the months and years he would never get back because he'd been overseas. Yesterday he'd realized his daughter was practically a woman. And with Colleen dead, the only women left in Naomi's life who could arm her with wisdom and encouragement were her two grandmothers. One was already a constant in her life; the other she saw only on vacations to Grand Cayman Island. But they were no substitute for a real mother.

His thoughts strayed immediately to Magdalena Alexandra. Would a woman like that consider taking on an adolescent?

Wow. He couldn't believe he'd just thought that. Just last night he'd wrecked the woman's rental, left a death threat, and now he was considering her as a potential mother to his child. *Am I really that delusional?*

No, just desperate. Honestly, when was the last time he'd had sex? He couldn't remember.

Hearing the telltale vibration of feet on the wooden stairs behind him, Jackson realized Toby'd returned from his three hour quest to find beer in the blue-law state of Maryland on a Sunday. He kept his eyes closed, even when Toby's shadow blotted out the sunlight.

"I hope you like Budweiser."

Jackson cracked an eye. Today Toby's T-shirt read: IF I AGREED WITH YOU, THEN WE'D BOTH BE WRONG. He wore his two hundred dollar sunglasses and a fake moustache.

Jackson sat up. "I take it no one recognized you."

"Nope." With a grimace, Toby ripped off the hair

glued to his upper lip. "You ready for a beer?" he asked, lifting the plastic sack while stuffing the moustache in his pocket.

"No thanks. Why don't you check to see if our password generating program discovered Lena Alexandra's password yet?"

Toby reached into the plastic bag, pulled out a cold one and twisted off the top, releasing a beguiling hiss. With a long swig, he surveyed the view with evident appreciation. "Place must cost an arm and a leg," he mused, ignoring Jackson's suggestion.

It was none of Toby's business how he spent his paycheck. "Beats the hell out of the National Center for Counterterrorism," he grated.

"Yes, it does."

"I'll be up in a bit," Jackson hinted.

"Sure, have a seat. Enjoy yourself," Toby countered sarcastically. "No, thanks," he answered himself. "I think I'll get right down to work." Saluting Jackson with his bottle, he turned and plodded back up the steps.

I am a dick, Jackson realized. "Hey thanks," he called over his shoulder.

"Take your time, Stonewall," Toby retorted.

Ignoring the Marine Drill Sergeant in his head who railed at him to get down to business, he stayed right where he was until Silvia called from the sliding glass doors that lunch was ready.

"That's our cue, Gnomy." The nickname Colleen had given Naomi had suited her when she was a baby and looked a little like a gnome. These days, she resembled a water nymph, all sleek lines and subtle curves as she waded out of the water.

My daughter is almost a woman. Panic banded Jackson's ribcage. If he blinked, would she sprout wings like a butterfly and flit away?

"Look, Dad!" Breathless and dripping, she showed him her bucketful of treasures—colorful shells and rocks and an earring made of real gold. "See, it says eighteen karats right there!"

"You're rich," Jackson affirmed. But a girl with no mother lacked the riches that mattered most.

Over a lunch of tuna sandwiches and dill pickles, Jackson watched Toby's eyes crinkle at the corners as he swilled down a second beer. Obviously, the ATF agent had stumbled onto something in Lena Alexandra's laptop that amused him.

With lunch finally over and Naomi settled up in the loft to read, Jackson made his way to their temporary office to see what Toby had found.

"Check this out," said the ATF agent as Jackson shut the door. Tapping a key, he enlarged a photo of Jackson as Abdul Ibn Wasi, tugging on a pulley rope. Unsettled, Jackson sank slowly into the second chair. The vixen *had* taken pictures of him that day, not that he needed any proof.

"And this," Toby added, clicking to another photo. "And this, and this, and this." Photo after photo of Jackson filled the screen, filling him with a mix of disquiet, heightened stimulation, and self-consciousness. She had zoomed in so close that he could see rivulets of his own sweat rolling from his temple to his jaw.

"Woman has the hots for you, Jack."

Toby's assertion made Jackson break out in goose bumps. "You think this is funny?" He leveled a glare at his colleague. "I am undercover, Burke," he reminded him, pitching his voice low so his daughter wouldn't overhear. "No one is supposed to take pictures of me, let alone a journalist. She knows who I am."

"Nah, I don't think so," Toby refuted, unfazed by Jackson's vehemence. "She took these pictures before she looked you up."

"She looked up me up on NCIC?" Jackson guessed, his stomach tightening.

"Relax. We erased the real Abdul's history, remember? She didn't find a thing."

"But that in itself looks suspicious."

Toby shrugged as he clicked through a series of action shots. The photos were taken in such quick succession that they formed a kind of motion picture.

Jackson' face grew hot. "Please tell me she took pictures of the other guys."

"Just this one," Toby returned to the main screen and scrolled up to a couple facial shots of Rupert Davis.

"That's the former cop," Jackson stated, his disquiet growing. He remembered Davis asking Maggie to meet him after midnight. She'd brushed him off. *Some other time.*

"She looked him up, too," Toby disclosed. "The man served eight of fifteen years at Arlington County Correctional facility. I think he's the reason she's here." Toby sat back and folded his arms across his chest.

Jackson thought about the two times the parolees had interacted with Lena Alexandra. The first day, she'd seemed intent on getting Sulayman to interview for her book, but not so eager that she was willing to spend time alone with him the other night. "What makes you so sure?"

"I saw his name on her email calendar. See?" He opened her Outlook calendar. On July 27th, Lena had written, *Rupert Davis gets out of jail.* "She obviously knows his real name," Toby stated. "He's the one she's hunting."

"No kidding," Jackson said, experiencing little relief in the knowledge that it wasn't him. "I wonder why"

"No idea. I put their names together in a search, but nothing came up. Davis is mentioned in a news article called *Dirty D.C. Cops*, but she didn't write it. But his getting out of jail obviously meant something to her."

"Maybe our analysts can find out," Jackson suggested.

"I'll request that right now." Toby sat forward to compose an email.

Ike had scheduled a 5 P.M. teleconference, after which time Toby would deliver Jackson back to Gateway. Jackson heaved a sigh. The weekend was getting away from him.

Toby glanced up at him. "Have a beer," he recommended. "Have two beers. Play a board game with your kid. *Relax,* Stonewall."

"I'm trying," Jackson muttered. It wasn't in his nature to relax, a fact that had driven Colleen absolutely crazy. Nor had he touched liquor since his wife drove headlong into an eighteen wheeler with a blood alcohol level of .18. Leaping to his feet, he went out into the living room and called up to the loft, "Hey, Gnomy."

"Yeah, Dad?"

"Do you still remember how to play chess?" He'd taught her several years ago while on leave from one of his deployments.

"Of course." Her eager face popped over the railing. "Is there a chess board here?"

"Sure there is." She darted out of sight then appeared again, coming down the spiral staircase with the board game under one arm and a grin on her face.

You'd have thought he'd just offered to send her to Disney World. Oh, wait, he did that last year. She had gone with her grandmother and a friend while he worked.

Colleen's plaintiff voice railed in his head. *Do you want to give up your life for your country, Jackson?*

No, he had resigned his commission from the Marine Corps to keep that from happening. Working undercover for the Taskforce was scarcely more dangerous than driving a car for a living, and yet he couldn't shake the fear that his sense of duty would get the better of him, yet, costing him his life and leaving Naomi parentless.

God forbid. With a private shudder, he ushered her to the table to play.

CHAPTER 7

Lena trailed the only customer out of Artie's and stared across the street. It was six o'clock on Sunday evening. The heat of the day was just beginning to wane. And if the official-looking sedans pulling in and out of Gateway were anything to go by, then the parolees were back from their weekend away. *Finally.* As much as she dreaded her face-to-face encounters with Davis, getting this business behind her was all she could think about.

Planting herself on the curb, she watched for the return of one man in particular. Soon Abdul Ibn Wasi would be finding out that his intimidation tactic hadn't worked. He would see that she was still here, by God, and she wasn't leaving until she'd made serious inroads into sending Davis back to jail.

Muhammed was the first parolee to catch sight of her as he popped out of a Dodge Charger. She raised a hand in welcome, and he shot her a shit-eating grin that mellowed her umbrage. At least some of the parolees amused her, instead of just creeping her out—or infuriating her, as in the case of Abdul.

A dark blue Crown Victoria veered abruptly off the

highway into Gateway's parking lot. Its brake lights flared, the back door opened, and Abdul Ibn Wasi rolled up out of the back seat. Just the sight of him set her heart pounding with a heady mix of exhilaration and resentment. As he turned his head, pinning her with a glare, a high-voltage charge seemed to arc across the four lanes between them, making the fine hairs on her body stand on end.

What? Not happy to see me? She raised her fingertips to her mouth and blew him an elaborate kiss. *Kiss this, Abdul.*

Thanks to him, she had spent all morning sweeping up ceramic and glass shards and resenting the fact that now she'd have to go and buy a whole new laptop.

At her overblown gesture, his eyes narrowed into slits. For a second, Lena quailed as she recalled his death threat. But then, with a shake of his head that was practically an admission of his guilt, he turned and stalked out of sight, freeing her to release the breath she was holding.

Ding, ding. Round one goes to me.

Smirking, Lena turned and marched back into the store. He would visit her tonight at Artie's—she was certain of it. She had to ensure he didn't tell the others who she was, especially not Davis. If he threatened to do that, she would let him know she still had pictures of him and she wasn't afraid to publish them, unless he kept her secret.

The others would likely visit her tonight, as well. She sure hoped so. But then she heard the muezzin wailing out the call to prayers just as it had on Friday night, and she heaved a frustrated sigh. Her next move would have to wait.

What now? Jackson asked himself as he shifted from one knee to the other while facing the *mihrab.*

Not only was Lena Alexandra still in the area, but thoughts of her were making it difficult to follow Ibrahim's sermon. The defiant way she had blown him that kiss made it obvious she knew he was to blame for the destruction of her rental and, therefore, the death threat, neither of which sat well upon his conscience.

He couldn't blame her for her fury. Hell, he and Toby had stolen the very tools of her trade. But the fact that she'd ignored his intimidation suggested she was both fearless and foolish, not to mention the most determined woman he had ever met. His and Toby's scare tactic should have made her flee in terror. Only, she hadn't. If anything, that kiss she'd blown him had been a smart-ass declaration of war.

Oh, fuck, Toby had exclaimed earlier when they'd both caught sight of Schlesser's Jeep in front of Artie's. With Jackson in the back seat, Toby had punched a button on his radio and used a hands-free connection to call their lead for immediate advice.

The memory of Ike's reply made Jackson grit his teeth even now. Stay away from her, Maddox. We're covering our asses as much as we can. For whatever reason, our analysts can't immediately connect her name and Davis's. Once we know why she's got her eye on him, we'll reassess the situation.

Stay away from her. *Right.* Just the sight of her drenched in the amber rays of sunset, her hands propped on her curvy hips, and her lips quirked into a sassy smirk had driven his testosterone levels straight through the roof.

He'd heard the men murmuring amongst themselves at the start of the service how they intended to visit her the minute it was over, and it'd taken all his willpower to block out their voices and tell himself he didn't give a shit.

He had a job to do, and staying focused on that job clearly required more attention than he'd mustered so far because Ibrahim was winding up his sermon and Jackson hadn't heard a damn thing.

"Then you," the imam was saying, gesturing at them from the height of the tower-shaped podium, "will become his army of courageous, sacrificing, and reform-seeking people."

The imam was quoting straight out of the pamphlet he'd issued on Friday.

Startled, Jackson glanced around at the men to see if they'd noticed. Given their vacant stares, it was obvious they hadn't even read the pamphlet, much less connected Ibrahim's words to the text in it. If Ibrahim wanted to rally an army to perpetrate some act of terror, he was going to have to do more than just preach scripture.

As the service drew to a close, Ibrahim descended the *minbar* and opened the wooden worship hall doors to bid the men goodnight. Jackson rose agonizingly to his feet. He did not join the others in following Zakariya to the outer doors in the foyer. Instead, he lingered in the emptying prayer hall. Here was his chance to question Ibrahim alone.

As the cleric pulled the doors shut, he drew up short to see him. "You are still here, Abdul?"

Jackson turned from pretending to admire the fancy inlay in the *mihrab*. "Yes, Imam." He approached the leader deferentially. "I was wondering, do you know when the *Mahdi* is coming?"

"I see you read the pamphlet. Good for you. In answer to your question...perhaps he is already here," Ibrahim stated mysteriously.

The savior of the world was already here? "How many years before Judgment Day will he be with us?" Jackson pressed. Ike had said there were three different translations: seven, nine, or nineteen year.

"Seven years," the imam answered confidently.

"Then, if the *Madhi* is already here, Judgment Day is very near," Jackson reasoned.

"Yes, very near." The cleric gave a nod.

Searching the man's bright eyes, Jackson wondered what it was that he envisioned.

"Do not be afraid," Ibrahim soothed, laying a hand on Jackson's right shoulder. "Allah has chosen you to fulfill his Will."

"Me?" Jackson's heart gave an irregular beat. "How will I help?"

"You will know when the time comes."

He was dying to ask about the Nation of Gods and Earths, but that would make him seem too inquisitive. Jackson gave an awkward bow. "Thank you, Imam."

"Sleep well, my son."

With Ibrahim's thoughtful gaze on his back, Jackson retreated to the foyer where he found Zakariya arming the alarm system. "Ah. I wondered if I had miscounted." With a tolerant smile and a warm good night, the junior imam unlocked the door from the inside and let Jackson out.

Out in the parking lot, Jackson was struck by how quiet the campus sounded. As he rounded the dormitory, he realized why. In the dark of night, the large glass windows that spanned Artie's facade framed a scene that made his innards cramp with envy and concern.

Several parolees were lined up along the check-out counter. Lena stood facing them, elevated by the raised platform that made her dark curls visible from a distance. Whatever she was telling the men kept them spellbound.

He knew the feeling.

Hovering on the edge of the highway, Jackson

grappled with his yearning to join them. Was it the competition that made him burn with envy or was he merely concerned for her safety? Suddenly, the Marine in him who had never questioned orders before was seriously considering defying them.

He knew why he should stay away: to keep Lena's curiosity about him to a minimum, which was clearly a priority.

But he could also think of several reasons why joining the men wasn't such a bad idea. What if she were telling them that Abdul had terrorized her? He could deny it on the spot, offer up a credible alibi, safeguard his reputation, not to mention her own. Didn't she realize her outrageous flirtation might incite a riot?

If he were over there and not standing on the edge of the road like an indecisive stag, he might even discover her agenda and what it had to do with Davis.

Oh, hell, who was he kidding? The real reason he wanted to be over there was because Lena Alexandra had raised his libido from the grave. Too bad that had no bearing whatsoever on his purpose at Gateway, which was to keep tabs on terrorism, not to get laid.

Turning his back on Artie's, he marched resolutely toward his dorm. It wasn't the first time duty put a damper on his sex drive.

"So, who wants to be in my book besides Muhammed and Jamal?" Lena projected her voice so that the others could hear it. Tonight the men were more subdued, less intent on trying to impress her.

"We should all be in the book," stated Hasan, one of the two parolees she'd just met.

"I'm in." Corey's eyes shone like new pennies behind his lenses. Only Davis still looked uncommitted, his expression as secretive and shifty as ever.

Nadim glanced uncertainly at the surveillance cameras. "I ain't sayin' nothin' in this place," he asserted in his Spanish accent. "Might get my ass sent back to jail."

Lena had anticipated his objection. "Oh, no. We'd go into the storeroom to talk," she assured him. "I hardly have any customers after eight, anyway. That way we'd have plenty of privacy and no cameras." She would definitely keep her pistol handy, though, in case any of the men got over-zealous.

The parolees eyed the rear room with interest. Several edged toward it to give it a closer look, even Davis. Lena's excitement rose. *The minnows are nibbling.*

"What would the title be?" Corey spoke up.

A bubble of guilt rose from Lena's belly as she noted his excitement. "Oh, I don't know. *Out of the Shadows,* or something like that? What about you, Sulayman?" she asked, eager to gain his compliance. "I bet you've got a story for me," she said in her sexiest voice.

"Oh, I got somethin' for you, a'ight." He licked his lips, giving his words a crude connotation.

Muhammed took immediate offense. "Man, don't be talkin' to Miz Maggie like that."

"Shut up," Davis told him. "I don't want my name in no damn book."

"What name? I only know you as Sulayman, and I have no intention of using your last name. There have to be thousands of converts named Sulayman. You'd be completely anonymous."

"Whatever," he said with a shrug.

That was enough of a commitment for Lena. She hunted for a scrap of paper and a pen. "Who wants me to interview them first?"

"I get to go first," Muhammed insisted. "I called it the first day."

"Muhammed's first," she agreed, jotting down his name. "Why don't you come in tomorrow, then, and we'll get started."

"Wait a second." Jamal frowned. "How you gonna write a book in just three weeks? We all leavin' after that."

"That's plenty of time to interview you. I just need an hour with each of you, say right at 8 P.M. That way you'll be done by curfew. Before you leave Gateway, we'll exchange contact information so we can keep in touch."

Jamal tried to negotiate a fifty-fifty split on royalties.

Lena smiled wryly. "Sorry, babe. That would compromise your anonymity." She jotted down the names of all the men present. "Where's Abdul?" she asked, casually glancing up at Corey. It had taken the wind out of her sails when he'd failed to show up tonight.

Corey shrugged and looked around. "I don't know."

"Ask him if he wants to be interviewed." A danger to her or not, they had to discuss the roadblocks he kept throwing up on her highway to justice. "Tell him I have a slot open this week."

Jamal elbowed Hasan. "You hear that? She got a *slot* open for Abdul."

"Man, shut up," Muhammad snapped.

Feeling her face heat, Lena fixed her attention on the schedule she was putting together. "Muhammed, Jamal, and Nadim, I have you down for this week. Corey, Sulayman, Hasan, and—what was your name again?" she asked the other parolee she'd just met.

"Shahid," he said.

"Shahid." She wrote his name down. "You four can

come next week."

"We can't do Friday nights," Corey reminded her.

"I already factored in your Friday night service. We even have an extra week in case I need to follow up with any one of you," she assured him as she handed each man a piece of paper with his appointment noted on it. "Give this one to Abdul for me?" she asked Corey. She still hoped to see him sooner than Wednesday night when she'd set aside time to interview him. But, if not, he'd at least get the message that she wanted to talk.

As Davis accepted his appointment, pinpricks trekked up Lena's arms and stabbed at her scalp.

She had done it! She'd secured an interview with her sister's killer. The next step—getting him to reveal incriminating evidence—was going to be the hard part.

"Here's your appointment time to interview for Maggie's book," Corey announced.

Stretched out on the bottom bunk, Jackson accepted the scrap of paper Corey offered him and glanced down at the decisively written *Wednesday, 8 P.M.* His pulse sped up at the prospect of a private interview three nights from now.

"She must like you," Corey noted with a pout. "I gots to wait till next week."

"You ain't serious," Jackson said, ignoring Corey's observation. "She expects us to talk to her under all those cameras?"

"Naw, man. She takin' us all into the *back* room, where there ain't no cameras." Corey tried to hide his grin of anticipation.

Jackson frowned. What the hell was Lena Alexandra thinking, boxing herself, alone and defenseless, into a small room with ex-cons? "Is

Sulayman getting interviewed?" he demanded, wondering if an interview with Davis was her real intent.

"Yeah. I think he go next week, right after me. Why?"

"No reason," Jackson muttered, looking away.

"You don't think she should be alone with him," Corey guessed. "I know, right. He ain't like the rest of us."

"No, he ain't," Jackson agreed. He wondered how far Lena would go to discover Davis's darkest secrets. What did they matter to her, anyway?

There were two ways to find out. One, the Taskforce analysts would eventually discover what linked Lena and Davis. Or two, Jackson could just follow his own instincts this time and ask her himself.

"So, you in?" Corey eyed him closely.

"I'll think about it," he hedged.

Corey chuckled. "Yeah, you playin' all cool about it. I know you ain't missin' that appointment." He ambled into the adjoining bathroom and shut the door.

As Jackson pictured himself sitting face-to-face with Lena, it occurred to him with starling clarity that, as a journalist, Lena would never conduct interviews without a camera handy.

Holy hell! He and Toby had completely overlooked the obvious. Her Canon Rebel wasn't the only camera in her possession. She had to have a hidden one, as well, which meant she probably still had more pictures of Jackson than those they'd already seized.

Son of a bitch! Where was the goddamn thing?

Sifting through his memories of her, he hunted for the kind of items that disguised miniature recording devices—something like a watch, an ink pen, or a hair clip.

What about her necklace? Dangling between her

delectable melon breasts, where he'd love to bury his face, it had caught his eye on more than one occasion. While the stone in the pendant varied, the setting was always the same—a tear-shaped bail with a scroll-pattern at the top, inlaid with a diamond chip. Only, he'd bet his next paycheck that wasn't a diamond chip; it was a fucking lens.

He threw an arm over his eyes. The pendant explained so much, like how she always seemed to stand with stiff shoulders and glide as she turned, like a jewelry box ballerina. He'd mistakenly assumed that she was flaunting her wares to her admirers, but it wasn't that at all. She'd been aiming her camcorder.

Christ, he had to take the thing away from her before she ruined his investigation.

Only, Ike would never agree to that. He knew exactly what kind of plan Ike would want to execute: Send Toby over to catch Lena unawares. Toby could grab her after work on her way to her car and rip the necklace off her throat. End of story.

All Jackson had to do was share his revelation with Ike, and it would be over.

He teased his ear bud out of his pajama pocket. In the bathroom, Corey had just turned on the shower. Jackson could give Ike a quick call. He knew Toby would be more than glad to address the situation.

On the verge of dialing the team lead, Jackson hesitated. He pictured Lena struggling in Toby's grasp. The mental image evoked both jealousy and reluctance. He didn't want Toby touching Lena. The thought of Toby bruising her or, worse yet, charming her like some dashing bandit, left a bitter taste in Jackson's mouth.

So, what now, Stonewall? demanded a voice in his head that sounded just like Toby's.

I'll take care of it myself.

No sooner did the thought cross his mind than the neon sign for Artie's flickered and went out. On Sunday nights, Lena closed at ten. If he wanted to catch her before she left, he needed to get over there ASAP.

Rolling out of bed, he scribbled a note to Corey on the same scrap of paper that held his interview time. *Be right back.*

He hoped to God Corey wouldn't blow the whistle on him for breaking curfew. Leaving the note on the book his roommate was currently reading, Jackson jammed his feet into his sneakers, pulled on a dark T-shirt, and let himself out.

CHAPTER 8

Floodlights at either end of Artie's kept Jackson hemmed behind the dumpster. His heart beat out a primal rhythm as he waited like a panther for Lena to leave the store, which should be any minute now. A moment ago, he'd overheard the locks at the front of the store scrape closed, which meant she'd be leaving via the delivery door at the rear of the store where the sabotaged surveillance camera had yet to be fixed.

Conscious of the anticipation zinging through his veins, Jackson realized he was blatantly defying orders for the first time in his life. While the ramifications made him nervous—who in his right mind would want to piss off Ike?—the physiological effect was highly stimulating.

Insane amounts of endorphins and adrenaline ricocheted through his body. No wonder it was human nature to defy the rules. What had obedience gotten him in the past but a shit-load of responsibility and a miserable, neglected wife, anyway?

It wasn't like Ike wanted Lena Alexandra toting around a hidden camera with images of his undercover agent on it. In seizing it himself, he'd save

Toby the trouble or, rather, the pleasure of stealing it himself.

If anyone was going to confront Lena, Jackson figured it should be the man who'd first laid eyes on her. Since that was him, he got dibs.

At the sound of the rear exit clanking open, he rounded the corner of the dumpster unseen by the woman moving briskly toward him. Up the alley she stalked, between the back of the store and the ivy-choked chain-link fence.

Two more seconds. Now. Walking out of the shadows, he intercepted her path.

With an audible gasp, Lena startled back, but to her credit, she didn't scream. The *chink* of coins as she clutched a pouch to her chest told him she was carrying money.

"Abdul," she exclaimed, recognizing him in the scant light that wrapped around the edges of the building. "What the hell do you want?"

Her hostile tone left no doubt that she blamed him for the wreckage at her rental.

"Why are you still in the area?" he demanded, acknowledging his guilt as he bore down on her.

She scuttled backward until her heels hit the wall, but instead of seeming afraid of him she glared at him fearlessly. "We need to talk," she stated resolutely.

Talking wasn't part of the plan. He'd come over here to reiterate his threats, confiscate her pendant, and leave. "I don't think so." He spoke in the same, cold voice he'd used for interrogating insurgents in the war. Too bad, insurgents had never smelled so damn delicious nor looked so damn hot. "You need to leave this place and not come back."

Her eyes flashed like road reflectors. "Who's going to make me, you?" she scoffed.

Her temerity amazed him, though he did elicit a

flinch as he dug his fingers into her shoulders. "Yes," he said. Transferring one hand to the slim, silky column of her throat, he encircled it with just enough conviction to elicit a tremor of fear. Beneath his palm, her pendant glinted in the dark.

She held defiantly still. "What are you going to do? Kill me with your bare hands?" she taunted, calling his bluff.

Curling his fingers around the sturdy silver links of her necklace, he readied himself to rip the chain off. But her enticing scent and the luscious curve of her lips sparked an overwhelming desire to steal a kiss first. He drew her closer and lowered his head, intent on crushing his mouth over hers.

But before their lips even touched, the cold, blunt tip of what felt like a pistol gouged his abdomen. Next came the unmistakable click of a gun's safety.

Where in hell had that come from?

"Step away from me, Abdul, or I'll drop you dead right here," she grated sweetly.

All Jackson could do was to stare at her in astonishment.

"You think I won't?" She gave a soft throaty laugh that stirred both his incredulity and his libido. "I can claim you attacked me for the money, and that I shot you in self-defense. You're an ex-con on parole, and I'm a helpless, solitary female. There isn't a jury in the state of Maryland that wouldn't support my right to defend myself."

Helpless, my ass, he thought, though truth was he could knock that little gun right out of her hands and overcome her in an instant. The pistol might just go off in the process, however, drawing unwanted attention to Artie's and possibly even injuring one of them. Maybe they ought to have that little talk she'd just mentioned.

"Let's discuss this," he said, wondering what the hell could be so important that she would disregard both a death threat and an assault in a dark alley.

"What a fine idea. Take three steps back," she ordered on a harder note.

Reluctant to relinquish his hold on her necklace, Jackson nonetheless let go and backed away three paces. He hoped she wasn't filming his humiliation. For the time being, though, his attention was focused on the pistol in her competent-looking grasp. "Easy, woman," he cautioned, when she leveled it at his chest.

"Don't call me that. I am sure as hell not your woman."

Yeah, that was the part of all this that bothered him the most.

"Now listen to me and listen well," she seethed, her fury returning. "I have no intention of leaving the area until my book is written, so get that through your thick skull now. Perhaps you'd like to know, in the meantime, that I still have videos of you in my possession, despite the fact that you stole my three thousand dollar camera and my laptop. I swear to you I'll put your face on every widely publicized forum in the country if you tell *anyone* what you learned about me from pillaging my laptop."

He glanced down at her pendant, certain that little sucker was the source of her so-called videos. Had she offloaded those she'd taken previously, or were they still stored in the pendant's memory?

"Tell me what you're after," Jackson demanded, struggling to fathom her plans.

"I just told you. I have a book to write."

That wasn't the whole story and he knew it. "Why all the pictures of me?" he persisted. "What do you want with Sulayman?"

The pointed question turned her rigid. "Considering the havoc you wreaked on my life the other night, I don't think I owe you any answers," she retorted. "You're damn lucky I don't just shoot you out of spite. In fact, I suggest you haul ass now before I change my mind."

Jackson considered lunging for the pendant first. Only he didn't trust her not to shoot him—probably not lethally but in a spot that would slow him down and force him to have to explain how he came by a bullet wound. He couldn't risk getting thrown out of Gateway for violating rules of behavior.

With a grin that promised retribution, he accepted that he had lost this round. "See you Wednesday, then," he tossed out with a grin that promised retribution. Before she could cancel his scheduled interview, he withdrew behind the dumpster. Darting through a break in the chain-link fence, he crouched behind the ivy to watch her jump into Schlesser's Jeep and peel out of the parking.

An incredulous chuckle sandpapered Jackson's throat as he recalled how she'd attempted to turn the tables on him. But then he pictured her having to do the same with a hardened criminal like Davis, and his humor evaporated.

She might be able to hold her own with Abdul, who was, in actuality, a law-abiding citizen, but Davis was another animal altogether.

What could be so important to Lena that she would ignore a death threat to get it?

As her taillights faded in the direction of the bank, he pushed to his feet and headed in defeat toward his dorm room. Tomorrow, he'd alert his colleagues to Lena's pendant and warn them that she was also packing heat. Hell if he'd tell them how he'd found that out, though.

* * *

With fingers locked around the steering wheel, Lena flew up the 235 to PNC Bank.

Dear God. A belated shiver of horror cascaded through her. Had Abdul really planned on strangling her to death?

For some strange reason, she hadn't felt like her life was actually in danger. She just didn't fear the man. Maybe it was the restraint in his long, warm fingers. Or the unspoken communication that seemed to exist between them assuring her that he was all bluster and no bloodlust. But, hell, if he could commit larceny, which he'd basically admitted to, what made her think he wouldn't stoop to murder?

Because he hadn't come close to inflicting the kind of punishment she'd experienced at the hands of angry criminals before police supervision interceded, that was why. And right before she'd pulled her gun on him, she could have sworn he was about to kiss her.

Careening off the highway under the bright lights of the bank drive-thru, Lena dropped the money pouch through her lowered window into the drop-off box. As she tugged the bar that swept it safely into the vault, her disposable phone buzzed. She knew it was Peter calling; no one else had this number.

"Hey," she answered, smoothing the quaver from her voice.

"Is everything okay?" he asked, surprisingly astute.

"Yeah, sure." If he knew what was really going on, he'd badger her to return home tonight. "You must be back from the beach already," she guessed, focusing the conversation back on him. "How was it?"

"Awesome. I'm a little sunburned, but I'm rested. How's your master scheme unfolding?"

"Terrific," she lied. Humid air wafted into the car

window, smelling of hot pavement and cow manure. She closed the window, cranked up the air conditioner, and pulled slowly away from the bright lights. "Davis has agreed to be interviewed," she disclosed, too distracted by the night's events to feel much of a victory. "But first I'm going to interview the others so he'll lower his guard while I get some practice in. That way I'm prepared to lead him to his execution. I won't question him till next week."

"Good idea," Peter said. "So everything's going as planned."

Not exactly. "Did you get my email?" she asked as casually as possible. "Something is going on with the office servers. I had to send it to your g-mail account."

"Yeah, the servers at work have crashed big time. I've got the IT guys working on it. That's actually why I had to come back early. I'll check my g-mail tonight, babe. What's up?"

"Oh, I just need your help identifying one of the parolees."

"Why don't you just look him up on the NCIC? I thought your friend at the DA gave you his log-in information."

"I did. This guy isn't there."

"How could he not be there? It's a national database," Peter pointed out.

"I know, but he's not. Plus, he's been trying to get rid of me from day one when he saw me with my camera."

"He saw you?" Alarm raised the pitch of Peter's voice.

She deliberated whether to tell him of the break-in; how else would she explain her missing equipment? "This guy actually broke into my house and stole my camera and my laptop. I'm having to use the computer in the store."

"What?"

He definitely didn't need to hear about Abdul's death threat.

"His name is Abdul Ibn Wasi, and he obviously has something to hide," she stated quickly, keeping him focused on the mystery and not on the danger. "Supposedly, he served time for running a pit-bull fighting ring and pocketing wagers, but I'm not buying that." She'd seen how the dog in Artie's parking lot had ceased to bark at his command, a behavior that connoted respect not fear. "It doesn't explain why his history has been erased."

"Maybe he's in some kind of witness protection program."

"Do you think you can find out?"

"Babe, I can find out anything," Peter said with egotism that grated her ears, but assured her nonetheless.

"Excellent." After the stunt Abdul had just pulled, he was going to rue the day he met her.

"I'll start making inquiries tonight," Peter promised.

Given all his myriad contacts in the law-enforcement community, Lena had high hopes he would find something soon. "I appreciate it."

"How's everything otherwise?" Peter didn't sound so optimistic.

"Perfect. I'm in with the parolees, I've still got my pendant, and I can always replace my laptop," she assured him.

"You sound a little shaken."

He knew her too well. "I'll be fine. Thanks for your help, Peter. I'll call you tomorrow." Before he could fill her mind with doubts, Lena ended the call and put her phone away. Talking on a cell phone while driving was illegal in Maryland, anyway, and coursing the dark highway and the even darker country road to her rental home required concentration.

With every mile, her tension mounted. She hoped to God she wouldn't be coming home to more destruction and death-threats tonight.

When the light on her front porch splintered the dark copse on her right, she breathed a sigh of relief. It didn't look like anyone had been here wreaking havoc in her absence. All the same, she held her pistol before her as she ventured inside, ready to shoot.

Jackson slipped on his running shoes and started for the door. He'd been waiting all damn day for this.

Corey looked up, startled. "You gonna run in the rain?"

"Rain don't bother me none," Jackson assured him, stepping out into the deluge.

It had been the longest damn day of his life. Between Ike's text advising him to rendezvous with Toby at nineteen thirty tonight and Imam Ibrahim's eye-opening lesson that morning, everything felt like it was up in the air. Plus, Ike must have found out something critical for Toby to be meeting him in person.

Pounding up the highway, Jackson arrived at the utility road in record time. By the time he bounded to the secure spot where Toby had played a practical joke on him previously, the rain had soaked him to the skin.

He slowed to a walk, silencing his breathing as he followed Toby's tracks in the damp earth. Last week, he'd been pegged by Toby's air soft gun. Hell if he would let the former Army Ranger catch him off guard again. Seeing Toby propped against a tree trunk in plain view took the fun right out of their ongoing game. So did the serious expression usurping Toby's habitual smirk.

"What's going on?" Jackson asked. His gaze flicked to the message on Toby's damp green T-shirt: I LICK ON THE FIRST DATE. *Jesus.*

"We know why the journalist is here," Toby stated, getting straight to the point.

Finally. "What took so long?"

Toby stuck his fingers into his pockets. "Her name isn't Lena Alexandra. She adopted that name when she started writing for *Crime and Liberty*. Her real name is Magdalena Anastasia Xenakis." He articulated every syllable as his eyes scanned the darkening forest, a habit from his Ranger days.

"Go on," Jackson urged, pleased that he'd guessed her first name correctly.

"Nine years ago, Davis was accused of murdering her fifteen-year-old sister, Alexandra."

It took Jackson a second to absorb the awful news. "The girl in the photo by her bed," he guessed, recalling how uncomfortable he'd felt wrecking Lena's bedroom when the eyes in the photo seemed to follow him. It disturbed him to think that the delicate, dark-eyed girl in the picture was dead. "Davis was a cop back then," he recollected.

"That's right. Alexandra had been walking home from an evening church service when she ran into a troubled teen named Curtis Vandaloo and his friends. They were high on coke and tried to talk her into snorting. Davis showed up and put her into his squad car under the pretext of getting her safely home. Curtis Vandaloo watched the cop drive away with her, and that was the last time anyone saw her alive."

Jackson's dinner of stewed lamb burbled inside him.

"When the girl's burnt body was found in a dumpster two weeks later, Curtis came forward. Unfortunately for him, he had a juvy record, so investigators initially suspected him of killing Alexandra, only he was seen by neighbors at his house around the time that the victim was murdered. Investigators swabbed Davis's cruiser for Alexandra's DNA and found nothing, suggesting it had been wiped clean, so with just Curtis's incriminating statement, they went ahead and pressed charges. Two weeks before the trial, the kid disappeared. His parents filed a missing person's report, and the city looked high and low for him, but he was never seen or heard from again."

The soft patter of rain filled the gloomy silence. "And that's why none of this is on Davis's rap sheet," Jackson guessed.

"Exactly. No witness, no trial. The charges were stricken from Davis's record."

A droplet of rain slipped under Jackson's collar to course his spine. Now he knew what had brought Lena Alexandra to Mechanicsville. Sure enough, her mission was personal, as well as dangerous enough to merit carrying a weapon. "So her cockamamie story that she's here to write a book is a cover, just like we thought," he considered out loud. "I think she's hoping to incriminate Davis without his knowledge." Recalling how masterfully she had manipulated the men so far and how she'd been garnering information over the years from various criminals, it was clear to see why she thought herself capable of such a daunting task.

"Using the hidden camera you suspect she's wearing," Toby finished, "the pendant. You want me to take it from her?" he asked, flashing an evil grin.

"I'll do it," Jackson insisted.

Toby raised an eyebrow. "I thought the boss told you to steer clear of her. It's only going to rouse her curiosity if you grab her pendant from her."

"Her curiosity's already roused. Let me handle the journalist. You break into Artie's tonight and hack the computer looking for my picture," he suggested, designating tasks to keep Toby busy. "She's bound have offloaded the contents of her pendant by now, and the store's computer is the likeliest destination."

"I see what you're doing." Toby's smile grew as he folded his arms across his chest. "You just want to jump the broad yourself."

Jackson scowled at him but didn't bother to deny it.

"Can't say as I blame you, Stonewall, but the boss ain't gonna like it," Toby pointed out.

"So don't tell him," Jackson bit back.

Both of Toby's eyebrows shot up this time. "You want me to lie? Damn, Stonewall, I didn't know you had it in you," he said with approval.

"It's not a lie," Jackson insisted. "Just don't tell him anything. I know for a fact Lena Alexandra won't leave this place unless we offer her something she can't refuse." He'd come to that conclusion just today.

"And what's that?"

"Davis's head on a platter. I won't tell her how I'd do it, just that I could help her bring about his ruin. Maybe that would be enough to send her on her way."

Toby scratched his chin and sent Jackson a dubious look. "Whatever, man," he finally agreed. "I won't tell the boss if you don't want me to. In fact, we never had this conversation. You said you had some news on your end?" he prompted.

The reminder of what had happened today dropped a heavy weight on Jackson's shoulders. "You guys were right about Ibrahim being a Five Percenter," he admitted, experiencing the same disillusionment he'd felt earlier that day. "He pulled seven of us into his office this morning, took down that book I told you about, and then proceeded to hammer his philosophies into our heads."

Toby grimaced. "How committed does he sound? I mean, the NGE can be a positive influence if it's not taken to extremes."

"This is extreme." Jackson swiped the rainwater out of his eyes. "He was skillfully brainwashing us, recruiting us to join him and his followers, and this wasn't his first recruitment, either. If you ask me, the majority of those men who attended last Friday night's service became Five Percenters years ago. That's what he credits their success to."

Ibrahim's words echoed in his mind. *God is you and you and you and every black man to walk this earth.* "He told us that on Judgment Day we would defeat the Devil and rule as we were destined to rule. I have to tell you, he's pretty damn persuasive. He had me sold right up to where the Devil was identified as the white man, the scourge of the earth. As annoying as I find you, Burke, I wouldn't go so far as to call you Satan."

Toby smirked. "How touching."

"Anyway, it looks like we've got a gang leader on our hands. I'll keep a finger on the pulse and keep you updated."

"Cool." Toby glanced at his watch. "You'd better head back, Stonewall."

"Right." Jackson made to turn away and then thought better of it. "Where's your gun?" he asked, raking his colleague with a mistrustful look.

Toby blinked. "Come on, do you really think I'd shoot you in the back, especially now that I learned you're a god?"

"Yes."

"You wound me, Jack," Toby said, clapping a hand over his heart. "We're partners now. You gotta learn to trust me."

With a final suspicious once-over, Jackson turned and ran.

Seconds later, a pellet whacked him in the right butt cheek, stinging like a son of a bitch.

"Prick," Jackson muttered, picking up his pace.

Toby's rumbling laughter echoed through the murky forest.

Emerging onto the rain-slick highway minutes later, Jackson's gaze went straight to Artie's neon sign. Under the weeping sky, its lights bled a rainbow of color.

He thought of the horrific crime Davis had inflicted on fifteen-year-old Alexandra Xenakis, and a cold wave of fear washed over him. Did Lena seriously believe she could elicit a confession from her sister's killer? If so, she needed a reality check. If Muhammed wasn't being interviewed by her at this very moment, he'd pound on the back door of Artie's until she granted him entrance.

Only what would he say that wouldn't expose him as an agent of the law? If he disclosed his knowledge of her agenda and offered to help her incriminate Davis, that might get her attention, certainly, but then she'd wonder how he knew.

He couldn't just tell her who he really was. She was a crime journalist, for Christ's sake, who wrote for a tabloid that railed against the abuse of civil liberties. Not only might she jeopardize his investigation but she could expose it to the percentage of the population who'd be most offended by the government's meddling.

On the other hand, turning a blind eye to her agenda was unpardonable. Davis would shred her like a rabid animal if he knew she had a bead on him.

Talk about being stuck between a rock and a hard place.

If only Ike had a means of whisking Lena to safety, like he'd done for Eryn. But, making Lena disappear for a couple of weeks wasn't an option. The parolees at Gateway would be the first to fall under suspicion if an employee at Artie's suddenly went missing. And Jackson needed scrutiny like he needed a hole in the head.

There was no apparent solution to his predicament. Somehow, someway, he had to convince Lena to abandon her plans without revealing how he'd come to know them. Plus he had to confiscate her pendant while tracking down the videos she'd possibly already offloaded.

It all sounded impossible.

Dealing with a resolute crime journalist was proving far more difficult than discovering Gateway's ties to terror.

CHAPTER 9

The rain had put a damper on the parolees' usual game of basketball. As he drew nearer to Gateway, Jackson spied the parolees taking shelter under the dormitory's overhang. Light from the windows behind them cast their dark forms into silhouette.

"Whassup?" Jackson asked, avoiding Davis's hostile glare as he joined them. A pungent cloud of body heat and body odor greeted his nostrils as he stepped under the portico.

"Yo, Muhammed's been over there for over an hour, dog," Jamal whined, nodding at Artie's with a look of envy.

"It's gonna take that long to tell his life story," Corey pointed out.

"Maybe we should go an' get 'im." Nadim shot Jackson a pleading look. "Ain't nobody gone into the store in all that time. What if he don't mind his manners?"

Jamal perked up suddenly. "Here he come now!"

Sure enough, Muhammed was darting across the highway with a ghostly plastic bag over his head. He whipped it off as he joined them under the overhang.

"How was it, brotha?" Jamal asked him. The men gathered eagerly around him.

Jackson remained on the periphery, feigning disinterest.

"Nice," Muhammed gushed. "Just like we was on a date." She gave me a hot dog and a soda. "We was in the back room, sittin' all close and shit."

Jackson's temples throbbed. Surreptitiously, he studied the faces of the men around him, especially Davis, for signs that they suspected 'Maggie' wasn't who she said she was.

"She look' good, too," Muhammed said, warming to his tale. "She had on a white shirt that was all tight and showin' off her stuff." The men broke into guffaws as Muhammed pretended his hands were breasts. He thrust them into Nadim's face and said in a falsetto, "'Tell me about your chil'hood, Muhammed.' Damn, I had trouble rememberin' my own name!"

The men roared with laughter.

"What kind of questions she ask?" Nadim wanted to know.

Muhammed shrugged. "All kinds. I tol' her what I done and how conversion changed the way I thought about myself and all."

The men lapsed into thoughtful quiet.

"Did you tell her everything?" Hasan wanted to know.

"Yeah, all I could think of," Muhammed admitted. "Hell, I got no shame. She ain't usin' our real names, no how."

As the men argued over how much of their shady pasts to divulge, Jackson slipped into his dorm room to peel off his waterlogged clothing. He'd heard enough to confirm that Lena Alexandra had successfully pulled the wool over Muhammed's eyes.

Plus she'd indulged him with just enough flirtation to announce to the others that they were going to get their turn at flirting with her, too.

Having read several of Lena's published articles, Jackson acknowledged that she'd interviewed murderers like Davis before. She knew what she was doing. Only, this situation was strikingly different. The men she'd interviewed had been incarcerated, with armed guards at the ready, not on parole. And none of them had butchered a member of her family. The more he considered it, the more convinced he became that her plan would backfire.

Davis would smell her fear, no matter how many parolees she interviewed first to prepare herself. As a former cop, Davis had questioned plenty of perps. He knew what a leading question sounded like. If he sensed her questions were geared to entrap him, he would react like the predator he was.

In good conscience, Jackson couldn't let it come to that. He had to supply a solution to Davis that didn't involve her interviewing him and, at a risk to his undercover assignment, he needed to do it tonight. Peeling off his sodden shorts, he cranked on the shower. Why waste another moment? His chilled, naked body tingled with anticipation. And it wasn't just the thrill of violating orders once again that egged him on. It was the prospect of going toe-to-toe with that feisty woman and seeing who came out the victor, this time.

Stepping into the narrow tub, Jackson soaped himself under the warm spray while imagining the look of dismay on Lena's face when he called her by her real name. After last night's showdown, he couldn't wait to turn the tables on her.

Feeling a tingling in his groin, he glanced down to find himself fully erect. He indulged in a moment of fantasy, stroking his sex and envisioning Lena pleading with him not to tell Davis who she really was.

"Please, I'll do anything you ask," she begged, her *eyes welling with desperate tears.*

"Anything?"

"Anything," she confirmed, sliding her palm over *the bulge in his slacks.*

Cut! Disgusted with himself, Jackson doused the lights on that imaginary vignette. Christ, was he that pathetic that he had to coerce a woman to have sex with him?

Don't answer that, he quickly warned himself.

But then a new scene evolved in his head. He was telling Lena that he knew men in powerful places; that he could help her find the evidence to put Davis behind bars for good. It felt better to play the hero.

"Are you serious?" Her eyes welled with tears of *relief.*

"Positive. You don't have to continue with this charade, Lena. I'll take care of Davis. You just take care of yourself."

"You'd do that for me?" she asked, melting against *him. Her breasts pillowed his chest. The kiss she planted on his lips ignited the kerosene in his veins.*

Suddenly, they were both naked and she was straddling his lap, guiding his cock into her liquid heat. She rode him with the same feisty bravado with which she'd wielded her pistol last night. Oh, baby.

Grinding his molars together, Jackson swallowed the groan issuing from his throat as pleasure stormed him. Ejaculate shot across the length of the tub, hitting the fiberglass wall as he succumbed to a climax so powerful he had to throw out a hand to steady himself.

Holy hell. The water continued to stream over him as he caught his breath. He dropped his hand with a touch of chagrin and a heavy dose of self-mockery.

One thing he was sure of: His encounter with Lena tonight wasn't going to go down like that, not at all. But a man could dream about rescuing a damsel in distress, even if that damsel refused to acknowledge she was in grave danger.

Lena peered through the dark drizzle. As tense as a hair trigger, she clasped the money pouch under her left arm while her right hand cradled the reassuring contours of the gun buried deep in the pocket of her purse.

When she'd arrived at work in a downpour that evening, her usual parking spot under the floodlights had been taken, forcing her to back into a space under the pecan tree and make a mad dash for the store.

Now she knew what a mistake it was to park so far away. The light cast by the floodlights didn't reach as far as the pecan tree, which meant that Peter's Jeep was sitting in total darkness. Considering Abdul had jumped her just last night, she shouldn't have been so careless.

But she neared the Jeep without mishap. No one leapt from behind the tree trunk to assault her. Her fears were a figment of her imagination. She relinquished her pistol for the car keys and slipped behind the wheel, locking the door and setting her purse and the pouch on the passenger seat.

She was combing her damp hair back from her forehead when fingers emerged like tentacles from the darkness behind her. One hand stifled the scream that erupted from her throat; the other pinned her right arm to her chest, keeping her from groping for her pistol.

"Shhh! Be still," commanded a deep voice she would have recognized anywhere. *Dear God, Abdul was going to kill her, after all!* She twisted violently, scarcely registering the words he spoke firmly in her ear. "Calm down. I am not here to harm you. Magdalena, be still!"

It was the sound of her full first name that penetrated her haze of terror.

"Breathe," he ordered, lifting his hand off her mouth and locking his arm loosely but threateningly around her neck.

As she dragged deep breaths into her lungs, her eyes wide with fear, she saw him take both the money pouch and her purse from the front seat and stow them in the back. So much for shooting him.

"What do you want?" she demanded in a voice that betrayed her by wobbling. "Why did you call me Magdalena?"

He removed his arm from around her neck and angled his chest between the two front seats. "Because your real name is Magdalena Anastasia Xenakis," he said to her profile with perfect pronunciation.

Shock paralyzed her body. How could he know that? Had she registered her laptop by that name?

"I know who you are," he stated with calm certainty, "and I know why you're here."

"Well, let's hear it then." She tried to sound flippant, but her thoughts were scattering in all directions.

"Rupert Davis murdered your sister, Alexandra," he said on a sober note. "You've come here to coax a confession out of him."

Lena couldn't breathe. If he told anyone else this, all her carefully crafted plans had the potential to crumble into dust. "How could you know that?" If Davis found out, he would hunt her down until she lay six feet under.

"Relax." Abdul's deep, musical voice steadied her erratic pulse. "So far no one knows but me. If you want to keep it that way, you need to do as I say."

He was blackmailing her, the SOB! It wasn't so fun being on the receiving end for a change. "How dare you," she seethed, conscious of the broad, warm shoulder touching hers.

"Calm down and listen to my offer. The first thing you'll do is surrender this." His fingers curled around her pendant.

"What are you doing?" Lena clapped a hand over his to keep him from tugging on it. "That's a family heirloom." She tried prying his fingers loose, but her efforts proved feeble against his superior strength. So that was why he'd had his hands around her throat last night. Just as she'd thought, he wasn't going to strangle her; he'd wanted her pendant.

"Bullshit. I know it's a camera, Lena. I know you've been filming me and the other parolees all along. Is it recording now?"

"Of course not. How would I have known you were waiting in the car? How did you get in here, anyway?"

"You left a window cracked. Take it off or I'll just break the chain," he warned.

Fuming silently, she lifted both hands to the back of her neck and unlatched the clasp.

"Are my images still in the memory?" he asked, sliding the pendant off the chain as it slipped loose from her neck. "Or did you offload them somewhere?"

In her befuddlement, it took her a moment to supply an answer. All she could think of was that after last night's victory, she was losing this round badly. "They're all still on there," she lied. "How was I supposed to offload them? You stole my laptop, remember?" She made no mention of the computer in Artie's where she'd offloaded all her files so far.

"Part two of my offer." He tried squeezing farther

between the seats so that he could look her in the eye, only the opening was too narrow. "Hang on a sec." In the next instant, he was out of the vehicle and rounding it to join her up front.

Run! Lena told herself, reaching for the door handle. Only where would she go? She tried to think of something, but then the passenger door popped open and Abdul slid into the seat next to her, having apparently moved at the speed of light.

"Who are you?" she asked, shuffling possibilities like a deck of cards. "How do you know so much about me?" She had purposefully kept her documents referring to Alexa and her killer on her home computer, but there must have been something on her laptop giving him a clue.

She could tell nothing from his shuttered look. "Who I am doesn't matter," he insisted, sliding the seat back to give himself more leg room.

"It matters to me!"

"Listen." His eyes resembled icebergs floating in a dark sea as he leaned intently toward her. "Do you honestly think you can get Davis to confess to killing Alexandra?"

"Alexa," she corrected him. "No one ever called her by her full name." His dubious tone made her burn inside. "And, yes. I wouldn't be here if I didn't," she insisted.

He heaved a sigh. "That's suicide. Davis is going to realize what you're up to, and when he does, he'll do whatever it takes to silence you."

A phantom of terror passed through her.

"Do your parents deserve to lose both daughters to the same killer?"

Her anger surged again. "Don't you dare bring my parents into this! Davis has no idea who I am, and unless you tell him, he'll never know," she insisted.

"What if I do tell him?" he challenged.

Her heart skipped a beat. "Why would you do that?"

"To force you to leave like I've been insisting you do for days."

"If you do that to me, I'll have someone else snap your picture and plaster it on the front page of every tabloid in the country," she threatened. "Why is it so important to you that I leave, anyway?"

He leaned closer, his breath warm and fresh against her cheek. "I don't know why," he said intently. "There's just something about you that makes me want to know you better."

All negative feeling vanished with that single phrase, replaced by a buoyant feeling inside.

"Plus, I abhor the thought of Davis hurting you," he added.

"I won't let him hurt me," she whispered automatically, but she wasn't evening thinking about Davis. Abdul had lifted a hand to cup the side of her face, and his tender touch seemed to travel through her body, zipping down every neural pathway.

"I'd like to date you one day," he murmured. "Would you agree to date me?" His thumb traced the curve of her lower lip, eliciting a shiver of overwhelming desire.

Her mouth went dry and her heart began to thud. "Okay," she agreed in a voice that sounded strange to her ears.

"Then go home, Lena," he pleaded softly. "Be safe. Once I'm out of this program, I will help you find the evidence needed to put Davis away forever."

Her sluggish brain had difficulty grasping his offer. What more did he gain by helping her with Davis than a chance to be with her one day?

"Who are you?" she demanded yet again. "Why isn't your criminal record in the federal database?"

"I can't tell you yet. Just trust me, Magdalena. Can you do that?" he urged. "Trust me to help you."

How could she trust a man with an alleged criminal past and yet no documented history in the mother of all data bases? Did that mean he wasn't really a criminal, or was his identity being protected so that other criminals, higher up the food chain, couldn't find him?

Oddly, when his lips settled over hers, they silenced her confusion. It didn't matter who he was. He was just Mocha Man, the star of her midnight fantasies, who tasted like a rum-laced piña colada.

She met his kiss with a whimper of defeat and the barest token of resistance. Deep down, she could not deny that she wanted him, too, that this moment had been inevitable since the day they'd met.

His tongue glossed between her parted lips, rushing into her like a wave. Retreating and returning, he coaxed her further into his arms, into the current of desire that tugged her out toward deeper waters. But she felt no fear. His kiss was a life ring, keeping her afloat, just offshore of their private, paradise island.

All too soon and with a ragged breath, Abdul severed the kiss, jarring her back to reality.

His deep voice rasped in the quiet. "Just think about my offer. I can help you, Magdalena. You don't have to do this alone."

To her sharp disappointment, he relinquished her. She watched him gauge the perimeter before rolling stealthily out of the Jeep. The passenger door gave a *click*. And then he was gone.

Lena fell back in her seat feeling like the world had tipped on its axis. *Cristemou!* Never in her life had she experienced such a perfect kiss!

Lifting fingers to her sensitized lips, she closed her eyes and replayed the interlude. Longing tugged at her anew. How unfair of him to kiss her like that then leave, with no explanation of who he was, or how he intended to help her solve a ten-year-old murder case?

Just trust me, Magdalena. Can you do that? Trust me to help you.

The words wrung her heart. He had to be sincere. No man could have conjured the passion that had leapt to life between them.

But then doubts overtook her certainty because they were more substantive than her feelings. What if his promise and his kiss were just a means of getting rid of her, something he'd been trying to do from day one? She should not forget that he had threatened her life, wrecked her cottage, stolen her livelihood, and assaulted her in a dark alley!

It was never more obvious that he was keeping secrets, things he didn't want a journalist to know.

Trust him? Hah. He was one to talk about trust when he had told her nothing about himself.

As he darted across the wet asphalt to his dorm, Jackson mentally patted himself on the back. That had gone as well as he could have hoped. He'd managed to convey his wishes and his concern *and* steal a kiss, all without giving away his identity.

And what a kiss it was, he marveled, chasing away the grin that split his face. The only thing that had caught him off guard was Lena's vulnerability. She wasn't the diva he'd thought she might be, wresting the reins of seduction from his grasp and leading him. Rather, she had clung to him like a drowning person clinging to a life preserver, making him feel all powerful and protective. And now he wanted to slay all her dragons for her.

Surely, now, she'd take him up on his offer and leave.

Seeing the light blink on in his dorm room window, Jackson drew up short. The night wasn't over yet. He'd thought he'd left Corey sleeping, only now his roommate was up and no doubt wondering where Jackson could be. He hadn't left a note tonight.

Scrounging up a lame excuse, he unlocked the door and casually let himself in. Corey looked up from the desk where he'd just cracked open his book. "That's two nights now you violated parole," he pointed out, pushing his glasses higher. "You got somethin' to tell me, Abdul?"

"I ain't doin' nothin' illegal, if that's what you're thinkin'," Jackson answered, locking the door quietly behind him.

"I figured that." Corey shut his book and laid it down.

"Can we turn out the light?" Jackson didn't want to draw any more attention to himself than he already had.

"I done figured out a lot of things about you," Corey continued, ignoring his request and stopping Jackson's heart with his words.

"Like what?"

"Like I know you ain't no ex-con," Corey said.

"What makes you say that?"Jackson strove for a belligerent tone.

"Come on, man. You ain't like the rest of us."

Worse and worse. If Corey announced his suspicion to the others, he'd be doomed.

"Since we met, I been tryin' to figure out what you doin' here, but now I know."

"What do you know?" He swam in a clammy sweat. Surely Corey hadn't accomplished a one-in-a-million feat and identified him as an undercover agent.

"You work for Imam Ibrahim, don' chu?" Corey asked, rising from the chair to face his roommate squarely. "You one of his Five Percent followers put here to keep an eye on us. You been reportin' to him each night. Ain't I right?"

Relief made Jackson lightheaded. "You is right," he acknowledged, even though the very thought repulsed him. "You got me. I work for Ibrahim. You gonna tell the others on me or what?"

Corey shrugged. "What I gotta tell for? 'Long as you don't get me into trouble, we cool."

"We cool," Jackson agreed. "You ain't no troublemaker."

"Jus' make sure you tell me the next time there's a room inspection," the young man said, turning toward his bunk.

"Why, you hiding somethin'?" Corey was the last parolee Jackson would have suspected of violating the program's regulations.

"No, but I know someone who is, only I ain't tellin' you."

Jackson chuckled. "Fair 'nuf." Snapping off the light, he made his way to the bathroom. "Thanks, man," he mumbled. If Corey was loyal enough not to tell on his smuggling friend, then hopefully he was loyal enough not to rat out Jackson to the others. His reprieve dried the clammy sweat on his skin.

Once in the bathroom, he flipped on the nightlight and regarded his tormented reflection in the mirror. This was his first job as a spy, and he was finding it tougher than he'd ever imagined. He hated lying to his roommate; hated pretending to Lena that he was someone he wasn't; hated being away from his family. The fastest way to shake off this undercover job was to find the evidence the Taskforce needed.

From now on, nothing would escape his notice.

CHAPTER 10

Lena sped toward Artie's with the Jeep's top down. Wind, smelling of the river and of rain-soaked leaves, whipped at her chignon. The Maryland countryside had a freshly washed look and feel now that the rain had given way to sunshine. She was days away from trapping her sister's killer. She ought to be ecstatic.

But as she neared Gateway, the memory of her run-in with Abdul last night made her confidence waver. His insistence that she was endangering herself, coupled with a kiss that left her yearning for so much more had her rethinking her plans.

Stripped of her pendant, she felt doubly vulnerable. What had once seemed a fairly straightforward process now seemed crisscrossed with trip wires. And on top of her sudden doubt, she was strapped with a nagging desire to get naked with an ex-convict.

The sight of a police officer lounging in a cruiser on the far side of Artie's parking lot, distracted her from her angst. The horse and buggy parked just off the narrow road behind him was nothing out of the ordinary. But why was an officer of the law hanging out in Artie's parking lot?

Lena rolled smoothly into her usual spot, happy to find it empty. Raising the Jeep's roof, she chased the Amish man's broad-brimmed hat into the store, while the officer watched her through narrowed eyes.

"Good afternoon, Bill," she said, pushing through the little gate that admitted her behind the counter.

"Afternoon, Maggie. I'm sure you've met Seth by now," Bill responded, introducing her to the man purchasing a scratch-off ticket. "Seth, this is Maggie."

"How are you?" she asked, as she stowed her purse.

Seth drummed his fingers on the countertop, sent her a shy nod, and kept quiet. Lena's gaze went to the black ink tattoo peeking out from under the rolled sleeve of his homespun shirt. She could just make out the letter "a." An Amish man with a tattoo—really?

"Anything else today?" Bill asked.

With a mumbled negative, Seth thrust the money at him, swiveled on his brown leather boots, and stalked out of the store, sending a frown at the watchful deputy.

Her curiosity piqued, Lena watched the Amish man climb into his buggy. "How long have you known Seth?" she asked Bill.

"Oh, 'bout ten years."

"Has he always been so moody?"

"Long as I've known him. He never did assimilate with the local Amish."

"Assimilate? You mean he's not from here?"

"No, he came down from Pennsylvania with his aunt and uncle, who died soon after. I reckon since he flouts the rules by playin' the lottery and such, he continues to be seen as an outsider."

"Huh." Lena's attention slid to the police cruiser. The man had stuck his brown-sleeved elbow out the window, in no apparent hurry to go anywhere. "And what's with the Sheriff's car?" she asked.

"Oh, that's Deputy Doug Hazelwood. Don't know, really. Something about the parolees coming over here so often."

Heat stole into Lena's face. She looked quickly away.

"I expect it's just a precaution," Bill said. "I should get that camera outside the back door fixed. You haven't had any trouble with those Gateway men, have you?"

Had he viewed the surveillance footage lately? "No, not at all," she answered, glancing gratefully toward her buzzing purse.

Bill nodded to the clock. "You've still got three minutes," he assured her.

Lena dove for her cell phone. It had to be Peter calling. Had he managed to identify Abdul? After last night's kiss, she was dying to know more about him. "Hey," she said, her hopes riding high.

"Hello, beautiful."

Ignoring the endearment, she concentrated on his tone of voice which told her he had news to share. "What have you got?"

"You're not going to believe this."

"What?" She stabbed a finger in her other ear so she could hear him better.

"Abdul Ibn Wasi lives in Baltimore with his wife and baby."

The announcement hit her like a punch in the gut. *My God, he was married.* "Does he?" she said stiffly.

"You don't understand, babe. He works full time as a janitor in a building owned by Homeland Security."

"What? I still don't get it."

"Listen up. The man you say is Abdul Ibn Wasi isn't. I'll send you this guy's mug shot when we hang up so you can see for yourself. He works in Baltimore and hasn't missed a day of work in the last week and a half. I found that out by calling his employer and pretending to be his parole officer."

"Okay," Lena murmured, conscious of Bill's curious glance. "So who's the guy I want to identify?" she whispered, moving toward the store room to ensure her conversation was private.

"That took me a little longer to find out. Everything pointed to the federal authorities being involved, so I called on a favor from a senator to get some information."

Senator? Federal authorities?

"The man calling himself Abdul Ibn Wasi is an FBI special agent, babe. His name is Jackson Maddox."

Astonishment rooted Lena to the spot. She gave a squeak of disbelief.

"He's working undercover," Peter added confidently. "The question is, what for? Not even the senator knows, but Gateway is an Islamic organization, so I'm thinking the Feds are alleging some kind of terrorism is being played out there, which is total bullshit."

Lena scarcely heard him. All she could think about was how blind she'd been not to guess the truth earlier. The signs were everywhere from Abdul's insistence that she delete his pictures, to his missing criminal history, to the cultured way he spoke when the others weren't around. Not Abdul, she corrected herself, Jackson Maddox. She repeated the name in her head, thinking it suited him.

"I'll be down there Friday night."

Peter's announcement plucked her from her deep thoughts. "What? Why?"

"I just told you. I'm tired of the Feds violating the Fourth Amendment. Someone's got to blow the whistle on them."

"Peter, no." Her protest was immediate. "You can't

do that."

"Of course I can."

"What would the senator think? You can't violate his trust."

"Oh, that's cute. Why do you think he told me, Lena?" Peter's voice dripped sarcasm. "He's not exactly a fan of the current administration."

"But you'll jeopardize the agent's safety if you expose his cover, not to mention other people's safety if he's investigating a crime."

"Relax. All I'm going to do is photograph him next to the mosque."

She'd taken a dozen pictures of the undercover agent in front of the mosque, but those had all been stolen along with her camera and laptop. "Why don't I do that for you," she offered, "since I'm already in the area?"

"I thought you said your camera was stolen."

He'd seen straight through her offer. "Oh, yeah."

"I'll see you Friday night," he reiterated.

She tried thinking of a way to stop him. Jackson would leave again on Saturday. All she had to do was delay Peter's arrival. "Better come down Saturday," she advised, thinking fast. "My cottage is tiny; I don't even have a couch for you to sleep on, plus you'll want to avoid the Friday traffic. It's hell in the summer." She held her breath, hoping he fell for it.

"Yeah, you're probably right. So I'll see you Saturday morning, then," he amended.

"Okay." Having protected the man who had her rethinking her future with a single kiss, she heaved a sigh of relief. Not all law enforcement personnel were wholesome. Lena knew that better than anybody. But the Adonis who'd captivated her imagination wasn't corrupt. She intuited that much the same way she was able to read his thoughts. Jackson Maddox was a good guy, not an ex-con with a shady past. She wished she'd known that when he'd kissed her. "Oh, send me that photo of the real Abdul," she requested before Peter could hang up.

"I'll do it right now. And if I learn anything else, I'll let you know. See you Saturday, babe."

The phone clicked loudly in her ear, followed by a chime as the image from Peter showed up in her messages. The dark-skinned, sullen looking stranger looked nothing like her Abdul—Jackson Maddox, she amended. And he wasn't *hers,* either; though that could change if they were both agreeable, couldn't it?

Just trust me, Magdalena. Can you do that? Trust me to help you.

A flame of hope flared within her as she'd considered that, with his FBI resources, maybe Jackson Maddox really could help her incriminate Davis. But then the flame flickered and went out. It had been ten years since Davis had murdered Alexa. Hell, if the PIs Lena had hired over the years had failed to find incriminating evidence in all that time, what made her think Jackson Maddox would have any more success?

Subdued by the reality of the facts, Lena returned to the register to relieve her employer and start her shift. Maybe if Special Agent Jackson Maddox rocked her world with another world class kiss, she'd be able to think more clearly.

"Man, what's that cop doin' over there?" Jamal groused. Tonight was his turn to be interviewed by Maggie.

Jackson peered through the chain link fence surrounding the basketball court. His gaze went automatically to Schlesser's Jeep, which he'd spotted the moment he'd stepped from the mosque earlier. So much for thinking Lena would abandon her plans and trust him to help her later. She'd apparently decided to stick it out, with or without his promise of help.

He'd had a feeling she would take that route. She was an independent woman on an important mission. As frustrating as it was, he could understand her reasons for not taking a blind leap of faith and trusting him.

The police presence at Artie's had been Jackson's idea. As he'd explained to Ike, who'd pulled the strings to make it happen, a cop in the parking lot would dissuade the parolees, especially Davis, from interfacing with Maggie. Then maybe she'd give up and go home. Plus Lena would be safer, over all. Hearing Jamal balk, Jackson inwardly celebrated.

"Man, whatchu got to be afraid of?" Muhammed gave Jamal a friendly shove. "You done served your time."

"You know cops can hear through walls, right?" Jackson spoke up, playing the devil's advocate.

Startled, Jamal looked back at the cop.

"Man, he ain't gonna spy on you," Muhammed insisted. "He listenin' to his radio. Can't you hear it?"

Jamal's eagerness to visit Lena apparently defeated his reservations. "You right," he said, hitching his basketball shorts and swaggering off the basketball court.

Damn. Jackson glanced at Davis, wondering what he thought about the cop. The man's scowl gave him hope that he'd stay away from Artie's from now on.

"With Jamal gone, you on our side now, Abdul," Corey informed him.

Jackson nodded and switched teams. He'd opted to play ball tonight after jogging just a short distance to leave the pendant for Toby to pick up from a pre-appointed location. Then he'd hurried back in time to join a game, and to monitor the officer's vigilance.

Beyond Artie's flat rooftop, the sky turned magenta. With a loud buzz, the halogen lights over the blacktop blinked on as the game continued under a darkening sky. An hour passed, and Jamal still wasn't back yet.

Jackson wiped a trickle of sweat from his brow and willed the lazy ass, screw-up of a deputy to get out of his cruiser and walk inside the store.

What idiot would miss Jamal's entrance coupled with Lena's disappearance for over an hour? But the cop couldn't seem to tear himself away from the talk radio show Jackson caught snippets of now and then. Only one customer had visited Artie's in all the time that she was alone with Jamal, and the man was still lounging in his cruiser listening to his radio.

Jackson reminded himself that she had pulled a gun on him. She could handle a mere convicted bank robber.

"Wake up, Abdul!" Shahid's admonishment snapped Jackson out of his reverie as the ball whizzed past him and bounced off the metal fence. "We gonna lose this game if you don't start lookin'."

"Sorry." At least they still had possession.

"Yeah, you is sorry," Shahid agreed with frustration, stalking to the sidelines with the ball. He bounce-passed it to Corey, who quickly passed it off to Jackson.

Seeing an opportunity to redeem himself, Jackson made a fast break down the court, where Davis defended the basket. Leaping higher than Davis could jump, he slammed the ball into the hoop. He was still in midair when Davis body-checked him, fouling him intentionally.

Jackson flailed like a cat trying to right himself. Unlike a cat, he landed on his back, not his feet, the wind driven clean out of his chest. *Oh, fuck, that hurt.*

Davis's face blotted out the bright lights. "Best watch yourself," he taunted before moving away.

Corey and Nadim bent over him.

"You okay, brotha?" Corey examined him with worry.

Nadim was grinning like a kid. "Man, that was dope, Abdul! I didn't know you could dunk."

Jackson's lungs re-inflated in painful little gasps.

At last, he was able to lift his hands and let the two men pull him to his feet. That was when he saw Jamal loping back towards Gateway. The grin on his face filled Jackson with envy. At least, his appointment was scheduled for tomorrow. As he'd warned her, he fully intended to keep it, even without Ike's permission.

"Switch sides again, Abdul," Muhammed called, as Jamal rejoined them on the blacktop.

"Yeah, we don't want no white Devil on our side."

At Davis's unsolicited comment, all the men turned and gaped at him.

"Half of my family's darker than you, Sulayman," Jackson countered with a hard look.

Davis stalked toward him with his fists balled.

"You got a problem with me, brother?" Jackson demanded, itching for the chance to thrash him soundly.

"I ain't your brotha," Davis spat. "You don't look like me and you don't talk like me."

Silence descended over the basketball court as the men formed a circle around the adversaries.

"Ain't you learned nothin' at this place?" Jackson spread on the dialect more thickly. "We all sons of Allah."

Davis jabbed a finger at his own chest. "I am Allah," he boasted.

Jackson shook his head. Ibrahim's lessons yesterday and today were already taking root in Davis's shallow mind. "You ain't nothin' but a fool."

With a growl in his throat, Davis pulled back a fist and swung. Jackson easily avoided the blow. The man was powerful but too slow to pose a threat to him. "Come on," he said, gesturing for Davis to attack him again.

Like an enraged bull, Davis lowered his head and charged. Jackson stepped aside at the last possible moment, gave him a push and sent him sprawling face-first onto the blacktop.

The men broke into uneasy laughter.

Just then, a flash of white beyond the cage caught Jackson's eye. He realized Imam Zakariya was making his way toward them. *Ah, hell.* Now he would pay for letting his emotions get the upper hand. "Hey, hey, quiet," Jackson hushed the others, nodding toward the gate.

As Zakariya stepped into the cage, Davis clambered to his feet, shooting daggers at Jackson. Under the bright lights, the cleric's robes shone as radiantly as an angel's.

"Peace be with you, my sons," he called, splitting a look of concern between Jackson and Davis.

"And with you, Imam," the men murmured uncertainly.

"There is no place for dissention here at Gateway," the clergyman stated on a gentle note.

"Yes, Imam," Jackson muttered.

"Look your brother in the eye," Zakariya urged. "And shake hands with him."

In Davis's dark eyes, Jackson read nothing but loathing. He extended his hand, all the same, earning a vice-like grip. The thought of that same hand snuffing out the life out of a child had him snatching his hand back.

"Reconcile," Zakariya insisted, giving Jackson an admonishing look for cutting short their handshake. "Now, I am sorry to disturb your free time, men," he continued, explaining his reason for interrupting, "but there's a truck due to arrive with important cargo, and I will need your help unloading it."

The men knew better than to complain. As they followed the imam toward the shed, Jackson gave Davis a wide berth.

The roar of a semi truck preceded the appearance of headlights. Brakes squealing, it slowed at Gateway and backed right up to the new shed.

The men stood nearby, breathing diesel fumes as Zakariya swung open the shed doors and snapped on a light. "Make a line," he instructed them. "You will pass canisters from person to person. Whoever is last in line will place them along the rear wall, understand?"

Curious to know the contents of the truck, Jackson took up the first position. The cargo door rumbled upward, revealing several dozen canisters of what looked like propane. The driver lowered one down to him. He passed the bulky canister along to Jamal, who passed it to Nadim, and so forth, then he reached up for another one.

"Man, wha's in these things?" Jamal huffed, weary after just three passes.

"Propane," Zakariya cheerfully confirmed. "You are going to warm the homes of your brothers in the city."

Jackson glanced at the warning labels as he passed the tanks along. *Danger. Flammable Substance.* Suspicion kindled his thoughts, leaping into blazing tongues of doubt. Older homes in the city might be heated with propane, yes. But if the Day of Judgment was near, then, Christ, this stuff was just as apt to be used for malicious purposes.

"You will deliver the gift of heat yourself," Zakariya enthused, "along with donations of food and blankets."

The imam's sincerity about their good-Samaritan efforts left Jackson wondering if he had aligned himself with Ibrahim's radical ideas or was completely oblivious to them. Was the propane's intended use really benign, or was it going to be used as an accelerant?

"In helping others, you will be a blessing to Allah and to all in your community. Thank you, my sons," Zakariya called as the truck revved and pulled away. With a reminder that their recreation time was a privilege and not a right, he took his leave.

"We got time for one more game," Jamal said, glancing at the sky to gauge the time.

Seeing Davis's vengeful glare, Jackson dismissed himself. He needed to text Ike about the propane right away. Given the donations to insurgents overseas and Ibrahim's radical preachings, the delivery of forty propane tanks took on a menacing connotation.

He longed to slip across the street to visit Lena tonight, but the police presence combined with Lena's refusal to leave as he'd requested convinced him to keep his distance for now. He'd done all he could do to keep her safe.

CHAPTER 11

By the next afternoon, Jackson felt his tension mounting like a rubber band pulled taut, and for good reason.

"Before I dismiss you for supper," Imam Ibrahim was saying as he paced before the same seven parolees he had pulled into his office three days in a row, "let me see how well you have listened to the first Supreme Lesson. Muhammed," he called, wresting that young man's attention from the window.

"Yes, Imam?"

"Who is the Devil?"

Put on the spot, Muhammed's initial panic gave way to confidence. "The white man is the Devil," he answered with a playful smile.

Davis snickered, casting Jackson a sidelong smirk. Earlier in the lesson, he'd asked why Abdul wasn't considered the Devil, being half-white. Ibrahim's assurance that Abdul's black ancestry purged him of evil clearly failed to placate Davis. His expression of loathing warned Jackson of impending reprisal for last night's embarrassment.

"And why does the Devil keep our people illiterate,

Jamal?"

"So he can use him as a tool or a slave." Jamal's tone conveyed his resentment.

"That is correct." Ibrahim's robes rustled as he paced across the Berber carpet. "Sulayman, what is the meaning of F.O.I?"

"F.O.I. is the Fruit of Islam, the name given to the Army of Muslim men in North America," Davis barked back like a Marine recruit.

"Also correct. You have listened well, my sons. What is the duty of the captain, Abdul?"

Jackson blinked. He'd been a Marine Corps captain for six years, but Ibrahim couldn't possibly know that. "The captain gives orders to the lieutenant, and the lieutenant trains the soldiers," he replied.

"Indeed. And because you have mastered just Lesson One out of one hundred and twenty lessons, you are only soldiers. And you will remain soldiers, continuing to learn the lessons long after you have left this place until, one day, you will have all of the Supreme Lessons memorized."

Jackson fought to conceal his disdain. In his wildest dreams, he could not have imagined the nonsense and ignorant talk to which he and the others had been subjected this week. Ibrahim's teachings completely negated the lessons of tolerance and forgiveness taught to them by Zakariya their first week here. Watching Jamal, Muhammed, Hasan, Shahid, and Corey drinking in the imam's words like they were the elixir of life sickened him. Davis, he could care less about. But for himself, if he weren't obligated to discover when and how Judgment Day would come about, he'd as soon stalk off in protest and find another way to give Ibrahim a wake-up call.

"For the New World Order to succeed," Ibrahim said, reclaiming Jackson's attention, "you must be obedient to your superiors. Do you have any questions for me?" he asked with a searching gaze.

Jackson averted his eyes and prayed one of the others would give voice to matters he sought answers to.

Shahid spoke up. "Who are our superiors, Imam?"

Good question. Jackson listened intently.

"Once they were as you are now." Ibrahim gestured at the men sitting before him. "They were poor, ignorant, and eager for power but not aware yet how to grasp it from the Devil. Today, they are lawyers, men of business, and political leaders. They have empowered the god within by heeding the Supreme Lessons and by helping each other.

"During Friday night's service, look closely at the men who walked these halls before you. They are now what you will eventually become—professionals, lieutenants, and even captains in the Fruit of Islam." Ibrahim's eyes burned with zeal. "Look at them and be inspired to follow in their ways. First you learn what it means to drive a truck for a living, to be responsible for your cargo and timely with your deliveries. While in transit, you will listen *only* to CD sets of The Supreme Lessons, and at the end of your shift your appointed mentor will contact you to quiz you and to discuss what you've learned. My lieutenants will counsel you and develop your strengths. In one year, you will take a written test of twelve hundred questions to prove your intellectual comprehension and worthiness."

Jamal groaned, and Ibrahim cut him off with a look. "Once you pass the test and are deemed a loyal follower," he continued, "your mentor will introduce you to his successor, and together they will guide you to a better means of making a living."

At last, Ibrahim had said something that gave him a

clearer picture of the NGE's scope and framework. The cleric gave every indication that his army was a well-established entity, with a hierarchy of levels that extended well beyond the populous of Friday night worshippers. No wonder he filmed his services and posted them on his website. He probably had more disciples than could even begin to fit into the mosque. How many were there, Jackson wondered: Hundreds? Thousands? He swallowed uneasily.

Ibrahim wasn't finished. "Having mastered the First Supreme Lesson, you are worthy to introduce yourself to just one of my lieutenants this Friday." Jackson was just thinking he'd get the names of as many service attendees as possible. "Choose the man you are most drawn to and tell him what you have learned here. Your words will identify you as a willing soldier. In good time, this man will become your mentor. Yet, it is important that none of you share the same mentor. Only one can offer you his guidance and teach you how to develop in stature and power until you fully realize your potential."

Why only one? Jackson wondered, but then he realized Ibrahim wouldn't want any lieutenant developing a following of his own. Competition wasn't good for any ruler.

An awe-filled silence had fallen over the group. Studying his peers out of the corners of his eyes, Jackson was struck by the eagerness shining in their faces, all but Corey, who merely looked thoughtful. He couldn't believe their willingness to put stock in Ibrahim's words.

Questions vied for articulation in his mind. He raised his hand, loath to draw attention to himself. But here was his chance to discover why the Taskforce hadn't managed to intercept communication between Ibrahim and his followers.

"Yes, Abdul?"

"If we on the road all the time, how we s'posed to talk to our mentors?" he inquired, striving for a humble tone.

Ibrahim's eyes focused on him intently. "Before you leave here, I will be issuing each one of you a new iPhone."

A gasp of appreciation swept through the room.

"Accepting it means you are committed to becoming a full-fledged Five Percenter. On the final Friday in the program, you will pledge yourselves in an elaborate ceremony and seal your commitment to the Nation of Gods and Earths, forever."

Jackson itched to hear more. But rather than take more questions, Ibrahim turned his back on the group, saying, "That is enough for today. You are dismissed to enjoy your supper." He pulled the door open. "Tomorrow we will discuss the Second Lesson."

Stunned and thoughtful, the men filed wordlessly out of the office.

Falling in line at the cafeteria doors, Jackson chafed to update Ike about the details of Ibrahim's vast, personal army. While choking down a dinner of tripe soup, cuscus and lamb, he watched Ibrahim speak amicably with Zakariya. If the lesser imam wasn't a Five Percenter, how could he be so blind as to overlook that Ibrahim was one? Or did he just accept it?

Polishing off his glass of milk, Jackson's thoughts shifted to another source of disquiet: Lena and her ill-conceived ruse to coax a confession out of Davis.

His pulse quickened as he realized his interview was a mere two hours away. He knew he shouldn't go. Ike would chew him a new ass if he knew Jackson had disobeyed the order to stay away from her—not just once but several times, already. Only, the opportunity to engage in another battle of wills and come out the victor, this time, was too tantalizing to overlook. The prospect of enjoying her company for an uninterrupted period of time unleashed a flood of hormones. He tried to minimize his arousal by coming up with the best possible strategy to gain Lena's trust. Her trust was what he really wanted. And not even the Fruit of Islam Army could keep him from trying his best to earn it.

"Excuse me," called out a red-faced woman standing at the counter.

Preoccupied by thoughts of Jackson Maddox and whether he would show up for his interview, Lena had failed to notice her customer. This was the second time her obsession with that man had distracted her from her duties.

Abandoning the coffee dispenser, she hastened behind the register to ring up the woman's milk. There were no quarters left in the tray, so she inexpertly cracked open a new roll. Coins scattered in all directions, several falling to the floor.

"Here you go. Sorry." Handing the customer her change, she waited for the woman to leave then stooped to collect the coins that had fallen.

"Everything okay here?"

The closely spoken, male voice startled her so badly she reared straight up, striking her head on the open register. *Ow!* Lena straightened, rubbing the knot rising on her crown, and found herself staring into the watchful gaze of Deputy Doug Hazlewood. This was his second evening babysitting her but his first time to come into the store.

"Didn't mean to frighten you," he said with a ghost of a smile. "I came in when the lady left," he added, explaining why she hadn't heard the door chime.

Without a word, Lena picked up the last lost coin as she sifted through her impressions of him. The officer was forty-something with a doughy face and a round belly that strained the buttons of his uniform. While his slovenly appearance and his partiality for talk radio made him seem like a lazy cop, his gimlet eyes hadn't missed one detail of her startled reaction. The man was more perceptive than he looked.

"You all right?"

"Of course." She smiled at him as she dropped the coins into the tray.

"I hear you're a real hit with the boys across the street," he stated.

She shut the tray with more force than necessary. "Is that why you park out front?" she asked, propping her elbow on the counter and her chin on her hand. She batted her lashes at him. "To protect me from the parolees?"

With most men, her rapt look was all it took to turn them into stuttering idiots.

Deputy Doug stared right back at her, seemingly impervious. "Those men might claim to have changed their ways, but you can't take the stripes off a zebra," he declared.

Having listened to Muhammed and Jamal spill out their guts and express their hopes for the future, Lena disagreed—except where Davis was concerned. One thing she was certain of, if she didn't get rid of Deputy Doug, Davis might never come to his appointed interview. She had to convince the deputy to abandon his dutiful post.

"What can I get for you?" she asked him sweetly.

He ordered two chili dogs, nachos, and a large soda, all of which explained why his belly bulged over his belt.

"May I ask you a question?" she inquired as she

took his money. Leaning closer, she exposed an extra inch of cleavage.

"Sure." Only, he didn't even look down.

"Whose idea was it for you to waste your law-enforcing talents just sitting outside these doors? Don't you have criminals to arrest?"

"I wouldn't be here if I didn't." With a thin smile that told her he saw straight through her, he slapped a five dollar bill on the counter. "Looks like you're stuck with me," he quipped, turning toward the soda fountain. "Keep the change, darlin'. Dinner's on the county."

Lena sighed with defeat and mumbled a greeting to the next customer stepping through the door.

Now, on top of all the obstacles she faced, she was being chaperoned by the only sentry in the world she couldn't manipulate.

Jackson gave the wide steel door at the back of Artie's a smart rap and stepped back. Every one of his senses was sharpened by the adrenaline pumping through him. He could easily make out the words of the talk radio show the deputy never ceased listening to, pouring out of the cruiser parked on the other side of the building. The dumpster nearby reeked of stale milk, and the asphalt under his thin leather soles still baked from the heat of the afternoon, even though the sun had already set. The sound of approaching footsteps made his heart race.

He positioned himself directly before the peephole. Hopefully she recognized him. In the dark, his skin tone could be a blessing or a curse, depending. Nor was she expecting him to show up at the back door. Why draw attention to himself by entering through the front wearing a fitted cap?

At least he knew the rear room was secure. Toby

had broken into Artie's before dawn, nabbing the files Lena had denied downloading from her pendant—little liar. Sweeping the space for bugs and cameras, Toby had declared the space secure. But there was still a risk that Lena had replaced her pendant with another spy camera. Funny how that didn't alarm Jackson the way it used to.

He could sense her gaze on him, affecting him like a heat rash, but she still didn't open the door. "Let me in," he whispered. If he was going to win her trust, they needed to be alone together.

Lena had wondered all day if Jackson Maddox would actually show up for his interview. Regarding him through the peep hole, she pressed a hand to her palpitating heart. Should she let him in, or not?

Considering all the man had done to frustrate her efforts, he deserved to be left standing in the muggy night air. Except that every atrocious thing he'd done was meant to protect his undercover status. After all, he was a special agent of the freaking FBI, a fact that continued to astonish her, though Peter had divulged his news twenty-six hours ago. He wasn't the ex-con she'd thought he was. Plus he kissed like a dream. So, how could she not let him in?

With a bracing breath, Lena pushed the door open.

"Hi," he said. His gaze traveled with evident appreciation over her clingy black blouse and matching skirt to the scarlet-tipped toenails peeking out beneath the straps of her high heeled sandals. Her impractical footwear felt suddenly worthwhile.

"I'm surprised you kept your appointment." He had even dressed up for it, she noticed, putting on his white shirt and gray slacks—for her? "I didn't think you wanted anything to do with my book."

Her comment elicited a snort. "Right. We need to

talk. You mind if I come in?"

At his curt tone, she was tempted to slam the door shut in his face, but curiosity got the better of her. "Fine," she acceded, admitting him into the cramped space.

The heat seemed to enter with him, and his scent, as he eased past her, gave rise to memories of Monday night's kiss, weakening her. Through eyes that finally saw him for what he was, she watched him absorb the details of the storeroom as if he were taking snapshots with his mind. The cinderblock walls, cement flooring, and wall-to-wall refrigerators were all noted and summarily dismissed. His gaze lingered longer on the square table pushed into the corner under a low-wattage light bulb where two chairs faced each other cattycorner, and his lips thinned.

Was he picturing Muhammed or Jamal sitting so close to her that their knees practically touched? Or Davis?

Transferring his gaze to the monitors over the store's computer, he noted the absence of customers in the building, crossed to the door that separated the store room from the front, and flipped the bolt. That simple action turned Lena's palms moist. Just what did Jackson have in mind that they required total privacy?

He turned to look at her. "Did you replace the pendant?" he asked.

Her resentment came surging back. "In forty-eight hours? I don't think so. That mini-camcorder was a gift, by the way. It cost over two thousand dollars."

"I'll see that it's returned one day," he surprised her by promising earnestly. "Just answer me this: are you filming me now?"

"Of course not."

He seemed to take her at her word because he

nodded. "Good," he said, visibly relaxing.

Lena tried taking control of the conversation. "Would you like a drink?" Her bracelets tinkled as she gestured to the refrigerators. "Something to eat?"

His gaze drifting over her had an effect similar to hot oil rolling down her body. "No, thank you. You look lovely, Magdalena."

The way he said her name, with that faint Islander accent of his, made her weak in the knees. She cleared her throat. "Would you like to sit down?"

"Not particularly. Why haven't you taken me up on my offer and left?" His blunt question ripped away the pretense that he was here for an interview.

"How am I supposed to trust you without knowing anything about you?" she shot back. If he were just up front with her about his own identity, maybe then she could trust him in return.

His jaw muscles jumped. "As much as I'd like to tell you everything about me, that's not an option for me." He took a step in her direction, notching her awareness of him higher. "But I can promise you that I'll help you find the missing boy, the one who saw your sister get into Davis's cruiser."

"Curtis Vandaloo." He seemed to know everything about Alexa's murder. "Thank you, but I doubt you'll have much luck. None of the PI's I've hired were ever able to find him. His parents said he disappeared while neighbors swore he went to live with relatives in Pennsylvania. Personally I think Davis killed him to keep him from testifying."

"And you're going to cloister yourself in a room with a man who would do that?" One of his dark eyebrows edged above the other. "I have news for you, Lena. Davis isn't going to confess with that deputy parked outside."

"Oh, so you did have a hand in that." She tossed her

head and sent him a bitter smile. "I thought you might have."

"Davis knows cops can listen through walls because he used to be one," he continued, ignoring her remark. "He's not going to tell you anything."

"All true. But he'll talk if the cop isn't here," she pointed out.

"And how do you propose to get rid of him?"

She shrugged. "I'll think of something. I usually do."

He briefly pinched the bridge of his nose. "Look, I'm trying to tell you that you don't have to. I know I haven't told you everything about myself, but I need you to trust me. Please."

Lena swallowed back the confession that she already knew who he was.

"I swear I can help you, Lena. In two and a half weeks when this program is over, we'll find the evidence together."

His tone was so convincing, his aura so confident that she was tempted to dump Davis's fate entirely into his capable hands. "How do I know you're not just trying to get rid of me?"

His gaze slid to her lips and her pulse spiked. "Getting rid of you is actually the dead last thing on my mind right now," he rasped. Her heart skipped a beat as he stepped abruptly closer, curling his hands about her upper arms. His palms, smooth but for a hint of calluses, gave rise to pleasant shivers as he lightly caressed her skin. "I meant what I said the other night. You're a lovely and desirable woman. The thought of Davis hurting you disturbs me more than you realize."

Enthralled with every word out of his mouth, Lena rolled up on her tiptoes and crushed her lips to his. He rewarded her initiative by hauling her against him and plunging his tongue between her parting lips, in a kiss that swamped her with longing. She found herself in a restless sea where white-capped waves of desire swelled higher as he severed their lips to suckle at her earlobe. Pleasure cascaded down her neck and over her shoulders, tightening her nipples into tingling buds that ached for his touch.

Desperate for skin-to-skin contact, Lena tugged Jackson's shirttails free of his slacks and funneled her hands beneath the cotton weave to luxuriate in the silky milk-chocolate texture of his skin. In a greedy quest to know him better, she explored the six-packs abs, his ribs, the thick flanks of muscle on either side of his back. It would take days, months, years, to memorize all the physical complexities of his body.

He pressed his lips to hers again, nudging her longing higher with heady forays of his tongue. In addition to the promising sweep of his palms skimming the swells and curves of her body, she could feel him gathering the slinky material of her skirt into his hands. Cool air swirled about her knees thrilling her with the suggestion that he was in pursuit of more.

Is this really happening? Or am I dreaming again? Either way, she would weep if he stopped. Thankfully, he seemed to intuit that, slipping a thigh between her bare knees and shifting his hands to her hips to rock her against him.

Dear God. The friction of his rock-hard quadriceps against her sensitive inner thighs made her arch toward him in desperate want. When he matched the massage to the strokes of his tongue, heat breached the surface of her skin. She moaned into his mouth and pressed her throbbing flesh against him as a signal of her need. Surely he could feel how wet she was becoming, how receptive.

In unspoken agreement, they gravitated closer to the table. When it bumped against her thighs, Lena settled her weight back on it and guided his mouth to her aching breasts. "Please," she whispered.

With a swift glance at the monitors, Jackson lowered his head over one of the twin peaks poking out the fabric and drew it into his mouth. An arrow of stark lust shot to Lena's womb as he suckled the stiff bud diligently, his ravishment all the more arousing for the wet fabric between his mouth and her flesh. Arching her back, she encouraged him to continue and prayed he wouldn't stop.

"Let me see you," he urged.

The tantalizing request had her pulling her the blouse off over her head in one swift movement and unlatching her bra without a moment's hesitancy. Nothing had ever felt more right that baring herself to him.

His eyes resembled half-moons under his heavy eyelids. "You're magnificent," he declared, sliding the straps over her shoulders. With a hiss of appreciation, he cupped the full mounds that spilled free. "Christ," he whispered.

Lena slid back until her shoulders touched the wall. In his large hands, her D-cup breasts seemed the perfect size as he held them to his mouth, flicking his tongue alternately over both taut tips. Entranced, she absorbed the erotic vision of their bodies touching. There was no blending of tones between his skin and hers, just a stark contrast that excited her beyond bearing.

She didn't care that she was sitting on a scarred, sturdy table in a musty store room. She had to have this man and she had to have him now.

"So soft," he marveled moving one hand to trace the curve of her outer thigh, then the tops of her legs, and finally the paler, softer flesh higher up.

Too tightly coiled to speak, Lena raised her hem to reveal the cream-colored lace panties that matched her bra. She had slipped them on that afternoon in a whim of fancy, wanting to feel sexy during Jackson's interview, never dreaming that he would actually see them.

A mask of desire tightened his features as she subtly spread her thighs.

"Touch me," she pleaded, shocked by her outspokenness but not the least bit penitent.

When he stroked his thumb over the nub tingling under the damp panel, her hips nearly came off the table. "Just like that," she breathed. He repeated the motion, and her head fell back. Again and again he caressed her, sending her into a realm of ecstasy.

Without warning, he edged aside the barrier, ducked his head, and replaced his dexterous digit with his open mouth.

"Oh, my God, Ja—Abdul!" she cried.

He stiffened, shooting a wary look up the length of her body.

"Abdul's not your real name," she said hastily. "Tell me what to call you when I come."

Her brazen distraction worked. "Call me whatever you want," he said thickly before plowing his tongue into the furrows of her flesh.

"Mocha Man," she breathed, scarcely capable of speech. "That's what your skin looks like to me. Dark, sweet mocha." Gripping the edge of the table, she teetered on the edge of an orgasm.

A deep resonant chuckle followed her comment. Traveling up inside her body, it called attention to the emptiness there. She needed more; something only he could give her. She pleaded with him to take her.

"Tell me you trust me first," he demanded between

flicks of his tongue.

Aware of what he was trying to do, she kept stubbornly quiet, causing him to still and lift his head with a challenging look.

"Oh, don't stop. That's not nice," she reproached him with a gasp of disappointment.

"Tell me you'll trust me to help you," he insisted.

Damn him. Was he really going to do this to her? "Fine, I trust you." Amazingly the moment his hot mouth resumed its magic, she did feel a surge of absolute trust, which made her pleasure that much more intense. "Oh, God!" It overwhelmed her unexpectedly. Gripping the table for dear life, Lena rode the caps of the tallest waves before plummeting into an orgasm that crashed over her, drove her deep into herself, spun her around, then deposited her gently onto a shore of sweet contentment.

To her confusion, Jackson straightened with a grimace and started tucking his shirt back into his pants.

"What are you doing?" she asked, flummoxed by his actions. Was he really going to stop now, in the middle of their tryst?

"Scrounging up some self-control." His grimace turned into a tortured smile.

"Why?"

"Because I want to give you more." He held out a hand, pulling her upright. "Dinner in a high-end restaurant, candlelight, a comfortable bed." He brushed a curl from her cheek. "I can't wait to date you. Just trust me to handle Davis my way and leave tonight, Lena. When I'm finished here, I will come for you." He looked deep into her eyes. "And then I swear I'll give you everything you ever wanted," he vowed hoarsely. "Everything you deserve, including Davis's head on a platter. I give you my word."

But Lena scarcely heard him for the blood roaring in her ears. "You seduced me on purpose," she accused. "You extorted a promise from me!"

His jaw tightened with frustration. "I only want to keep you safe. It's that simple."

What if it was? He seemed sincere enough. Lena bit her lower lip uncertainly.

When the chime of the front doors reached her ears, she didn't immediately react, but Jackson did, swiveling toward the monitors.

"It's the cop," he announced, snatching up her bra and thrusting it at her. "Quick, get dressed."

"You'd better leave," Lena warned, scrambling off the table to put herself together.

Jackson backed toward the exit. "Magdalena?"

In the process of redressing, she glanced up at him. "What?"

"Remember that you can trust me," he said, holding her gaze captive as he pushed the door open behind him. "My word is all I have to give you now, but I swear it's all you need."

CHAPTER 12

The sharp knock on the door right next to Lena drowned out the sound of the service door closing as Jackson slipped out the back.

"Just a minute!" she snapped, struggling to hook her bra.

From the other side of the door, Deputy Hazelwood demanded, "Why's this door locked?"

"No idea!" Flustered and furious, Lena tunneled into her top, grimacing at the damp patch over one breast as she tugged it down. Making one final adjustment to her twisted skirt, she stepped toward the door, took a deep breath then snatched it open. "What do you want?" she asked with all the grace of a defiant teenager.

"What are you doing?" His gaze went straight to the wet spot on her blouse.

"Stocking the refrigerator," she bit out.

Craning his neck to see inside, he took a good look around. "Keep the door open next time."

"Who appointed you my keeper?" she groused, aware that she was taking out her temper on the hapless deputy. She already knew Jackson was responsible for the police presence at Artie's.

"*No idea*," the deputy tossed back, using her own words against her as he swiveled toward the hot dog grill.

Lena stalked into the store after him. Lathering her hands with antibacterial gel, she grilled the hotdog he ordered on autopilot while deliberating Jackson's ultimatum.

Not only had he sworn to help her implicate Davis in her sister's murder, but he'd pledged to woo her like a gentleman the next time they met. All she had to do was leave tonight.

The dilemma made her stomach churn with conflicting impulses.

My word is all I have to give you now, but I swear it's all you need. Was it really? She had nothing in writing, nothing to guarantee he would fulfill his promises. From the fateful night she'd learned that her sister had been murdered by a cop, she'd trusted no man—not even one she intuited was a good guy.

Desire gave way to cynicism. Maybe if she still believed in fairy tales and princes in shining armor galloping to a fair maiden's rescue, she'd take Jackson Maddox at his word. But she'd moved well beyond that stage in life.

More than that, she was this close to catching Davis on her own. How could he expect her to turn her back on everything she'd accomplished so far, all in the hopes that he had the integrity he said he did?

Jackson stared up at the springs checkering the bottom of the bunk above him. Corey's snores abraded his raw nerves. He couldn't sleep. His body still hummed with sexual awareness. Visions of Lena, virtually naked and lying spread-eagle on the table top flickered before his eyes like an endless X-rated movie. The only way to loop his thoughts off the erotic film track was to picture her interviewing Davis. His blood ran alternately hot, then cold.

Twelve years of active duty in the Corps had accustomed Jackson to going without sleep, but if he didn't keep his senses sharp and his guard up on this undercover job, he'd make a fatal error. Having stayed up late the last two nights, he already felt like he was running on fumes. Unless he got rid of this hard-on, sleep would continue to elude him.

With chagrin, he loosed the string on his pajama bottoms and took his steely erection in hand.

This was twice now in just days that he'd had to masturbate. For a man who hadn't thought about sex in months, even years, his current state was nothing short of a resurrection. Not only had Lena brought his sex drive back to life, but she'd ratcheted it to the highest setting, making him as horny as a nineteen-year-old.

Picturing what he would do to please them both next time, it took mere seconds to whip himself into a critical state.

I've fallen for her, he realized with mixed dismay and euphoria. The one woman in the world with the potential to expose him as a fraud now had him by the balls. Worse than that, she gave so little consideration to her own safety that he had every reason to fear she wouldn't make it out of Mechanicsville alive.

Envisioning himself buried in her tight, slippery sex, he swallowed a groan of sublimity as he came in a powerful rush, wetting his own bare chest. A pleasant, sleepy stupor ambushed him immediately. He barely had the energy to grope for the T-shirt that was balled up under the bed.

Please leave town tonight, he willed as he wiped himself dry. The plans that were forming in his head about the future hinged on Lena remaining safe, and very much alive.

The next evening, Lena pushed out of the store in the hopes of dispelling her agitation. Turning her back intentionally on Gateway, she admired the lavender sunset on the western horizon and dragged warm country air into her lungs.

"Howdy," called Deputy Doug Hazelwood out the window of his cruiser. "Nice evening."

She sent him a tight smile and a barely perceptible nod of agreement. Concentrating on the scent of freshly mowed grass and a gust of summer air, she was nonetheless aware of every cell in her body clamoring for Jackson to come visit her again tonight. Only, she knew he wouldn't.

He had given her an ultimatum—to surrender her plans for Davis or else never again experience the intoxicating thrill of getting to know him intimately. Of course, he hadn't worded it in such black and white terms, but she was fairly certain that it was Jackson's way or the highway.

The only sure method to get what her body and heart yearned for was to pack her bags and head for home.

Still, she wasn't leaving. Maybe if she got some kind of promissory note that would hold up in a court of law, she thought wryly, but probably not even then.

If she could just explain to Jackson that it wasn't strictly a matter of trust. She was days away from her interview with Davis, an interview she'd imagined countless times in the past ten years. How could she just walk away after all she had done to prepare for his entrapment? Especially when she fully believed in her ability to make him say something incriminating. She couldn't just give it up.

Nor could she shake the sinking certainty that, as a consequence, she was letting something extraordinary slip through her grasp.

What if Jackson never sought her out again because she'd rejected his offer and therefore *him?* Would this longing inside eventually subside? Or would she end up looking for his face in every crowd, wondering what might have happened between them if she'd just acceded to his wishes?

Even now, she fought the urge to turn around and search for him on the blacktop, where she could hear a basketball being dribbled. Pride alone kept her from stealing a peek as she whirled around and marched for the door.

But then a lone figure jogging on the shoulder of the highway snared her attention and, with lurch of her heart, she recognized the runner as Jackson. Slick with sweat, his limbs gleamed like oiled teak as they pumped in graceful rhythm beneath him, carrying him closer. Envisioning him driving his powerful body into hers, she gave a moan of lament before she squared her shoulders and forced herself to look away.

I didn't come here to fall in love, she reminded herself. The four-letter word leaped so lightly into her head that it made her heart stop. *I came to catch my sister's killer.*

"Maggie!"

Hearing her other name called, she glanced back to see Nadim, hustling across the highway on his way over to be interviewed. Pasting a smile onto her face, she held the door for him and waited. "Glad you could make it," she said when he reached her side.

"I wouldn't miss it for the world," he exclaimed with Hispanic flair.

His words prompted a powerful pinch of remorse. What am I going to miss, she wondered, by refusing

Jackson's offer?

At last, the packed Friday night service ended. Ibrahim stepped to the edge of the *minbar* to issue a final blessing which Zakariya repeated from a lower platform opposite him.

"*Maa'assalama*," Zakariya called. "Go in peace, my sons and brothers."

Rolling up his prayer rug, Jackson tucked it under one arm, careful not to whack any of the men that pressed in on either side of him.

The service had been as heavily attended tonight as the prior week, with Five Percenters and parolees crammed together like sardines into the prayer hall. Again, Ibrahim's sermon had been filmed to be uploaded to his website. But, unless he'd spoken in a code Jackson couldn't decipher, the imam had said nothing to suggest that Judgment Day was at hand. Catching the eye of the powerful-looking stranger who'd kneeled beside him, he proffered a hand.

"*Assalamu alaikum*. My name is Abdul Ibn Wasi. I am a soldier of the Fruit of Islam."

The unsmiling giant looked him over dubiously as he came to his feet. At last, he clasped Jackson's hand in a daunting grip. "I am Mr. Rakeem," he responded in a stentorian voice. "Welcome to your future, Abdul."

Mr. Rakeem seemed to be establishing his dominance with their handshake. "Thank you." Tugging free, Jackson sought something else to say. "Did you come through Gateway?" he asked, knowing the answer already.

The powerful stranger nodded. "Seven years ago when the doors first opened. I was once a thief," he added on a note of self-contempt. "Now I run a school for boys."

Terrific, Jackson thought, picturing a school full of dark-skinned boys being taught that the white man was the Devil. "What's the name of your school?"

"Rabia," came the terse reply. "Ask less questions and you will learn more."

Unimpressed with the man's arrogance, Jackson gestured at their feet. "May I put away your prayer rug for you?" he asked to placate the man. Without a word Mr. Rakeem stepped back while Jackson stooped to roll it up.

"You are a quick study, Abdul," Mr. Rakeem relented as he straightened with the rug. "Tell me what you have learned about the First Supreme Lesson."

Jackson summarized the gist of the lesson quickly. It was Mr. Rakeem who needed to offer information, not him. "When is the Day of Judgment?" he tacked on to his last statement.

The man's dark eyes glinted. "Is that a question, Abdul?"

Jackson's hopes nosedived. "I'm jus' curious," he persisted.

"What you are is a soldier," the man corrected. "It is not a soldier's place to know these things." He clapped Jackson hard on the arm. "We will meet again," he predicted, moving abruptly away.

I'll be there when the judge hands down your jail sentence, Jackson thought as he watched Mr. Rakeem walk away, his chin at a regal angle. Then Jackson cast his gaze about to find Muhammed, Corey, Shahid, and Davis in deep in conversation with their future mentors. Jamal and Hasan had finished talking to theirs.

If he and Toby didn't find the evidence needed to indict Ibrahim while searching the imam's offices tonight, then all seven of Ibrahim's chosen, himself included, would be initiated into the Five Percent Nation on the last Friday in the program. While Ibrahim hadn't mentioned it yet, there were severe consequences for trying to leave a gang. Once pledged, new recruits were members for life. Deserters were beaten to death, or drugged and set on fire to burn alive.

Jackson swallowed the sour taste in his mouth. He could never wish that on the men he'd come to know, least of all on his soft-spoken roommate. All he could was do was try to get Ibrahim incarcerated before that happened. But even jailed leaders were known to wield their positions of power from behind bars.

Nothing I can do about that, Jackson told himself. His job was to secure the evidence the Taskforce needed to put Ibrahim in jail. Once he'd accomplished that much, he could take some well-deserved time off and spend the remaining weeks of summer with his daughter. What he absolutely would not do was cave into his obsession with Magdalena Xenakis who, despite his best efforts to convince her otherwise, was stubbornly proceeding with her plans.

Oh, she had given him her trust when she wanted something from him, but the very next day she'd shown up at Artie's like their interlude had never happened, like his word wasn't worth shit.

His blood boiled with frustration. He'd been so certain he'd finally persuaded her to leave town. The fact that she remained, that she refused to trust him, left them nothing to discuss. How stubborn could one woman be?

Among some of the first men to leave the mosque, Jackson stalked to his dormitory, averting his gaze from the bright lights across the street. Just the sight of Schlesser's black Jeep parked out front made his jaw ache. And that discomfort was nothing compared to the hollow sensation in his chest or the throb of disappointment in his groin. He had hoped...well, it didn't matter what he'd hoped. Tonight, her presence was a distraction he couldn't afford.

Stripping off his dress clothes, he donned his dark pajama bottoms and paired them with the black T-shirt he would wear in his reconnaissance of the mosque. Corey came into the room shortly after him. Directing an astute look at him that made him feel a flash of transparency, Corey switched on the desk lamp. "Mind if I read?" he asked.

"Go ahead."

Corey parked himself at the desk and buried his nose in a book. Jackson brushed his teeth and rolled into his rack.

He heaved a sigh. With the light on, he doubted he'd fall asleep any faster than he had the last few nights. Christ, he was tired—tired of this investigation, tired of being away from his daughter, tired of trying to bend Magdalena to his will.

Rolling toward the wall, he punched up his pillow and closed his heavy eyes. In a matter of minutes, his sleep deficit sucked him straight into an unconsciousness state.

He slept soundly, for hours, his dreams unmemorable. Then, suddenly, he was back in Fallujah, leading his platoon down a debris-strewn alleyway hemmed by bullet-pocked walls. Their mission: to clear the city of civilians. Every one of his senses was set on high-alert when a bullet whizzed out of nowhere.

"Sniper!" Jackson shouted, diving for cover. A tingling pain lanced his hip. *Oh, shit, I've been shot!* He looked down at himself in horror. Blood spurted out of him, forming an ever-widening ring around him, despite his best efforts to stem the slippery flow.

He could feel himself going into shock.

Oh, God, Naomi. He'd been terrified that this would happen, that he'd be killed before he could return to her. And now she would have no one but her grandparents to look after her. He'd failed her.

Tears of remorse scalded his cheeks as the dark screens of unconsciousness began to surround him, shrinking his field of vision like a retracting camera lens. He thought of Lena, whom he'd never get to court, slowly and methodically, the way he wanted to, while relishing every new discovery about her.

He was going to die in this God-forsaken, war-torn city, and for what? Because he'd put duty to country above his family. Hadn't he learned his lesson the first time? Hadn't Colleen's senseless death taught him anything?

A tingling in his palm tugged him back toward consciousness. Why was his palm burning when it was his hip that was shot? Forcing his eyes to open, he found himself in bed, one hand pressed over the cell phone in his pocket, which emitted an electrical charge, not too painful, but not pleasant, either.

Hitting a button on the side, Jackson acknowledged Toby's silent summons and sat up slowly.

Above him, Corey mumbled in his sleep. A glance at the room clock showed it to be 2:08 in the morning already. Damn, Toby had probably been calling him for eight minutes now.

He eased out of bed, wriggled his feet into his tennis shoes, and slipped outside.

Heavy cloud cover smothered the stars and enveloped the campus in darkness. The night air felt so humid that it dampened his pajamas and muffled the cricket-song as he picked his way through tall grass to the back wall of the mosque.

As planned, Toby awaited him by the mosque's rear

exit. Dressed in midnight camouflage with his face painted black, Jackson wouldn't have seen him at all if he hadn't leveled a glare at him, the whites of his eyes flashing.

"Little out of practice, aren't you, Stonewall?" Toby mocked, but then he let Jackson's tardiness go. "Bossman says the alarm's disabled, so we're good." He handed Jackson a helmet rigged with night vision goggles.

"Sorry," Jackson mumbled, setting the helmet on his head. What could he say? He'd been sleeping like the dead, for a change.

Toby took out a silent, battery-powered picklock, the same tool he'd broken into Artie's with, and headed down the five steps to the basement door. Meanwhile, Jackson surveyed the deserted perimeter through his NVGs. He heard the picklock purr as it lifted all the pins in the deadbolt. The lock clicked open. Toby cracked the door, took a peek inside then held it open for Jackson.

Backing down the steps, Jackson leapfrogged his position. Once they were both within the long, basement corridor, Toby secured the door from the inside while Jackson waited at the entrance to the stairs.

As they'd practiced at Quantico prior to the investigation, they crept up the steps together keeping five yards between them. Arriving at an unlocked fire door on the main level, they emerged just outside the imams' offices.

Jackson surveyed the empty hallway through the neon green and gray lenses of his NVGs. It made sense to start their search in Ibrahim's office, where the evidence was most likely to be found. As far as Jackson could tell, Zakariya seemed to have no affiliation whatsoever with the Five Percent Nation.

Toby made swift work of unlocking Ibrahim's door. As they swept inside, Toby headed straight for the computer to install a keylogger, a gadget that would forward every stroke Ibrahim typed on his keyboard to the National Center for Counterterrorism. That would allow Taskforce analysts to record Ibrahim's passwords, giving them access to all his files.

Jackson, meanwhile, flipped up his NVGs and riffled through the metal filing cabinet with a penlight.

Cupping the light to keep its beams from escaping out the window, he scanned the alphabetized names looking for the file belonging to Mr. Rakeem. "There's paperwork here from the first year of the program," he observed, finding the file and pulling it.

"Seven years' worth of information," Toby muttered. "We oughta find something."

Seven years. The phrase echoed in Jackson's head. Seven was a mystical number in Supreme Numerology. It was also the number of years Ibrahim had said the *Mahdi* would dwell with his people prior to Judgment Day. *Coincidence?*

Working his way backward through the alphabet, Jackson looked for references to the Five Percent Nation or any common thread that tied the graduates together.

With two hours in which to accomplish their search, he took his time to be thorough, making sure he overlooked nothing of significance. He had just finished searching F through N when the distinct thud of a door closing made him freeze. Toby snatched his head out from under the desk. "What was that?" he whispered.

"Someone's coming."

As the sound of spry footsteps grew louder, both men scrambled up and moved to either side of the closed door. Jackson handed Mr. Rakeem's file to

Toby, who shoved it in the large pocket on his thigh. Catching Jackson's questioning gaze, Toby shook his head, signifying that he'd never witnessed this kind of behavior while logging the imams' nighttime rituals.

"And he tells me not to forget to set the alarm," a tenor voice muttered.

Zakariya, Jackson realized, breathing a small sigh of relief. Keys jingled as the imam unlocked the next door over. A weak strip of light appeared at the bottom of the door where the agents remained poised. On just the other side of the wall, the imam scraped back his chair. A faint hum told Jackson he had started up his computer.

They had to get the hell out before Zakariya realized he had company. Only the imam had kept his door wide open, and it was directly across from the stairs, which meant they were better off leaving a different way.

Jackson pointed to the window and, with a nod, Toby crossed the room.

The sound of hip hop music, so unexpected in the sanctity of the mosque, pulsed suddenly through the wall. Jackson hesitated, cocking his ears to listen. With surprise, he recognized the distinct sound of the band, The Slangers. Why would Zakariya be listening to The Slangers at this ungodly hour?

In the next instant, Toby was standing beside him again, conveying with gestures that the windows didn't open.

Jackson looked over at the glass panels in disbelief. What was this place, Fort Knox?

Toby pointed toward the stairs as the closest, most viable exit. *Let's go,* he signed.

But Jackson had just recalled that many hip hop artists professed to being Five Percenters. Nodding absently, he tried to identify the music. Toby, meanwhile, cracked the door. The loud music muffled his footfalls as he darted across the hall and slipped behind the fire door, keeping it cracked for Jackson.

Jackson was just about to follow, when The Slangers arrived at the end of their rant and the mosque fell eerily quiet. Freezing, he hardly dared to breathe as he waited for the music to resume. Thankfully, it did, this time with a rap being belted out by Native Threat.

Several of the words reached his ears. The lyrics were unmistakably a call to violence. What reason did peace-loving Zakariya have for listening to this stuff?

With his heart thudding in counterpoint to the beat, he signaled to Toby through the cracked door. *Wait.* He wanted to be able to pick out this song later.

Toby gestured impatiently. Jackson held up a finger. *I said, the top is comin' down. 6th and H. Every State. Every Great. Dropped to dust till we stand back up.*

He had it. With the refrain memorized, Jackson started furtively across the hall. Suddenly the music stopped again, and in the utter silence, the stealthy tread of Jackson's sole sounded as loud as thunder. Zakariya whipped his attention toward the door.

"Who's there?" he yelped.

Go! Jackson waved Toby ahead of him and flew toward the closing fire door to catch it. He slowed only long enough to shut it quietly behind him before throwing himself down the dark stairwell, moving so fast his feet scarcely touched the steps.

In a matter of seconds he had overtaken his partner, who waited at the door below him. "Nice going," Toby whispered. Light chased them as the fire door above them yawned open.

"Stop! Thief!" Zakariya's voice echoed off the cinderblock walls as he and Toby burst out of the basement exit. They tumbled up the back steps without slowing.

"Go," Toby urged, snatching the helmet off Jackson's head. Sprinting in the opposite direction, he was gone from view by the time Jackson arrived at the corner of the dormitory and glanced back. Every light in the mosque was coming on, one by one.

Hoping to beat the alarm that would be raised at any moment, Jackson stole into his dark room, crawled stealthily into bed, and lay there with his heart thrumming. The fact that Corey wasn't snoring kept him from feeling any real relief.

CHAPTER 13

Through the open windows of her cottage, Lena heard the crackle of pine needles being crushed by the tires of a car. She glanced at the clock on her laptop and smiled grimly: 10:30 A.M. By now, the parolees were long gone from Gateway. Just as she'd hoped, Peter had arrived too late to photograph Jackson.

Getting up from the vanity she used as a desk, she went to the door to greet him. The happy grin he sent her as he stepped out of her Jaguar made her confidence waver, especially when he held up his camera and said, "I got what I came for."

Her stomach dropped. "What do you mean?"

"I got to Gateway right when he was walking out with his parole officer. Followed him nine miles down this road to a house on the river."

Now she was more confused than ever. "What?"

He joined her on the front stoop. "The parolees must go home on weekends. I'm surprised you didn't know that," he stated with a glint in his gray eyes. "Except Jackson Maddox doesn't go all the way to Baltimore. He's renting a riverfront house just down the road."

As he nodded in the direction of the river, Lena

considered his news and found that she wasn't too surprised. "Did he see you taking pictures?" she asked Peter.

"Please." He shot her a patronizing look. "I'm not an amateur."

Implying that she was, of course, since Jackson had seen her taking pictures.

"Did you get another laptop yet?" he inquired with excitement.

"Yeah." She'd bought herself a Mac just yesterday.

"Come on. I'll show you the pictures."

Lena balked. She'd spent hours trying to find out who Abdul Ibn Wasi really was. Knowing he was a federal agent was enough for her. She didn't care what his purpose was at Gateway. She wanted nothing to do with exposing Uncle Sam for meddling in the private lives of U.S. citizens. She wished Peter would just go home and leave Jackson alone.

On the other hand, the prospect of seeing where Jackson spent his weekends was awfully tempting, especially since he'd intentionally kept his distance these past couple of days, punishing her silently for rejecting his offer and giving her plenty of time alone in which to relive the pleasure of his company, both mental and physical. It seemed like an eternity since their interlude in the store room. "It's in my bedroom on the vanity," she heard herself admit, and Peter marched into her house like he owned the place.

In her bedroom, he took his top-of-the-line Nikon from its case, attached it to her laptop, and with a couple of key strokes, uploaded his recent photos, enlarging them on her monitor so they could both see.

Peter sat on the stool. Leaning over him, Lena feasted her eyes on pictures of Jackson crossing Gateway's parking lot with his parole officer, getting into a familiar looking Crown Victoria. To her astute gaze, he struck her as tired and listless this morning.

"I'm sure the other guy's an agent, too, since they're staying at the same house," Peter commented.

A couple more shots showed the Crown Vic pulling out on the highway. "This is where I followed him," he noted.

The next photos were of a large A-frame structure with cedar siding and expansive windows. The glimmering swathe of blue behind it suggested it stood on a bluff overlooking the Patuxent River.

"So that's where he stays," Lena guessed with a stab of envy.

"Yep. It's a rental owned by a real estate tycoon. I determined that much on my way home." Peter forwarded to pictures of two vehicles parked out front—the agents' car and a white Volvo. He had zoomed in to photograph the Maryland state tags. "I'm going to call my buddy at the DMV and find out who owns these cars," he determined, taking out his cell phone.

As he rattled off the license plate numbers to a guy named Rich, Lena paced the length of her room. "Is that all you took?" she asked when Peter hung up.

"Nope. Got a few more here." He continued the slide show.

The image of a copper haired girl, twelve or thirteen years of age, rooted Lena to the spot. The photos were blurry since Peter had been taking them while turning around at a cul-de-sac, but once the driver's side window paralleled the yard, the photos came out clearer. The girl had turned to regard him curiously. Her eyes were so strikingly familiar that Lena gasped.

Peter glanced up at her sharply. "What's wrong?"

"He has a daughter," she croaked.

"Who? Jackson Maddox?"

"Yes. She looks just like him."

Peter gave a disinterested grunt. He forwarded to the next photo, where the leg, chest and chin of a woman were just visible as she stepped out of the house to join the girl.

"Who is that?" Lena pointed, but it proved to be the last picture Peter had taken. "Did you see this woman? Is she the girl's mother?"

"Probably," he said, unconcerned. "I bet she drives the Volvo and meets up with her husband on weekends."

Lena gripped one of the bed posts to keep the room from reeling.

It was too disturbing to contemplate. The man who'd coerced her into declaring her trust for him had a child and was probably married. *The son of a bitch.* No wonder he hadn't gone all the way with her.

Peter finally took note of her silence. "You okay?" He craned his neck to look back at her.

"Yeah."

She closed her eyes in gratitude when his cell phone rang.

"That was fast," he said, taking the call. It had to be his buddy at the DMV. "Awesome. Whatchu got?" He opened a Word document and started typing. *Dept. of Homeland Security, year-long lease,* Lena read. "That's it? No names?" Peter dabbed at the beads of sweat glistening at his hairline. "What about the other car?"

She held her breath as Peter typed the name *Silvia Shultz*. Jealousy, as green and sour as the skin on a Granny Smith apple made Lena's lips pucker. Peter typed *DOB:* and the date *7/19/1949*, and her jealousy morphed into relief. No way could Silvia Shultz be Jackson's wife or the little girl's mother, not at sixty some years of age. *Themou efharisto.* Thank you, God.

However, that didn't mean he didn't have a wife tucked away somewhere, she cautioned herself.

With a word of gratitude and a promise to take Rich out to lunch soon, Peter hung up.

"Are you thirsty?" Lena asked. Her throat was parched.

"Definitely."

She went to kitchen and poured two iced-teas in the new drinking glasses she'd purchased. A fresh wave of resentment plunged through her as she chugged her glass. Returning to the room with the other, she found Peter reading an online news article.

"Can you open the window any farther?" he asked her, taking his glass. "It's hot as hell in here."

"Sure." She wrestled the window all the way open. "No air-conditioning," she apologized, flicking on the overhead fan.

"I don't know how you stand it." He put his empty glass down with a thud. Armpit stains ringed his short-sleeved shirt. "Plus your internet is slow as hell."

"It's DSL," she explained. Funny how sweat looked sexy on some men and not on others. She shifted her attention the article he was reading. "What'd you find?"

"I paired Silvia Shultz's name with Jackson Maddox, and this is what came up. It's her daughter's obituary."

The relief that washed over her left her feeling shamed. His wife was dead.

"Colleen Shultz Maddox was killed in a single-car collision in 2009," Peter quoted, unaware of her response. "She is survived by her husband Captain Jackson Maddox, United States Marines Corps, blah, blah, blah. None of this tells me what he's investigating now." He closed the page before she could read past the first paragraph. "I'm better off returning to the office where I have broadband."

With rising panic, Lena watched him put away his camera. The certainty that Peter was going to blow Jackson's cover made her stomach cramp. She laid a restraining hand on his shoulder. "Peter, you promised you wouldn't expose the agent's cover," she reminded him.

He looked up at her like she was crazy. "No I didn't." Zipping up his camera case, he stood up and shouldered the strap.

"What if he's at Gateway to prevent an act of terror?" she argued. "You could be jeopardizing thousands of American lives."

He eyed her in disbelief. "Why are you defending him? This guy broke into your house. He stole your camera and your laptop, for God's sake."

She thought it best not to mention that the pendant, which he'd given her last Christmas, had been taken also.

"Who cares if his fucking cover is blown?" Pushing past her, he stalked into the living room.

Lena chased after him. "We're talking about national security, though," she persisted, blocking his path to the door. "The FBI wouldn't have an agent masquerading as a felon unless something serious is happening at Gateway."

He drew up short. "And why would anything bad be happening at Gateway?" he sneered. "Because it's run by Muslims? That's racial profiling, Lena. And it ought to be illegal."

"You can't be certain Gateway doesn't have terrorist ties."

"It's a highly esteemed reintegration program," he shot back. "Ninety percent of its graduates do not reoffend and are contributing to society."

"But what if there's some link to terrorists, and people die because you exposed a government investigation?"

"No one is going to die."

"The agent could, Peter! They'll consider him a traitor. Who knows what they'll do to him in reprisal."

Peter jerked the strap on his shoulder higher. "Not my problem," he said shortly.

She wished she had never asked his help in identifying Jackson in the first place. "So that's it? You're just going to take this story away from me?"

"If I let you have it, then there won't be a story," he predicted. "Sorry, this one's mine." With a tight smile, he elbowed her out of his way and marched outside.

"Peter, please!" she shouted off the porch. "Just give it two weeks before you run your story." That way the session would be over, and Jackson would be safe.

"We'll see." He halted suddenly en route to his Jeep. "I want my car back," he announced, returning to the house to hand her back her keys.

He would go and make this even more difficult for her. Seething, Lena stormed inside to fetch his key ring. They met on the porch. "What's Davis going to think when I show up in a fifty thousand dollar car, and what's my small town convenience store boss going to think?"

"Tell them your Jeep broke down, and the Jag's your dad's."

"Fine." She thrust his keys at him and snatched hers out of his hand.

"Come on, babe," he coaxed, eyeing her flushed face. "Don't take this so hard. I'll give you credit for the story, I promise."

"No! I don't want credit. Don't you dare link my

name with your article." It was bad enough that Jackson now ignored her; she couldn't imagine how she'd feel if he blamed her for ruining his investigation.

"Whatever. I thought you were a journalist first and foremost, but I guess I was wrong." Turning his back on her Peter marched to his car.

Stung by his words, Lena had to remind herself that not long ago she had planned to discover Abdul's secret and use it against him. For the first time ever she found herself on the other side of the fence, emotionally involved with the subject of a story—not that Jackson reciprocated her emotions. He'd had no apparent difficulty shutting her out of his life.

She watched Peter climb into his Jeep and pull away. Glancing back at her once, he shook his head. It was obvious he thought she'd lost her touch.

The black Jeep disappeared over a hillock. Disappearing with it was glimmer of hope that Jackson Maddox might one day be an integral part of her life. When *Crime and Liberty* declared him an undercover agent and paired an article with a photo of him taken from the vantage of Artie's freaking parking lot, who would Jackson blame, but her?

If she'd just left town when he'd first asked her to, none of this would have happened.

Ike Calhoun's scowling face loomed on the company laptop. "All clear?" he rapped.

Jackson heard the kitchen door thump shut as Silvia followed Naomi outside. His team lead had called an immediate, top secret conference requiring anyone in the house who was not a Taskforce agent to step out. The fact that it was required to be top secret suggested Ike had critical news to share.

"All clear," Jackson affirmed, annoyed that he

hadn't even been able to greet his daughter properly.

Toby shot him a sympathetic grimace and sank into the chair next to his.

"What the hell happened last night, Maddox?" Ike demanded. "I want your version."

Obviously, Toby's version hadn't appeased him.

Chagrined, Jackson relayed how Zakariya had caught them by surprise by varying from his usual routine, and what they'd seen and heard before Jackson accidentally betrayed their presence. He even admitted how the local police had awakened all twelve parolees to question them, only to leave the campus scratching their heads.

"You realize," Ike retorted, using whip-lash syllables that made Jackson flinch, "that the imams are going to tighten security from now on."

They'd fucked up and Ike was right; the investigation would now be that much harder.

"I think we should look at the music he was listening to," Jackson suggested. "Something tells me it was encoded."

Ike sent him a hard look. "Our analysts report that he was visiting a music site, but they have no way of knowing what he listened to."

"But I remember." Jackson imbued his tone with confidence. "I'll look up the songs and send them to you."

Ike did not look mollified.

"I have an idea," Toby said, earning Ike's hard stare. "Have the fire marshal check on Gateway's compliance with NFPA Code 58 regarding the storage of propane. If they're in violation, we could get warrants for Ibrahim's arrest and then search his office."

"I'll think about it," Ike replied, jotting himself a note. "That's not all," he continued, his rough voice raising the hairs on Jackson's forearms. He should have guessed something else was going on, here, besides a royal ass-chewing.

"At zero five hundred hours today, Greenwich time, the Algerian rebels who received funds from Gateway last year rammed a boat packed with explosives into a luxury cruise liner, causing it to catch fire and to sink. There were dozens of casualties including six American tourists."

Jackson felt suddenly sick to his stomach.

"Whether that stunt could have been pulled off without Gateway's financial backing is a moot point. Attorney General Wilkes wants to prosecute the leaders, only he knows he won't win his case without substantive evidence. It's our job to find a link between Gateway and terror."

Toby scrubbed his face with his hands. "I hate fucking politics," he muttered under his breath.

"Maddox, this is the halfway mark in the program," Ike reminded him. "I need you to pull out all the stops and goddamn find what we're looking for."

"Understood," Jackson answered.

"Identify that music, and I'll have our analysts study it for hidden meaning." Ike jabbed a key with a long finger, and the screen went black.

Jackson slowly exhaled.

"He busted my balls last night," Toby offered consolingly.

"The man's under a lot of pressure," Jackson said in Ike's defense. Though, come to think of it, he had seen the Taskforce lead under unprecedented pressure before, and Ike had never once lost his cool. Could pressure from the AG really be stressing him out, or was something else going on, maybe in his private life?

"Let's find the music," Toby suggested.

"Right." Sitting forward, Jackson went to YouTube to hunt down the two songs he'd heard snatches of the previous night. "This was the first one." He turned up the volume as The Slangers, three young men draped in chains and gesturing angrily, stalked up and down the stage spewing, *Think you can step on me, spit on me, lock me up, quit on me? Think you can hide from my Colt 45 double-action revolver, problem-solver?*

Toby raised his eyebrows. "Sounds like a threat to me."

Jackson embedded the YouTube link in his email to Ike and hunted for the second song he'd heard. A throbbing beat filled the office as he identified it by the lyrics. "This one's by Native Threat."

I said, the top is comin' down. 6th and H. Every State. Every Great. Dropped to dust till we stand back up.

Jackson hit pause. "Those are the lines Zakariya played." He backed up the video and played them again.

Toby cocked his head, listening. "Did they just say 6th and H? That's an intersection in D.C."

Jackson played the lines again. "6th and H. Every State. Every Great," he repeated, pondering the meaning behind the words.

Toby sent him an electric look. "How many roads in D.C. have state names?"

Jackson's mouth went dry. "All of them."

"And what about Every Great? What could that be?"

Jackson shrugged. "Makes me think of the great men in history."

"Could be a reference to the Lincoln and Jefferson Memorials." Toby nodded at the computer. "Play the next line."

Jackson hit play and they listened one more time.

"Dropped to dust sounds like a reference to a bombing, don't you think?"

"We can't just assume that," Jackson warned. "Rap's always been an outlet for socio-political dreams and frustrations."

Nonetheless, as he imbedded the second link into his email, he tingled with the suspicion that they'd stumbled on an important component of NCE communication. In the subject line he typed *Encoded?* And then he sent the message off to Ike.

Toby snorted. "Of course it's encoded." He leapt to his feet. "I bet you Zakariya was pushing code to his Five Percenters on that music site. He sure as hell wasn't listening to it for his own kicks," he added, heading for the door.

Jackson mulled over Toby's assertion as he logged off. Out in the kitchen he heard the refrigerator open and close, heard the familiar hiss of a twist-off. Toby wasn't wasting any time enjoying the rest of the weekend.

So why am I still in the office?

He followed his colleague onto the sunbaked balcony. Toby sat in the lounge chair nursing a beer. Beyond him, at the bottom of the long run of stairs, Naomi and Silvia stood in water to their ankles.

"Hi, Dad!" His daughter caught sight of him and waved. Her bright hair lifted in the warm breeze. "Come on down."

"In a minute," he promised.

Drawing a deep breath of air, he tried to shake off his growing sense of foreboding. The air smelled of brackish water and sunscreen. He imagined it might have smelled similarly aboard the cruise ship that was attacked by rebels that dawn.

No one vacationing on that cruise ship would have expected the attack. It made Jackson wonder if equally unforeseen violence was about to break loose on U.S. soil.

Not a soul had entered Artie's in the past hour. Gateway stood deserted. Out in the darkening parking lot, Deputy Doug Hazelwood had fallen asleep in his cruiser, his head lolling against his head rest, one arm flopped outside his open window. Sweeping the linoleum floors with an electric Swiffer, Lena sought to pass the time while contemplating Peter's intent to accuse the government of infringing on civilians' rights by spying on them.

Rounding the end of an aisle, she was startled to find herself staring at a pair of scuffed boots. Snatching her head up, she recognized the man standing silently in front of her. "Seth!" Her heart pounded at the false alarm. "I didn't hear you come in." Turning off the appliance, she hurried behind the counter to get him a scratch-off ticket.

It wasn't until she stood directly opposite the Amish man that she caught a whiff of whisky on his breath. He clutched his straw hat to his stomach as he held the edge of the countertop, using it to keep his balance. Astonished and fairly positive that Amish folk were forbidden to touch liquor, Lena went through the motions of ringing him up while wondering if there were any Amish rules Seth didn't break.

"Having a rough day?" she worked up the courage to ask.

When he raised bloodshot eyes at her, Lena realized he'd never looked directly at her before. She was startled to discover his eyes were a vivid green. With his beard wildly disheveled, he looked a little like a madman. She instantly regretted her impulse to reach out to him but then, surprisingly, he answered her.

"Yeah," he admitted on a gruff note. "You?"

Because he asked, she told the truth. What the heck. "Yeah, me, too." If it weren't bad enough that Peter's anti-government campaign was going to put Jackson in danger, all hope for reconciliation between them was doomed, which sucked. Every moment she had ever spent with him had been fraught with exhilaration, something that had never happened to her before, not with any man. What if he was meant for her and she'd blown her one and only chance at finding the love of her life?

Seth grunted. He opened his mouth as if to say something, changed his mind and handed her his payment, instead.

Sensing he was on the verge of actually confessing something and that he could benefit from unburdening himself, Lena gave him a nudge. "So I noticed your tattoo the other day," she said before he could get away. "Is it a girl's name?"

He looked down at his right arm. Today the tattoo was hidden under the sleeve of his homespun shirt. "Yeah."

"Old flame?" she asked.

He seemed confused by that remark, but then his brow cleared. "Oh, no. I didn't...love her," he admitted. "I just—" With a far-away look in his eyes, he cut himself off.

His Lotto ticket was paid for, but he still didn't leave. Lena felt sorry for him. He had to be lonely, cut off from the other Amish folk. "You don't really fit in here, do you, hon?" she asked, curious to know more about him.

He loosed a humorless laugh. "You noticed?"

"I don't know of any Amish who play the lottery." She didn't know any other Amish, period, but that was beside the point.

He smoothed his wild, wiry whiskers, his eyes

downcast.

"So, what happened?" she asked, betraying the journalist in her. "Did you do something that branded you an outcast?"

He glanced up, and his glassy eyes filled with tears that darkened them to a lovely emerald green. She suffered a sudden sense of déjà vu. Hadn't she seen that effect before, on someone else with green eyes?

"'S not what I did." Seth's words slurred together. "'S what I didn't do." Pocketing his scratch-off ticket, he swiveled on his heels and staggered out the door.

Struck by his remorse, Lena watched him stumble off the sidewalk, waking Deputy Doug with his muttered curse. His words reverberated in her mind: *'S what I didn't do.*

She thought immediately of Jackson and of what might happen to him if she didn't warn him of Peter's intent. So what if Jackson blamed her for tipping off Peter in the first place? Not warning him would be an act of cowardice. The last thing she wanted was to be like Seth and regret all her life that she hadn't acted when she should have.

Her heart began to pound as the thought took hold. How should she get a hold of Jackson? She didn't have a number. *Should I call the FBI?*

Then suddenly she knew. She could find the house Peter had photographed this morning. First thing in the morning, she'd locate it and confess everything.

A feeling of calm resolve filled her as she made up her mind. Jackson might possibly never forgive her. On the other hand, her warning had to count something. If there was even a slim possibility that he'd offer her a second chance, she was willing to take it.

CHAPTER 14

Jackson glanced over at his daughter, who eyed him sleepily from the kitchen table. "You sure you don't want blueberries in your pancakes?"

With Silvia away that weekend, he was the one cooking their breakfast and attempting to whip himself into a more cheerful mindset. But between the tragedy off the coast of Algeria and the aborted search of Ibrahim's office, everything in his life seemed to be going to shit. And that included his relationship with a sherry-eyed beauty who'd opted to stick to her own path of justice rather than rely on another individual. And in so doing, she had denied them the possibility of a future together, one that had seemed so fraught with possibility.

What more could he have promised her that he hadn't already? He'd gone over it in his mind a thousand times. Obviously she wasn't as drawn to him as he was to her or she'd have taken him up on his offer. For days now, he'd felt drained, incomplete. His zest for life—so recently rediscovered—was crushed.

"Gross," Naomi said in answer to his question. "Blueberries are mushy and they turn your pancakes purple. Why can't we have chocolate chips?"

"Because blueberries are better for you." He winced at his own surly tone.

Just then the sound of a car, rare because of their location at the end of the street, had him glancing out the window. He didn't immediately recognize the sleek, burgundy Jaguar circling the *cul-de-sac* outside, but his sixth sense urged him not to dismiss it.

"Honey, have you seen that car before?" he asked when it slowed and parked, its rear fender facing the house so he couldn't see the driver.

Naomi looked out the window by the dinette table. "Oh, yeah. I saw it here yesterday. A man was taking pictures of the river."

Jackson's antenna for danger shot straight up in the air. *Taking pictures?* In the same instant, who should step out of the car but Magdalena Xenakis Alexandra?

Speak of the devil, he thought grimly.

Watching her strike out toward the house in jeans that fit her shapely body like a glove, his hormones immediately started celebrating while his brain cautioned him that she was probably up to no good.

"Toby!" he shouted, turning off the stove before he burned breakfast. "Naomi, go wake up Mr. Burke." He waved her toward the back hall when she balked. "Go on." The minute she was out of sight, he stalked toward the door and snatched it open.

Lena pulled her hand away from the doorbell and took a healthy step backward.

"What are you doing here?" He raked her gauzy blouse for any signs of a hidden camera. She must have left her purse, and hence her pistol, in the car, and he didn't see anything on her person that could conceal a lens, but he didn't put it past her to not be wearing a wire.

"We need to talk...Jackson," she said with wide,

watchful eyes.

The sound of his name on her lips made his heart stop before it took off galloping. "Come inside." He didn't leave her much choice. Hauling her into the kitchen, he shut the door behind her, spun her around and thrust her against the door's facade in order to thoroughly frisk her.

Memories of Wednesday night and how sexy she'd looked with her breasts bared and her thighs spread scorched his senses, making it nearly impossible to keep his touch impersonal as he patted her down. Dipping his fingers into her jeans pockets, he discovered a set of car keys. He felt up under her gauzy blouse for a concealed listening device, but the only things his hands encountered were full, soft breasts encased in a snug tank top.

At her sexy-sounding gasp, he swung her about and caught her chin in his hand, turning her head from one side to the other to examine her earrings and the silver choker at her throat. Neither looked capable of concealing a camera. He even gave her sequined sandals a cursory glance.

"Satisfied?" she asked when, at last, he let his hands drop to his sides.

"Hardly," he grated through clenched teeth. Christ, just standing before him, exuding her seductive scent, she had an arousing effect on his body. If not for Toby and Naomi's presence, he would take her, right here, right now against the wall.

Just then, Toby barreled into the kitchen with his hair disheveled, stubble on his jaw, and a yellow T-shirt that read: ALCOHOL, TOBACCO, AND FIREARMS. WHO'S BRINGING THE CHIPS?

"We have a visitor," Jackson announced to Toby's astonished face. "She's clean." Curling a hand around her elbow, he marched her unceremoniously through the living area. "Stay inside while we talk to our guest," he instructed a wide-eyed Naomi.

Lena let herself be escorted through sliding glass doors onto a shady deck. Jackson's colleague joined them, pulling the door shut to keep the preteen out of earshot.

"Sit," Jackson said, pulling a chair away from the wrought iron table topped by glass and an open umbrella.

Wincing at his suspicious tone, Lean stiffly obliged. He dropped into the chair opposite hers, while the other agent chose the chair between them. A moment of tense silence ensued, and then Jackson said, "Talk."

Lena narrowed her eyes at him. "I am not a dog." She had expected him to be upset, but was common courtesy too much to ask?

"Amen to that," drawled the other agent, shattering the hostile atmosphere with a wolfish grin.

Jackson shot him a look that said, *Shut the fuck up.* "Tell us why you're here," he commanded. "Please," he tacked on.

Lena shivered under the cool shadow of the umbrella. Eyeing Jackson's hard face, she wondered, with a pang, where the man was who'd sworn to woo her with a fine meal and a soft bed.

"I'm here to warn you, that's all," she told him stiffly, "I don't want to jeopardize your situation at Gateway. I swear it."

The mistrust radiating off him scarcely seemed to subside. Lena glanced hopefully at his colleague, who had yet to be introduced. That man, at least, seemed to be withholding his condemnation.

"Warn me of what? How long have you known who I am?" he tacked on before she could answer his first question.

"Less than a week—though I've questioned your

identity from the start." Her gaze skittered over him. Dressed in a heather-gray Polo that matched his silvery eyes, she had to admit the preppy look suited him far more than a sleeveless T-shirt. "Even when you dress like a thug, you don't look like one," she said.

At this, the other agent threw back head and roared with laughter.

Jackson glared at him again, his eyes shooting fire.

"I would never betray your cover," Lena rushed to assure him. "I might have at one time, but things are different now…between us."

Emotion flickered on his face and was gone. Then he asked in the same cold voice, "What do you want to warn me about?"

His tone left her with little hope of reconciliation. "When I couldn't find any criminal records on Abdul Ibn Wasi, I made the mistake of sending your image to my boss," she admitted. "This was right after you broke into my place. I was royally pissed and hungry for retaliation."

Her news met with ominous silence. Lena looked down at her bracelets and idly turned them. "I asked him to help me identify you." Biting her lip for courage, she looked up and met Jackson's chilly stare without flinching.

"So your boss identified me," he guessed, with crisp consonants that betrayed his disgust. "Did he say how?"

"With the help of a senator."

The agents shared a baffled look.

"Which senator?" asked the other man.

"I don't know. Peter never said. But now he's all worked up about Gateway being under federal investigation. He thinks Uncle Sam is violating the civil rights of Muslim Americans, and he's going to blow your cover, Jackson. He took pictures of the two of you leaving Gateway yesterday. Then he followed you here and took pictures of your vehicles and your daughter."

Jackson visibly paled beneath his tan. "No," he exclaimed, pointing a finger at her. "You get those pictures the hell away from him. I won't have Naomi targeted by Five Percenters trying to get back at me."

"It's okay—"

"No, it is not okay!"

"The pictures of her are all blurry," she assured him. "Plus, he's not going to publish them. Peter might be a jackass, but he's only trying to make a political statement; he would never put a child at risk."

Jackson's jaw muscles jumped. "You'd better be right about that."

"I am." She pushed the apology through a strangled throat. "And I'm sorry, about everything." The disillusionment radiating off him made her want to crawl into a dark corner and cry. "If I'd had any idea this would happen, I swear I never would have asked for Peter's help in the first place. I take complete responsibility. And, if it's any consolation, I can warn you when Peter's exposé is on the verge of publication."

"How long do we have?" the other man asked.

Glancing at him, Lena was relieved that he wasn't looking at her as if she'd initiated a countdown to Armageddon.

"It depends how deeply he wants to dig before he goes public. But I'll find out," she promised.

Jackson shoved his chair back without warning. "You should have left the area when I goddamn asked you to." For a moment, he loomed over her like he had something else to say, but then he left without a word, stalking into the house and sliding the door forcefully shut behind him.

Stung by his condemnation, Lena crossed her arms to ward off her sudden chill. Tears of self-pity and remorse stung her eyes, but she refused to shed them with the other agent eyeing her so closely.

"So, you want to stay for breakfast?"

The hospitable inquiry drew her attention to his crooked smile. His devil-may-care attitude might have cheered her if she weren't so stricken by Jackson's condemnation.

"I should go." She started to rise.

"Stay." He came up out of his chair just far enough to lay a hand on her shoulder and push her back down. "The damage is done," he reasoned. "Might as well stick around and watch the day get better."

"That's very philosophical but—"

"Tobias," he introduced himself, holding out a hand for her to shake.

She did so, noting that his hands were powerful and square, just like the rest of him.

"Nice to meet you, but I really think Jackson would rather I leave."

"Don't be so sure," he said with a wink.

Just then, the glass door opened, and Jackson stood at the threshold looking back and forth between them. "Might as well stay for breakfast," he said tersely.

Eyeing him in surprise, Lena read nothing in the rigid lines of his body but betrayal.

"I don't want to intrude on your family time," she balked.

"Stay," he repeated in a tone that brooked no arguments. "Toby, go tell Ike what's going on." Swiveling toward the kitchen, he left the door wide open.

"Be right back," Toby said to Lena as he jumped up

to do Jackson's bidding.

Alone, Lena took in the view. The Patuxent River, calm and cerulean blue, kissed the sandy beach at the end of a long run of steps, where folding chairs and a red plastic bucket suggested happier times. Considering how furious Jackson was, it was gracious of him to invite her to breakfast. Or was he merely holding her here while he waited to see what the powers that be wanted him to do with her? That was probably it.

Sensing she was being watched, she glanced back at the glass door and found Jackson's daughter standing just inside staring at her.

"Hello." Lena summoned a friendly smile.

"Hi." The girl managed a shy smile of her own. "You're very pretty."

The comment evoked a bitter laugh. She didn't feel pretty at the moment. "I'm sorry for intruding on your time with your father," she apologized.

"That's okay. I'm used to him being busy."

The girl stepped cautiously out onto the balcony. Her fresh face and wise-looking eyes reminded Lena of Alexa. A knot swelled in her throat.

"Are you going to have breakfast with us?" the preteen asked.

"If that's okay with you."

"Sure. Then maybe you can come down to the beach with us afterward."

The offer just proved how unaware she was of the circumstances. "Maybe," Lena answered.

"You could borrow one of my grandma's swimsuits. She went home to water plants this weekend."

"We'll see." At least Silvia Shultz wasn't around to formulate a negative opinion of her. It was hard enough to cope with Jackson's censure.

"Orange juice or milk?" he asked from the open

door.

"Orange juice, please. Here, let me help."

"Talk to Naomi," he said shortly. He looked at his daughter who said she wanted milk, and then he disappeared.

"Naomi, that's a pretty name," Lena commented.

"Thanks." Naomi slipped into the chair Toby had vacated.

"How old are you?" Lena asked.

"Twelve and a half."

"So grown up. Let me guess: You're going into seventh grade?"

The girl grimaced and sighed. "Yeah."

"You don't look too thrilled about it."

"That's 'cause there's so much drama in middle school. You don't even know who your real friends are."

Lena's heart sank. That was probably the way Jackson felt about her right now. How would she ever redeem herself?

The more Jackson dug into his plate of pancakes the more he had to fight to hold onto his resentment.

Damn it, Lena had compromised his cover by involving her boss! *But that had been done unwittingly,* argued a voice in his head. Watching her interact with his daughter across the table on the deck, he admitted he still wanted her, not just physically but in every aspect of his life.

You love her, a little voice inside his head accused, causing him to realize their changed circumstances hadn't altered his feelings for her.

Nor was he the only one basking in Lena's company. The dimple flashing on Naomi's right told a similar story. He hadn't seen his daughter work so hard to impress a stranger since he'd taken Eryn ice skating the winter before Ike came home injured from Afghanistan.

"You're not married, are you?" Naomi blurted.

Jackson felt his face heat and quickly hid that fact behind his coffee mug.

"No." Lena wiped her mouth with a napkin as she shook her head.

"Have you ever been married?"

"Naomi," Jackson warned.

"That's okay," Lena assured him, though her face was distinctly flushed. "No, I've never been married."

"My dad was married to my mom," Naomi said matter-of-factly, "but she died in a car accident."

Jackson laid down his fork.

"I'm so sorry."

Lena's sincerity cut straight to his heart. He couldn't bring himself to look at her and see her pity. "I know what it's like to lose a member of your family. My sister died when she was just few years older than you."

"How'd she die?"

The pancakes in Jackson's stomach were turning into concrete. "Sweetheart," he firmly interrupted, "how would you like to take Lena to the beach while Mr. Burke and I have our morning conference?" Ike had scheduled a 10:30 teleconference even before he'd gotten word of Jackson's cover being blown. The Taskforce lead didn't want Lena to walk out the door before they all discussed what to do about her.

"Yes!" Naomi cried, giving up all pretense of eating. "You want to play at the beach?" She didn't wait for Lena to answer. "Let's go!" Gathering up her plate and utensils, she started to carry them inside. "I'll find one of Grandma's suits for you to wear."

Looking bemused, Lena rose more slowly. "Does

this mean I'm being held for questioning?" she asked the men as Naomi slipped into the house.

Jackson blinked. He'd like to hold her hostage for an eternity. "Don't know yet," he retorted. Right now he liked having her on the end of his hook, squirming and groveling for his forgiveness. "Toby and I have a phone conference with our boss. Once we've spoken to him, I'll know where we stand. We shouldn't be long, and Naomi could use your supervision."

"Okay," she agreed. Looking anxious but resigned, she followed Naomi inside.

"You scheming SOB," Toby murmured with glint of approval in his eyes. "You're just keeping her here in the hopes of getting some action later."

Jackson sent him a long, hard look. "I cooked, so you get to clean up," he declared, ignoring Toby's evil chuckle as he left him to clear the table.

Sequestered in the office to browse his emails, Jackson admitted to himself that Toby was right. Lena might have jeopardized their investigation, she might have rejected his vision for the future, but he still wanted her, desperately.

At least she'd warned them of her boss's intent, he reminded himself. A lesser woman might have just walked away and let the dice fall wherever they rolled.

He swiped a hand over his face. With so much uncertainty, it was impossible to know what the future held for anyone.

Toby pushed into the room just as Ike's image appeared on the screen, accompanied by a warning chime. "We caught a break," Ike announced, getting right to the point. "And it was the hip hop music like you suspected, Maddox. Job well done."

Toby shot Jackson a told-you-so grin and hit him hard on the back. "Atta boy!"

Ike wasn't done. "We knew Zakariya had a habit of visiting a certain music site, but we didn't realize, until you suggested it, that the music he was putting down as his top ten picks was encoded. This is how the imams have been flying under the radar. They call the music God's Hop."

Jackson's dark mood lifted. Maybe he'd be leaving Gateway sooner than expected, and it wouldn't matter if his cover got blown.

"We are now fully certain that this group is planning a revolution."

Ike's announcement tethered Jackson's hopes.

"But our expert is an encryption specialist, not a Five Percenter. He's not familiar with the Supreme Alphabet or Numerology, both of which they use to encode certain information. This afternoon, I'm going to visit an incarcerated rapper Kid Prophet. Decoding the music buys him a lighter sentence. Let's hope he sheds some light into the details we're missing."

Ike raked a hand through his silver buzz cut and sighed. "Here's the bad news: Over twelve thousand website visitors acknowledged Zakariya's top picks, which suggests the imams have more of a following than we ever suspected. The majority are located on the east coast, with the largest concentration, not surprisingly, in the D.C. area."

Foreboding reared its grizzly head, chasing Jackson's optimism back into hiding. Judgment Day was beginning to sound more like a reality than a doomsday prophecy.

The team lead's gaze shifted to Toby. "At your suggestion, Burke, the fire marshal will descend on Gateway tomorrow at midday. I doubt the leaders are violating any laws, but you can use that distraction, Maddox, to search Zakariya's office this time. Try to find out where those propane tanks are headed. If the addresses match any of the domain names of those following Zakariya's playlist, then we'll have enough implication to start arresting and questioning suspects. That'll strengthen our case against the clerics."

"You got it."

"And, by the way, gentlemen, I'm going to be a father in February."

The addendum elicited an astonished silence. Ike no longer looked into the camera. The tips of his ears turned pink as he pretended to wipe dust off his keyboard.

Toby broke the awkward moment with a, "Hooah! Way to go, boss."

A slow smile split Jackson's face. He suddenly realized why Ike had been so damn cranky for the past couple weeks. The specter of fatherhood had obviously terrified him. Eryn had shared with him that Ike's parents had left him to be raised by an abusive older brother. She must have been working on Ike's confidence lately, enough that he was now feeling sufficiently positive to share his news with the team.

"I'm happy for you, Ike," Jackson said, grinning at the mental picture of Ike toting a baby in one arm, his favorite long-range rifle in the other. "You'll make a great dad."

"Yeah, well…" The team lead scratched his chin and changed the subject. "About the journalist—"

"Magadalena."

Ike shot him a look with his eyebrows raised. "Right, her. You tell her we will hold her personally responsible if your identity is leaked to the press."

Jackson forcibly exhaled. "It's out of her hands at this point."

Ike persisted. "Tell her we want twenty-four hours' notice, at least. The second she learns her boss is going public with his disclosure, she contacts Toby, and he pulls you out of there. I don't care what's going on, Maddox. I'm not going to leave you in there to defend yourself against those thugs and the clerics' reprisal. And now that we know a senator's involved, there's no stopping this exposure."

"I appreciate that, sir, but like you said, we need enough evidence to guarantee the imams' indictment."

"And we'll get it. This week," Ike assured him.

"Good luck with Kid Prophet," Toby tossed out.

The incarcerated rapper was the one who needed luck, Jackson thought as Ike ordered them to enjoy their day and disappeared.

Jackson logged them out. He knew he ought to be fretting that his cover was about to be blown; instead, his thoughts were down at the beach where two important females awaited him.

He was out of his chair and opening the door when Toby drawled, "If you don't get a piece of that today, Stonewall, I swear you're going to have some competition."

In the blink of an eye, Jackson was leaning over his colleague and breathing fire. "Don't even think about it," he warned.

Toby's dark blue eyes mocked him. "Relax, man, I would never trespass on your territory. But seriously, I'll watch the kid for you so you can give it your best shot."

"Don't be crass," Jackson said, striding out of the office and across the hall to his room.

A minute later, they bumped into each other out in the hallway, Toby in his Hawaiian shirt and cut-off jeans, Jackson in his swim trunks. Toby raised an inquiring eyebrow, and Jackson felt his face heat. "I accept your offer," he said, shortly. "Give me half an hour."

"Half an hour?" Toby rolled his eyes. "A body like

that should be hammered for at least an hour str—"

Jackson stuck a warning finger in his face. "Don't say it." Disgusted by how easily his colleague pushed his buttons, he stalked toward the sliding glass doors, ignoring Toby's wicked snicker.

"My mom was always sad," Naomi divulged, her shovel sliding into the sand as she carved out a castle moat.

Lena tore her gaze from the dancing water to the profile of the girl sitting next to her, head bowed in concentration. She had promised herself she wouldn't exploit the child by asking questions, but, as it turned out, Naomi didn't need any prompting. Her words suggested all kinds of tragic situations.

Maybe Lena could allow herself one *tiny* question. "Why was she sad?"

Naomi shrugged. "She missed my dad, I guess, 'cause he was in Iraq. But whenever he did come home, my mom got mad and sometimes she'd cry or go for walks by herself."

Oh, dear.

"He thinks you're hot, you know," the girl volunteered, squinting against the sun to smile up at her knowingly.

Pleasure tingled to the ends of Lena's extremities only to fade away with a throb of regret. Whether Jackson could forgive her now depended, in large part, on what happened with his investigation. She had her own concerns to fret about—her interview with Davis, whether Peter would blow Jackson's cover, whether she and Jackson would ever have the chance to reconcile.

It seemed ludicrous to hope for any kind of a relationship between them now, sexual or otherwise.

"I think I'm ready to wade," Lena decided, hoping

to raise her flagging spirits.

Naomi scrambled to her feet. "I promise it's not muddy at all unless you go out deep," she encouraged, running into the shallows and diving under the surface.

Lena took off her tulle blouse and draped it over a chair. Wearing just her royal blue tank top and jeans rolled to her knees, she waded cautiously into the water which closed with welcoming coolness about her calves. "Wow, this feels great," she admitted, wondering if she'd done the right thing to turn down the offer of Silvia's swimsuit.

Movement up at the house had her glancing up. Her heart leapt to see Jackson, bearing an armload of towels on his way down. Toby followed him carrying a cooler, but Lena only had eyes for Jackson, whose smooth bare torso made her heart race.

As Abdul Ibn Wasi, he had appealed to her in a powerful, but illicit way. As Jackson Maddox, there wasn't any dimension of his being that didn't strum a chord of admiration and desire.

"You're staring," Naomi taunted.

"Am not." Lena turned and splashed her. Naomi splashed her back then gasped in remorse when she realized she had soaked Lena's tank top. "It's okay. I can get this shirt wet." She looked back up at the stairs.

The memory of Jackson's skilled tongue turned her bones to Jello as she watched him come closer. To think that just the other night she had gripped the table and begged for his possession. A shiver of longing rippled through her, pearling her nipples and heating her face.

There was no hiding her response from Jackson's sharp gaze as he stepped off the last set of stairs. Blocking Toby's view of her, he deposited their towels on one of the folding chairs and strode into the water toward them.

"You two having fun?" he asked, his gaze dipping toward her sodden top.

"Yes," they chorused.

Compunction at not accepting Jackson's ultimatum wrung Lena's womanly parts. *Say it's not too late,* she begged silently. Seeing him like this, in his off-duty life, interacting with his daughter, he appealed to her so powerfully, she simply had to have him, had to learn all there was about him, to feel him possessing her utterly and completely.

"Swim with us, Dad," Naomi ordered, tossing water on him.

With a mock roar of outrage, he charged his daughter, tackling her into the shallows. They fell together with a splash, and the displaced water billowed toward Lena, soaking her jeans to her thighs.

Shocked, she returned Toby's mocking gaze as he settled into a chair to salute her with his beer. *Oh, what the hell.* She was probably going to get a lot wetter before she got dry again.

She dove in after them.

CHAPTER 15

"FYI, it's 3 P.M.," Toby called, having glanced at his phone.

Lena, sitting in the lounge chair next to him, looked down at her clothing, which had repeatedly been soaked and dried in the scorching sun, over the course of the day. Now, she was wet again. Thanks to the cold beer she'd sucked down, she felt both wonderfully content and sensually stimulated as she watched Jackson draw Naomi about on her float.

She could not remember a single day in the past ten years that she had enjoyed more. Having frolicked for hours in the river with the two of them, sharing comfortable conversation and a picnic of chicken salad sandwiches and strawberries, the last thing she wanted was to return to the reality she'd created for herself these last two weeks.

At Toby's remark, Jackson looked over at her, his expression conveying reluctance. "You should probably head out," he commented. Leaving Naomi to sunbathe on her float, he waded out of the water. Sunlight glimmered on the droplets snaking down his powerful chest, making him look like a dark-skinned

Poseidon.

Lena's heart expanded. Was it possible for him to appeal to her any more than he did? Everything he had said and done today had an immediate, corollary effect on her pulse and her emotions.

Naomi's head popped up. "Oh, man! Can't she stay a little longer?"

Can't I? asked a plaintiff voice in Lena's head.

"We both have to get ready for work, sweetheart." Jackson's firm yet gentle tone made arguing pointless.

Lena admired his assertiveness, while his words elicited a pang of compunction.

"Plus, your grandmother will be here within the hour," he added, unwittingly providing her the impetus to leave. "Stay here with Mr. Burke while I find Lena something to wear and see her on her way."

"But there's nothing to do," Naomi protested, flopping back on her float.

Toby stood up unexpectedly, whipped off his sunglasses, tossed aside his straw hat, and started tackling the buttons on his colorful shirt. "I'll tow you to the other side," he offered.

Naomi squinted at the opposite shore. "You can't swim that far."

But one glimpse at Toby's broad bare back, and Lena was pretty certain that he could.

"Let's go," Jackson urged as Toby dived into the water and seized Naomi's raft.

"Daddy," she shrieked with mixed delight and terror. "He's kidnapping me!"

"You'll be safe," Jackson called with confidence. "Say good-bye to Lena."

Good-bye as in they'd never see each other again?

"Bye!" Naomi called out.

With a poignant farewell, Lena recalled how she'd

never gotten to say good-bye to Alexa. "Good-bye, Naomi. I had a great time today."

As Jackson draped a towel over her shoulders, he sent her a searching look. "You okay?"

"Yeah." She dredged up a smile. "Naomi's great. I like her a lot."

He cut a glance at his daughter, who lay back, smiling up at the sun as her float moved farther into the slow-moving river. "I missed too much of her childhood," she heard him say in a gruff voice. "But that's going to change."

Regarding his pained expression, Lena realized she was seeing his vulnerable side. Her heart seemed to crack in half. "Do you miss your wife?" she blurted.

His startled gaze made her curse her inquisitive nature, but then his words reached her ears and she was glad to have asked.

"Honestly, since we met, you're the only woman I think about."

The sand burning the soles of Lena's feet was the only indication that she wasn't floating inches off the ground. The time had come to bury her pride, once and for all. "Can we start over again, Jackson?" she pleaded.

A slow smile drew back his lips and carved dimples into his cheeks that turned her giddy. "I'd like that," he agreed.

In the next instant, he caught her hand in his and tugged her toward the stairs. Feeling like a teenager, Lena hurried up the zigzag staircase at his side, wondering with a pounding heart, what starting over would look like.

He led her into the cool hallway at the back of the house. "Come on in," he said, waving her into a tidy bedroom with a queen-sized bed. She knew it was his by scent alone. "You need to get out of those wet clothes. I'll find you something to wear home."

He started sifting through his drawers then froze as the door clicked shut and Lena dragged her tank top off over her head. Fire leapt in his gaze as it jumped to hers, then dropped to her naked breasts, following the path of her jeans as she peeled them deliberately over her hips and down her legs, dragging her underwear off with them. "I need you to finish what you started the other night," Lena requested, in a voice thick with longing. Something about Jackson brought out the tigress in her, and she could care less about modesty at the moment.

If he didn't make her his, right here, right now, she would self-combust.

Thank you, Jesus, Jackson thought. Shutting the drawer he'd been riffling through, he approached her wordlessly, backed her against the door, and crushed his mouth over her questing lips.

The kiss was as blistering as the sun outside. With their tongues entwined, Jackson cupped the cool, soft mounds pressed against his chest. Circling the velvety peaks with his thumbs, he brought her nipples into stiffness, eliciting a sexy whimper that drugged him with desire.

Somewhere along the way, his plans to court her slowly, while savoring every moment, had gone up in flames. With Lena, self-control and planning ahead were proving impossible. Breaking off the kiss, he stroked the length of her arms, twined his fingers with hers, and drew her toward the bed.

She followed him willingly. With a hint of color in her cheeks, her eyes sparkling with anticipation, she sank gracefully onto the mattress and scooted to the center to make room for him. The vision she made, with her legs slightly parted, tan lines highlighting her private parts, made him pause just long enough to strip off his swim trunks and take a mental picture. He would savor the memory later. Fully naked, he crawled over her, using his upper arms to push her legs apart. "So beautiful," he muttered drinking her in.

"Jackson." She arched in languorous invitation.

With a growl, he lowered his mouth to her naval, swirled his tongue into the hollow there and tasted salt from the river. He measured the cradle of her hipbones with his lips, lathed the brackets between her thighs and her vulva, approaching the tempting pink flesh that peeked out between the plumper mounds. When he finally licked the tender petals, her cry of satisfaction hit him like a drug being mainlined to his veins.

If only he had all the time in the world to learn what pleased her most. For now butterfly flicks of his tongue and the finger he stroked into her dewy opening seemed sufficient. When she drove her hips eagerly against his hand, he added a second digit. Her muscles gripped him, betraying her eagerness.

"Please, I want you inside me this time."

He wasn't about to deprive himself again. Retrieving a condom he had found in his shaving kit, he ripped into the wrapper with his teeth. "It's been a while," he confessed, embarrassed by his fumbling hands. Prophylactics never seemed big enough. But her eyes, wide and luminous, were mercifully focused on his face.

With the condom covering him, he settled between her open thighs and gazed down at her. Breathing fast, she kneaded his shoulders as if caught up in the immediacy of the moment. He could see the pulse beating at her throat.

"Magdalena," he murmured, watching for the least hint of discomfort as he advanced his penetration inch by inch. "Talk to me. Tell me what you need."

"More." Her lusty answer was almost his undoing. He stilled, afraid of coming too soon.

She undulated, drawing him deeper still.

Pleasure wicked up Jackson's spine and nearly made his head explode. "Promise me," he rasped, "this won't be the last time." As much as he didn't want to think of Davis right now, he was terrified of what the future held in store for both of them. "Promise me you'll be careful."

Her eyes locked with his. "I promise."

Surrendering himself to sensation, he pushed all the way inside her.

Lena had to be in heaven. She'd never experienced this sense of absolute, delectable fulfillment. It was shockingly titillating, outrageously erotic. A primal rhythm pulsed at her core, emitting a slippery heat that allowed them to defy the laws of geometry. God, he so felt incredible inside her!

"You okay?" he asked.

"Oh, yes."

He moved, igniting a relentless craving in her to be driven over the brink. "Take me there, Jackson," she pleaded, coaxing him to keep up with her.

What he made her feel when he moved transformed her into a creature of impulse and appetite. Every foray of his body into hers, whether fast and hard, or deep and slow, was exactly what her body wanted.

"Perfect," she breathed when he shifted to a different rhythm. A light layer of sweat coated them both, enhancing the slippery collision of their bodies. "Don't stop," she begged him as he fought for control. "Don't ever stop, baby."

But her senses could only take so much. With a cry of ecstasy, she gave into the current that swept her toward the brink of release. At Jackson's answering growl, they plummeted over the edge together, crashing into a pool of bliss where they sank deep beneath the surface, pummeled by pleasure, until they floated gently toward shore, secure in the circle of each other's arms.

Peering through her lashes, Lena was almost surprised to find herself in the same place as where they'd been twenty minutes ago, though the room was distinctly warmer and perfumed with the scent of sex. Jackson's stunned and blown-away expression had to be a mirror reflection of her own.

What they'd shared had been sublimely, frighteningly perfect.

With tender fingers, he brushed a damp tendril from her cheek. His heavy sigh seemed to correlate with the pressure that descended suddenly on her chest. She didn't want to leave him, was terrified to let him waltz back into Gateway knowing his safety now rested in her hands. What if Peter refused to tell her before he went public? "I'm scared for us both," she admitted.

His arms tightened around her, holding her more securely. "It's not too late for you to go home," he reminded her.

"And leave you here alone? I don't think so."

"As long as you tell us when your boss takes his story public, I'll be fine. You're the one who's in danger here."

"I'll be fine," she tossed back, using the same words.

They lapsed into quiet, an uneasy truce between them.

"What are you most afraid of, Jackson?" she asked, her fear getting the better of her, ruling the words that slipped off her tongue.

He drew a deep breath then let it out all at once.

"You really want to know?"

"Yes." She wanted to know everything there was to know about him, to carry those details around in her head like love letters to be taken out and examined later.

"All right. I'm terrified of dying in the line of duty. I never used to be afraid of that, and it makes me sound like a coward."

"Not at all," she assured him. "What would Naomi do without you?"

"Exactly. I should put my family first."

A warm gush of emotion filled Lena's heart and sent tears rushing into her eyes. She had never fallen in love before, but if she had, she imagined it would feel like this.

The unmistakable thump of a car door closing caused them both to start. "Naomi's grandmother's back." Jackson's tone was gruff with reluctance.

The tears in Lena's eyes abruptly dried.

"Don't worry," he assured her, reading her expression of chagrin accurately as he scrambled from the bed. "I'll go talk to her." Rifling through his drawers, he produced a pair of drawstring pants and T-shirt. "You can wear these home," he said. He snatched his swim trunks off the floor, dropped a swift kiss on her forehead, and headed for the door. As he crossed the hall into the bathroom, Lena dressed in his overly large clothing, rolling up the pants and tucking in the voluminous T-shirt.

She heard him retreat down the hallway and speak to the grandmother in the kitchen. Feeling awkward and uncertain, she gathered up her damp clothes, took a deep breath, and walked through the living room into the kitchen.

The middle-aged woman standing at the counter looked up at her and beamed. "Here she is," she exclaimed, taking in Lena's flushed dishevelment without so much as a blink.

Bemused, Lena allowed herself to be hugged as Jackson introduced them. "Silvia, this is Magdalena. Lena, this is Naomi's grandmother."

"Nice to meet you," Lena murmured. Her face felt like it was on fire. She glanced at the kitchen clock, "but I do have to get going."

"I'll walk you to your car," Jackson volunteered. Having grabbed her sandals from where she'd left them by the sliding doors, he placed them by her feet.

"Hope to see you again soon," Silvia called as they passed back through the kitchen and out the door there.

"You will," Jackson said on Lena's behalf.

In comfortable silence, they crossed to her Jaguar. Lena unlocked the doors remotely.

Warm air wafted out as he opened her driver's side door. "Make sure you have Toby's number," Jackson reminded her.

Toby had called her cell so she'd have his number on her caller ID. Reaching into the car, she pulled her phone from her purse. "Area code 202?"

"That's him."

Glancing up, Lena caught Jackson studying her intently. The feelings that had overpowered her earlier rose up in her again, and she took a quick step toward him, laying her cheek against his chest to hide her surfaced emotions. His arms folded tenderly around her. *I could just stay right here,* she reflected.

"Remember what you promised me," he rumbled overhead.

He had made her promise that they would be together again; that she'd be careful.

"I won't forget." Forcing a smile, she eased away from him and slipped into her car. Despite the heat in the vehicle a chill formed on the top of her head as she realized she'd be facing her sister's killer in just two days.

It'll be fine, she told herself. She'd made Jackson a promise, and she intended to keep it.

As the wail of a siren penetrated the glass in the cafeteria windows, the parolees and imams looked up from their bowls of lentil soup. The interruption wrested Jackson from memories of the extraordinary contentment he'd experienced yesterday, memories that caused him to get lost in abstraction when he could least afford it. He realized now that the fire marshal had arrived for their surprise inspection. The time had come to search Zakariya's office.

With identical frowns of confusion, the imams rose from their table and hurried outside to investigate. The parolees all looked at one another then abandoned their own lunch to follow them.

This is it, Jackson told himself.

Dawdling, he was the last to reach the exit. Instead of heading outside, he doubled back and hastened to Zakariya's office. The door was shut but thankfully unlocked, saving him the hassle of having to pick the lock.

Slipping into the sunlit office, Jackson shut the door and looked around. Unlike Ibrahim's office, Zakariya's personal space was cluttered with books and paperwork. Finding the evidence he sought would be like looking for a needle in a haystack.

Through the window blinds, the red lights cast by the fire truck glittered on the shed's new shingles where the roof rose over the flat-roofed dormitory. The reassuring sight encouraged him to sift carefully through the paperwork piled on Zakariya's desk. Finding nothing of interest there, he pawed through the drawers and came across a letter which made reference to "a struggle." There were receipts from the purchase of what looked like ammunition and a rental agreement between Zakariya and a storage facility in Washington D.C. More propane tanks might be stockpiled there.

Making a quick decision to copy the evidence onto one sheet so he could hide it inside his pocket, Jackson crossed to the copy machine. A glance outside prompted a spike of alarm. The reflection of red lights on the shed's roof had disappeared. Either the fire trucks had left already or they leaving were soon.

Lifting the lid of the copier, he went to place the originals on the glass, removing the sheet that was already there. He laid the bits of paperwork face down, closed the copier, and hit start. Only then did he glance at the paper in his hands, and did a wide-eyed double take.

Yes! He was looking at a list of forty names, one of which immediately caught his eye: *Mr. Ali Rakeem, Country Club Way, Unit 1000.* Every other name was also listed with an address and an apartment number beginning with the #1. That couldn't be a coincidence.

As the copier spit out a shingle sheet, he overheard voices nearing the mosque. He threw open the lid, swiped up the originals and made a quick copy of the list of names while he stuffed the evidence haphazardly back into Zakariya's desk. As he passed the copier en route to the door, he snatched up the two copies he'd made and slid them up inside his T-shirt.

He had just enough time to dart down the hall before the corridor filled with voices.

"Abdul," Imam Ibrahim reprimanded, catching sight of him. "Where have you been?"

Jackson swiveled, holding his hand over his

stomach to keep the paperwork in place. "I had to use the bathroom," he replied. "I think the soup disagrees with me."

The cleric's suspicion visibly eased as he glanced at Jackson's hand. "Are you still unwell?"

"I feel a little better." Having discovered the destination of the propane tanks, he actually felt better than he had in a very long time.

Catching sight of several parolees crossing Artie's parking lot, their voices raised in excited chatter, Lena handed Seth his daily scratch-ticket and took his payment. A second glance out the front windows confirmed that Jackson was not among the men ambling defiantly past Deputy Doug Hazelwood's cruiser. Beating back her disappointment, she bid Seth a fine evening.

"Sorry for the other night," he muttered. "I don't usually drink."

She dragged her attention from the window. "That's fine. You don't owe me an apology, Seth. In fact, I'm glad you shared what was troubling you." If he hadn't stated his lamentations last night, she might never have taken the initiative to warn Jackson about his cover being blown. It was because of Seth that she'd given Jackson a heads-up. Plus she'd secured Peter's promise to give her twenty-four hours, before publishing his exposé.

Seth frowned, obviously trying to remember what he'd said to her.

In the next instant, Muhammed, Shahid, Hasan, Jamal, Davis and Corey all tumbled into the store, still snickering over some snide comment about the deputy, who openly glowered at them.

"Hey, Miz Maggie." Muhammed was the first to salute her, showing every tooth in his mouth when he smiled.

Seth had stiffened at their entrance. With a suspicious look on his face, he slid to one side of the counter and started scratching away on his ticket, something he had never done before. It occurred to Lena that he was reluctant to leave her alone with the parolees. How sweet was that?

"Hi, fellas," she said, taking note of their contented expressions. "What's going on? You all look like you won the lottery or something."

Muhammed held up a hand, showing her a shiny black cell phone. "Look what we all got today." If possible, his smile widened.

"They gave you new cell phones?"

"Sho'nuff. Now we can give you our phone numbers, and you call us, you know, when you need more for the book."

"Okay." She'd had no intention of calling any of them, except maybe Corey to whom she felt she owed an explanation for defaulting on her promise. All the same, she laid a sheet of paper and a pen on the counter. "Go ahead and jot your numbers down," she said, handing the pen to Corey first as she expressly wanted his number.

"Muhammed hopes you gonna call him up and ask him out," Shahid mocked as Corey handed Muhammed the pen to go next.

"Man, shut up. I never said nothin' like that." Muhammed scribbled down his new number.

"Both of you boys talk too much," Davis interrupted, snatching the pen from Muhammed's grasp.

At the sound of his deep voice, Seth's head swiveled in his direction. His face drained of color and his green-as-grass eyes bugged as he staggered back a step or two. Then, without a word, he turned and bolted out the door, leaving his scratch-off ticket on the counter.

"Seth, your ticket!" Lena called, but he was already halfway across the parking lot, and Deputy Doug was climbing out of his cruiser with a strange look on his face.

"What the fuck's his problem?" Davis demanded, shoving the pen at Hasan.

"Now, look what you done," Muhammed groused. "Cop thinks you done chased him off."

"I didn't do shit."

Hasan and Shahid had just finished jotting down their numbers when Deputy Doug swept into the building, setting off the chime. Raking a critical look over the motley crew, he planted his feet apart, crossed his arms over his protruding belly and asked, "Everything okay in here, gentlemen? Maggie?"

"Of course," Lena said brightly. "The men were just showing me their new cell phones."

"I think they've lingered long enough." The deputy hooked his thumbs in his pockets, putting his right hand conveniently close to his pistol.

Honestly, that was fine with her. Corey should have come over alone for his interview. But it was unusual for the deputy to interfere when the parolees loitered in the store just to chat. Tonight, though, he obviously intended to chase them all out.

"Well, you guys heard him," she said. "Off you go. I'll see you soon enough." Catching Corey's eye, she leaned across the counter to whisper, "I'll call you to reschedule."

"Shoot, we ain't no threat to Miz Maggie," Muhammed protested as he swaggered past the cop.

Deputy Doug's response was to rest his hand casually on his gun holster.

Grumbling under their breath, all six men filed

outside, brought up at the rear by Corey. It was Davis who looked back, though, shooting her and the officer a suspicious look.

"Go ahead and fetch your keys," Deputy Doug instructed quietly. "I want you to lock up now and stay that way till my replacement shows up."

"Why, what's wrong?"

"My wife's been in an accident. I need to get to the hospital," he said without inflexion.

"Oh, I'm so sorry." Feeling beneath the counter, Lena located the keys.

With the deputy standing outside the building, she locked the doors from within. "I hope your wife's okay," she called through the glass. He tipped her a tight-lipped nod, hurried to his car, and sped away.

It was only quarter to eight on a Monday night, and she'd heard nothing to indicate when the deputy's replacement might show up. In the meantime, unable to meet customers' needs, she dimmed the lights at the front of the store, leaving the neon sign over the highway illumined so that customers with credit cards could still buy gas. Then she looked around for something to do. She could spend the time restocking the refrigerators and searching for the video file that she'd apparently misplaced on the store's computer.

With a tingle of anticipation, it occurred to her that tonight would be the perfect opportunity for Jackson to swing by for an evening tryst. She hadn't caught so much as a glimpse of him since yesterday. While that was scarcely more than twenty-four hours ago, time had slowed to a crawl since. It felt like days since she'd last felt his arms around her.

Cristemou, if she weren't convinced she wasn't the type to easily give her heart away, she might have to conclude that she was already deeply in love with the man.

CHAPTER 16

Two hours later, it dawned on Lena that the videos she'd saved on Artie's computer weren't missing; they'd been *removed* by either Jackson or his colleague. As much as she cared for the man, he had routed her efforts at every turn! With a groan of annoyance, she threw herself out of the chair and went to the front of the store to count the money in the register.

The view out the windows displayed brightly lit gas pumps and an empty parking lot. Deputy Hazelwood's replacement had never shown up, and neither had Jackson. With his cover already in jeopardy, she figured he couldn't afford to violate curfew; still, she viewed this as a wasted opportunity.

Doubts percolated in her mind. What if Jackson didn't feel the same intense yearning to be with her as she felt for him? The possibility paralyzed her until she recalled that he'd wanted her to promise their time together wouldn't be the last. Her fear dissolved into mere disappointment.

By the time she finished counting and bagging the cash, it was 10 P.M. The Gateway campus stood entirely in darkness. With little hope that Jackson might still show up after curfew, she made up her mind to leave the store when a quiet knock at the service entrance made her heart leap with joy.

Dropping the money bag on the counter, Lena smoothed the sundress she had worn just in case Jackson came to visit and flew through the back room to let him in.

A quick peek through the peep hole revealed his dark, powerful silhouette. With the blood singing through her veins, she unlocked the door and pushed it wide open. Her welcoming smile froze into a grimace of terror as she recognized Davis, not Jackson, standing like a dark specter in the alleyway.

"Wh-what are you doing here, Sulayman?" Her voice came out high and thin.

"You expectin' someone else?" he accused.

"No. No, of course not. I just…came to see who was knocking. What do you want?"

"What'chu think I want? I figured since that cop ain't comin' back, you should interview me tonight."

"Tonight?" She tried to swallow but her throat was too dry. Was he serious about the interview or was he planning to attack her? "I really can't. I-uh-I left my laptop at home and all my questions and my notes are on it," she said, speaking faster than she could think.

"You'll make do." With that prediction, he bulldozed his way inside, forcing her to scuttle back while blocking her only exit. As he took a good look around, she fought desperately to rein in her runway panic.

My God, I'm alone with my sister's killer and no cop outside!

Common sense advised her to arm herself and to keep calm. Like the predator he was, Davis would sense her fear if she let it get the best of her. "Fine, you want to do this now?" she said more firmly. "Wait right here. I need to get a notebook."

As she hurried up front, her gaze traveled longingly to the front doors. Either she could slip out that way like a coward, or she could interview Davis now and get what she'd come to Mechanicsville for.

Considering all she'd gone through to get to this moment, the decision was daunting but not hard to make.

Drawing her purse out from under the register, she flipped the switch in the lipstick-case clipped to one side, activating her new spy camera. She'd procured it on the same day that she'd bought her new Mac. With trembling hands, she transferred her micro pistol to the voluminous left pocket of her sundress. Grabbing up a notepad and a pen, she willed her heart to stop pounding.

In order to pull this off, she had to be convincing.

I can do this. Plus, with Deputy Doug Hazelwood out of the picture, Davis just might actually tell her what she wanted to know.

She thought of Jackson and her promise to be careful. She thought of Alexa and the justice she deserved. And then she slowly and deliberately turned toward the store room.

Rupert Davis scrutinized sexy Maggie. Her red and white sundress had a high waist, a low neckline and a short hem that showed more of her smooth, tan skin than it covered. Silver jewelry shimmered at her pulse points. Women who dressed the way she did deserved to get what they were asking for.

He licked his lips. She sure had it coming.

He hadn't returned to Artie's so much to be interviewed as to relish his plans for her. Her tale that she was writing a book was just an excuse to lure men one-by-one into the back of the store, anyway. She claimed to be a writer, but she was just a slut like any other woman, the strong-willed kind that didn't break when things got rough. But when the time was right, he'd show her who had the upper hand.

"Have a seat," she offered, nodding at the chair cattycorner to the one she pulled away from the table. Situating her purse, pen and notepad on the tabletop, she smoothed the shapeless fabric of her dress and sank into her seat, crossing her legs at the knee. A whiff of her perfume and a glimpse of bare thigh clouded his thoughts momentarily.

Not yet, he cautioned, feeling his dick swell. Later, when he lured her to the abandoned meat plant on 15th Street South East, where all trace of her struggles could be eradicated, he would take what he wanted. And then it would be the tangy sweet smell of her fear that excited him, not her perfume.

As he wallowed in his anticipation, she picked up her pen, started scribbling a note, then laid it promptly down.

Only, too late. He had seen her fingers trembling.

Excitement boiled inside him as he noted, too, the rapid pulse along her slender neck. The telltale signs of her fear goaded him to attack her now, to shred her clothing and throw her to the floor beneath him.

But then she met his stare with such a direct look that he questioned his perceptions. Maybe the bitch was turned on by him, not afraid.

"Tell me about your childhood, Sulayman," she calmly requested.

Confused by mixed signals, he obliged her by describing what it was like growing up in Ward 8 public housing. He had been a member of a street gang. Bodies were being bagged and carted away, sometimes daily. "Cops told me I could testify against my friends or go to jail with them. So I testified. That's when I realized whose side it paid to be on," he recollected.

"How old were you then?" she asked him.

"Fifteen."

"If you could talk to the boy you used to be, what would you tell him?"

He had to think a moment. "Trust no one," he finally decided. "Not your mother, not your so-called friends. It's every man for himself. Write that down," he added, proud of the way he'd phrased his thoughts.

She jotted his words down quickly. "You mentioned your mother," she noted, her pen now steady in her pink-tipped fingers. "What did she do to break your trust?"

Davis snorted his derision. "All that cunt was ever interested in was how to get her next fix."

"So, you're saying she was a drug addict," Maggie inferred, with little trace of empathy.

"And a whore," he added, reliving the first time he'd seen his mother with a man. He had recoiled that first time, but after years of watching perverts exploit her filthy body, he'd realized she deserved every minute of her torment.

"Do you mean that was her profession? Or is that just your opinion of her?"

"Both," he spat.

"Has your mother affected your view of all females?"

"Whatchu think?" Her fixation on is mother was beginning to annoy him.

"What about your father? Where was he?"

"Who the hell knows? I never knew him."

"I see. How old were you, then, when you became a police officer?"

"Nineteen. I went to the academy right out of high school."

Her assessing gaze fell to his broad shoulders. "Would you say you were an asset to the force?"

He sat up straighter. "Hell, yeah. Because of me, Ward 8 became a decent place to live."

"Did you end up having to arrest your friends? People you knew?"

He shrugged. "Had to. So what? That was the only way to clean up my neighborhood."

"What was your strategy?"

"I owned the drug dealers," he admitted, experiencing the same heady power he'd felt back then. "Hell, I owned the whole damn city. See, crime is always gonna be there. Key is to make it work for you. I made 'em fear me." He paused, remembering his glory days. "Someone's got to rule. That was me. That's what I did."

"I guess the system didn't see it that way," she drawled, all inflection smoothed from her voice. "Or you wouldn't have gone to jail."

He could have cared less what the system thought. "Bet you the streets are crawling with vermin now," he predicted darkly.

She heaved a sigh, laid down her pen, and sat back.

"What?" he demanded, sensing her disappointment.

She raised her eyebrows at him. "I don't know, Sulayman. I guess I'm looking for more substance to my book, you know? My goal is to tell gripping, true-life stories about the other side of crime, but drug trafficking doesn't interest people. It's not like abduction, or rape, or murder. That's the stuff that sells." She sent him pleading look. "And so far, I haven't gotten anything like that from any of the others. I was hoping to get it from you. I mean," her gaze skittered over him, "you just seem so much more experienced."

Her words filled him with satisfaction. "So what if I am?"

She spread her hands. "Then here's your chance to show people how the world really works. People need a reality check. You've seen the darker side of life, and you mastered it. Prove yourself the master."

He liked the word she used—*the master*. It reminded him of what Ibrahim insisted, that he was Allah; he was God. As such, he could do whatever the hell he wanted.

"Come on, now." Her voice grew husky. "You must've have gotten away with some awfully naughty things as a cop. Am I right?"

The way she touched her tongue to her teeth made his dick tingle. He'd gone so long without pussy in prison that he doubted he could ever get enough to make up for his deprivation. His plan to lure her to the abandoned meat market two weeks from now seemed suddenly too distant. "Shit," he drawled, stalling to think through his options. "I wouldn't know where to start."

Her eyes shimmered with excitement. "Are you that bad of a boy?"

Her effect on him was too much to ignore. "Why don't you sit your pretty little ass in my lap and I'll show you just how bad I am," he growled, drawing attention to his hard on as he rubbed himself through his pants. Problem was, if he took her here, he might lose control, leave a DNA trail that couldn't be covered up, and then he'd be back in the slammer before he knew what hit him. They would have to go somewhere else for what he had in mind.

"I want a rape story," she requested unexpectedly, keeping his fire lit with her bold request.

"Why?" Seeing his hard-on must have excited her.

"You like it rough?"

"Maybe," she hinted. "Do you have one for me?"

"I might." She didn't know how rough she was going to get it. It was becoming more difficult by the moment to think clearly. Maybe if they got in her car and went somewhere…

"Women have a weakness for a man in uniform. A man with a gun." She ran her gaze over him. "I'm sure you had all the ladies throwing themselves at you."

"Let's go for a ride," he suggested. Surrounded as they were by miles of farmland, how hard could it be to find a place where no one would find any evidence if things went south? Some women acted like they liked it and still pressed charges later. And others fought like they'd never led on like they wanted it— the bitches.

"I'll think about it," she replied, sliding a hand causally into the folds of her dress.

He cut her hand a suspicious glance. Was she hiding something down there or playing with herself? He couldn't tell what she was doing with the tabletop blocking his view.

"Maybe you just need more incentive," she suggested.

Her words snatched his gaze up. "Like what?"

"What if I offered to pay you money?"

Just the mention of money made his mouth water. Fresh out of prison with no finances to speak of, money was second to what he wanted most, sex being the first. Money bought cocaine, which he could always sell at a profit. "How much?"

"Up to five thousand dollars," she promised smoothly, "if you tell me a really good story now."

Suspicion wicked into Rupert's brain. Why was she so desperate that she felt the need to buy him? "Where you gonna get money like that?" he asked.

She shrugged. "My daddy's rich. You've seen my new ride, haven't you?"

The sleek Jag outside had caught his eye on Sunday. Hell, who cared where the money came from? Having a small fortune to invest in drugs was a broke ex-con's dream-come-true. He couldn't afford to turn her down.

A rape story huh? He had so many of those he wouldn't know which one to pick. One in particular stood out, though, because he'd almost been caught— but not really, because he'd known what he was doing and he'd outsmarted the system, something he could have done forever if some rat hadn't ended up squealing on him.

Maybe she'd pay even more for a juicy story like that.

"Well..." He paused, measuring the risk. There'd been no evidence to indict him then. Ten years later, he ought to be safe in coming clean. "One time stands out because I did almost get caught, though the bitch turned out not to be worth the trouble."

Her expression seemed to freeze. "You almost got caught?"

"There was this school girl I picked up one night on patrol. Found her bein' harassed by the wrong kind of people, if you know what I mean. I was gonna take her home to her parents, but then I thought, what's this schoolgirl doin' out alone at night? And then I knew; she was out looking for action, just like any other whore. So I decided to give it to her good and ha-"

A rap on the door behind them cut him off.

Davis leapt to his feet. The story he was on the verge of confessing made him react like a hunted man. "Who's that? You got someone listening outside?"

She cut him an innocent but frazzled look. "No, I have no idea who's out there."

Paranoia flooded his mind. What if the cop was back, listening through the walls with some newfangled technology?

Something wasn't right about this whole set up. His skin had been crawling for ten minutes straight. The scheming bitch had to be up to something. Lunging at Maggie, he caught her by the neck, plucked her out of her seat and dragged her to him, pinning her back to his chest so he could use her as a hostage in some worst-case scenario.

But then he heard a familiar voice on the other side of the door calling, "Sulayman, open up!" And he realized it was only Corey—that studious do-gooder. What the hell did he want?

With Maggie's soft ass pressed against his hard dick, Davis found himself incapable of letting go. Giving himself a taste of what he'd do to her next time, he squeezed one of her big tits and stabbed his tongue into her ear. The way her body locked up in protest turned him even harder. But then Corey knocked on the door again, distracting him from his pleasure.

"Mother fucker." With parolees looking for him, there was no way in hell he'd get to satisfy his compulsions tonight.

No worries. He still had plans for Maggie. Now he knew exactly how to lure her to the meat market. It'd be easier than it might have been. "Keep it quiet," he warned her, slowly removing his hand from her throat. Shifting to see her better, he savored his power over her as she gagged and sucked in air. "You want to hear the rest of my story?" he asked, as her fit subsided.

Lifting wide, watering eyes at him, she gave a nod.

He snatched the pen off the table. "Write your number on my hand," he requested. "I'll call you in two weeks. You come with the money and you'll have that story and more."

Fingers trembling uncontrollably, she scrawled a D.C. phone number onto his palm as he raked her curvaceous body with dark anticipation. "We'll finish this when I'm done at Gateway," he vowed.

Striding to the door, he thrust it open, knocking the steel panel into Corey's face as the man had his ear to the door.

"Watchu want?" he growled, herding him away from the building.

"Ibrahim's lookin' for contraband," Lena heard Corey murmur just before the door clanged shut.

Overcome with relief to find herself alone and in one-piece, Lena sank bonelessly onto the dusty floor where she battled the impulse to vomit.

Diavolos!

One minute she'd been euphoric with the realization that Davis was confessing to her sister's murder; the next, she was writhing in pain and in mortal fear as he overreacted to the interruption.

The certainty that he would have sealed his own sentence of guilt made the ache in her throat all the more unbearable. Acid burned her esophagus as she realized she could still feel his saliva in her ear. She scoured it with her sleeve, shuddering in disgust.

Damn Corey for undoing her hard-earned work in an instant! And damn Davis for reacting like the guilty beast he was and cutting short his confession at the most critical moment.

She felt her neck for permanent damage. A fraction harder of a squeeze, and he'd have cut off her airway completely.

But the physical discomfort was nothing compared to the crushing knowledge that all the effort she had poured into this project was for naught…unless, of course, she met Davis when he called her looking for the money.

There was still that option. Except just thinking of it made her sick to her stomach.

A soft knock at the door snatched her head up. She winced and scrambled to her feet. Had Davis come back? God, no!

Drawing her micro pistol from her pocket, she flipped off the safety and aimed it wildly at the door.

The knock came again, urgently.

Could it be Jackson? She didn't want him seeing Davis's handiwork.

A soft whirring sound replaced the knocking, and the lock on the door shivered. In the next instant, the lever turned and the door swung open. Lena's grip on the pistol tightened, only to relax again as Jackson's colleague, Toby, surged into the room.

Wresting the gun from her grasp, he set it aside. His horrified gaze locked on her bruised throat. "Christ, Jackson is going to kill me."

"What are you doing here?" she asked, confused by his presence.

"He texted me. Said you were over here alone with Davis. I had to talk him out of coming over here himself—not a good idea, what with the bad blood between him and Davis. I got here as fast as I could. It was his idea to send Corey in the meantime."

"What?" Then it was Jackson's fault Corey had interrupted her interview.

A pounding at the door startled them both. "That's gotta be Jackson." Toby crossed to the door to let him in. "She's alive," he said on a reassuring note as

Jackson barreled past Toby to get to her.

"Lena!" His reaction to the marks on her neck was identical to his colleague's. "That sick son of a bitch," he raged through clenched teeth. He whirled on his partner. "What took you so long?"

"I was on the other side of Mechanicsville!"

Frustration and fury exploded in Lena without warning. She shoved Jackson with all her might. "You arrogant jerk!" she grated hoarsely. He staggered back and she pursued him. "I had him!" she cried, striking his chest with her balled hands. "I had my sister's killer eating out of the palm of my hand. He was telling me exactly how it happened, and it was Alexa he was talking about because he mentioned her school uniform, and that's when Corey knocked on the door and interrupted his confession. All because of you and your meddling. How could you!"

Stone-faced, Jackson caught her wrists as she continued to pummel him. "Stop it," he insisted. "Calm down."

"Calm down?" Tears scalded her eyes, blurring her vision. "You have the gall to tell me to calm down when you just ruined everything? Get out!" She jerked her chin furiously at the door. "Just go. I don't want to look at you right now."

At her harsh words, Jackson freed her wrists abruptly. "You're being unreasonable."

"Unreasonable? How do you expect me to behave? I told you I could do this. I promised I would be careful. You demand me to trust you, but you didn't trust me. How does that make *me* unreasonable?" She swiped an impatient hand over the tears now leaking from her eyes.

"He was in here alone with you," Jackson countered. "Look at your neck. He could have killed you, for Christ's sake!"

"I had my gun the whole time."

"That puny thing? He could have knocked it right out of your hands, just like I could have done that night in the alley when you pulled it on me. You're lucky to be alive, Lena. Why don't you get that?"

"I wasn't in danger until Corey started knocking," she insisted. Whirling on him, she crossed to the table where she flipped open her lipstick case and switched off the camera. To think that she'd been a hair's-breadth from capturing Davis's full confession! The only real evidence she'd recorded was his vicious attack. And that would get him—what?—a couple of months in jail, at most.

Out the corner of her eye she saw Toby and Jackson share a look as they realized they had both been caught on video.

"Here." Unsnapping the small pouch, she turned and thrust it at Jackson. "I don't need this anymore. Congratulations, you've finally gotten rid of me," she added, snatching her gun off the table where Toby had set it and dropping it in her purse. "I'll be out of here tomorrow, so you can continue your investigation without any distraction."

"Lena," Jackson protested, but his tone couldn't completely hide his relief. "Why don't you stay at the river house with Naomi and Silvia?" he offered.

Memories of the perfect day spent with him and his daughter filled her with sorrow. But, like she'd told him once before, she was not that quick to forgive. Right now, she just wanted to retreat and lick her wounds in isolation.

She shook her head refusing the offer. "I have to go. My work is finished here." She'd put all her eggs in one basket, and now the basket was dropped, the eggs all broken. Her only hope was that Davis would call to request a rendezvous in two weeks. Not that she was looking forward to it.

"You need to get back," Toby said to Jackson, who continued to ignore him.

"Lena," he called as she turned her back on him, marching into the unlit store to fetch the money from the counter. She still needed to drop the pouch off at the bank.

Ignoring the cameras in the store for once, he caught up to her by the register. Catching her elbow, he swung her around. "Lena," he said in that firm voice he used with Naomi. "Look at me."

Steeling her heart against the pull of emotion she knew she would feel, she raised her eyes reluctantly to his. Even in the dark they shone like stars at dusk.

"Make sure you put ice on your neck the first chance you get." His gruff concern was palpable as he cupped either side of her face, holding it captive. "You promised me," he reminded her on a note of disappointment.

She hadn't forgotten. But right now, there was no future, only the past, and every dream she'd harbored in the last ten years had just been swept down the drain.

"You'd better go before you're missed," she whispered, her heart hard and cold.

He stroked his thumbs lightly over her cheeks, clearly hoping for some softening of her expression, only she refused to relent, and he stepped away from her with a sigh. "Toby will make sure you get home safe tonight, and he'll stay in touch. I *will* see you again, Magdalena," he added on a firmer note. Then he turned and disappeared into the storeroom.

He and Toby exchange terse words before the door shut quietly behind him.

Lena picked up the money pouch. Feeling numb, she jotted Bill a note of apology, letting him know that she wouldn't be back. Then she took one last look around.

She'd intended on leaving this place with everything needed to bring closure to her sister's death. Instead, she had nothing but a bruised neck and a broken heart to show for it.

CHAPTER 17

Jackson awoke in the middle of the night, his heart thudding unevenly, a lump in his throat. Plagued by disturbing dreams, he'd done nothing but surface sleep for the past several hours. Whenever he lapsed into unconsciousness, he dreamed of Lena with her neck ravaged, glaring at him accusingly.

Colleen used to look at him like that, but for entirely different reasons. At least he couldn't be blamed for neglecting Lena also. If anything, he'd been overprotective. But what kind of concerned citizen would leave her alone with Davis in a closed, locked store? If he hadn't alerted Corey who'd come up with the idea of warning Davis about a room inspection, who knew what Davis might have done to Lena? His imagination supplied an appalling answer.

Christ, he'd never fall back asleep if he kept up this line of thinking.

Things will get better, he assured himself, now that the Taskforce had sufficient evidence to start arresting people. Toby had let him know that between the list Jackson had found on Zakariya's copier, the information Ike had extorted from the incarcerated rapper, and the files they could now access on Ibrahim's computer, the Taskforce had pieced together a clear and chilling picture of the imams' vision of Judgment Day.

Those receiving the propane were all original graduates of Gateway. For seven years, Gateway had been supplying each man with propane. While records stated it was to be used for heat, the apartment buildings were all upscale residences heated by natural gas and occupied by mainly white, upper-middle class professionals. That left only one viable use for the amassed propane.

At a designated date and time, to be conveyed in code through Zakariya's top ten music picks, all that volatile accelerant was to be released at once and ignited via remote detonators, instigating explosions throughout the city. Forty apartment buildings would collapse as a result, causing widespread death and injury.

In the ensuing chaos, Five Percenters would arm themselves with the weapons Ike had found in the storage facility in D.C. and take to the streets to kill or maim any white man or woman in positions of power. Jackson shuddered at the thought of all those weapons in the hands of brainwashed ex-cons.

Worse than that, documents in Ibrahim's computer detailed plans to attack federal buildings, banks, and institutions of higher learning, not just in Washington, D.C., but throughout cities on the east coast. If Ibrahim's diabolical plan unfurled as he had architected it, the nation would be stood on its head, as the so-called gods of the Earth wrested the reins of power from those who presently held it.

As long as the Taskforce took quick, decisive action to tear down the infrastructure of the Five Percent Nation, to confiscate their tools of war and stifle their communication, then Ibrahim's plans for Judgment Day would never get off the ground.

At last, given the mass of evidence now in hand, the Attorney General was seeking warrants for both imams' arrest. It could all go down in a matter of hours now. In the meantime, Jackson was to keep a low profile and not make waves.

Heaving an unsettled sigh, he willed himself to fall more deeply asleep. *Ride it out,* he told himself. *It'll soon be over.*

Lena blinked her bleary eyes and looked around. After nearly three weeks in her rental cottage, it came as a shock to awaken in her tastefully appointed Alexandria apartment, just across the river from the nation's capital.

With its modern furniture and central air, the room was startlingly plush compared to what she'd gotten used to. Wincing at the stiffness in her neck, she turned her head to eye the bedside clock. She had slept until early afternoon.

After last night's fiasco, she'd packed up her possessions and driven straight to the city, even though she knew it would be nearly dawn by the time she arrived. Crawling into bed, she'd tossed and turned, her mind too full of frightening visions of what Davis had in mind for her when she met up with him next.

At 4 A.M., desperate for rest, she'd taken a sleeping pill to knock herself out. Now half the day was gone, and she felt miserable and hung-over.

A composite of Jackson's face, looking both determined and torn, loomed large in her mind. Yearning wracked her heart and made her body throb with want. They'd shared a passion unlike anything she'd ever experienced. Only, he'd gotten in the way of the one thing that meant most to her—putting her sister's killer behind bars. How could she ever forgive him?

Yet, the fact that he was still neck-deep in his own investigation made her feel guilty for even thinking that way. She might not forgive him, but she dreaded the thought of harm befalling him.

Rolling toward her bedside table, Lena fumbled for the landline phone. As tired as she was, it took a couple of tries before she punched in the number to *Crime and Liberty*'s main office correctly. Clearing her hoarse throat, she identified herself to Peter's secretary and asked to be put through.

He came on the line several seconds later.

"I just wanted to let you know that I'm back in the city," she croaked. "My investigation's over," she added with a pang.

"What's wrong with your voice?" he asked. "Are you sick?"

"It's just a cold," she insisted. "I got a partial confession," she added, in answer to his first question. "Would have had everything but we were interrupted."

He was quiet for several seconds. "Well, I'm sorry it didn't work out for you," he said with a question in his voice.

Regret wrung her heart anew. She wasn't in the mood to provide Peter with details. "Thanks."

"So, will you be coming into the office any time soon?"

"Maybe next week." Her neck would look worse before it looked any better. "How's your research coming on the investigation at Gateway?"

"Oh, great," he said on a note of disdain. "Get this: the Feds think the leaders there are backing Algerian rebels."

"How do you know they're not?"

"Oh, come on. Do you know how easy it is to plant that kind of evidence? I told you, Lena, they're trying to frame the Muslim leaders because they deplore diversity."

"Whatever, Peter. Just remember that you promised me a week's notice."

"No worries. I'm not going to run the piece until October."

Why would Peter wait that long? But then she thought of the senator who'd helped him identify Jackson. "Let me guess. You're counting on your article to impact the Presidential election?"

"Of course. This is the perfect example of how paranoid the President is. If you're a Muslim and a former prisoner, then you're automatically a terrorist."

"I doubt it's that's simple, Peter. Do me a favor, if you change your mind and run your story any earlier, I want you to call me, okay?"

"Why?" he asked, ever the journalist.

"I'll explain later. Just remember who brought this to your attention in the first place," she pointed out.

"Fine, I'll call you."

"Thanks. Listen, I have to go." Her head had started throbbing. Without waiting for his good-bye, she dropped the phone into its cradle and rolled out of bed to find her cell phone. Toby would probably like to know that Peter wasn't running his story for another two months.

Jackson slipped out of his dorm room into a balmy evening to jog to the forest and meet up with Toby. No sooner had he shut his door than a local sheriff's car, driven by the deputy who'd guarded Artie's, swerved into the entrance at Gateway right in front of him. Two official vehicles from another district followed right on his tail. All three cruisers were moving fast and displaying their lights.

Jackson blinked in surprise. The logo on the sides of the second two cars told him they were D.C. Metropolitan Police. What the hell? Was the Taskforce arresting the imams without giving Jackson so much as a head's up?

Postponing his run, he chased the cruisers around the dormitory and found them blocking the gate to the basketball court. Ten or so parolees had frozen in the midst of a game to gape at the lawmen popping out of their cars with pistols drawn.

"Hands up and spread out along the fence!" Deputy Hazelwood shouted. He and three Metropolitan police officers approached the cage. Two of the four edged into the enclosure just as the halogen lights, operating on a timer, flickered on.

"Which one of you men is Rupert Davis?" the larger officer demanded.

Stunned and curious, Jackson inched closer.

None of the parolees spoke up to rat out Davis, probably because none of them knew him by his birth name, but Davis took a wary step backwards, drawing attention to himself.

"You're Rupert Davis?" demanded the Metropolitan police officer, honing in on him.

Under the bright lights, Davis's skin shone with a film of perspiration. "My name is Sulayman," he snarled, his gaze shifting left, then right.

Jackson smiled, anticipating the sight of his arrest.

Just then Imam Ibrahim came rushing out of the mosque, his sleeves flapping like the wings of a stricken bird. "What is going on here?" he cried.

Jackson strained to hear Deputy Hazelwood's reply.

"We have a warrant for the arrest of Rupert Davis."

"On what charge?" Davis asked, no longer denying

who he was. "I ain't done nothin' wrong."

"For the murder of a fifteen-year-old girl," answered the cop approaching him.

"Those charges were dropped ten years ago," Davis protested, the whites of his eyes more evident than usual.

"New evidence has cropped up," the officer stalking him said.

Jackson couldn't believe his ears. What new evidence? Even if Davis had finished confessing to Lena, which he hadn't, she'd surrendered her spy camera to the Taskforce agents. She didn't have the proof to instigate this kind of action.

"Hit the ground, Davis," the officer continued. "You know the drill. Arms behind your back, legs spread. The rest of you put your backs to the fence and stay there."

Eyes rolling, Davis hunted for an escape route. But the fleeing felon rule that authorized police to shoot persuaded him to drop stiffly to his knees. In the next instant, he lay face down on the asphalt.

Watching the officer put a knee into Davis's spine and cuff him, it was all Jackson could do not chuckle with satisfaction. With all eyes focused on the activity on the blacktop, he stealthily retreated. No one had taken any special note of him.

As he turned toward the highway, his attention fell on the Amish man standing at the corner of Artie's, watching the action from across the street. The protected soul had probably never witnessed an arrest before.

Relief lightened Jackson's step as he raced down the quiet highway, running as fast as he ever had. The peach-colored sky and the cooler air lifted his spirits to new heights as he pictured Lena's overjoyed response to Davis's arrest. As long as the new evidence that had come to light kept Davis behind bars, Jackson had reason to believe she might finally let go of the past and concentrate on the future—*their* future together.

Turning off the highway, he sprinted beneath the power lines. On either side of the cleared track, the last rays of sunlight turned the leaves of the trees to green flame, but the trunks were already lost in shadow. He didn't immediately see Toby until the ATF agent detached himself from a tree trunk to intersect his path. If he was carrying his air soft gun, Jackson couldn't see it.

An earring glinted in Toby's left earlobe. Today his T-shirt read: *I HEAR VOICES IN MY HEAD, AND THEY DON'T LIKE YOU.*

Jackson stopped in front of him, holding up a finger for Toby to let him catch his breath. He put his hands on his knees for a moment and then straightened. "Okay. What's going on?"

"The warrants are being processed. We're arresting the imams tomorrow," Toby announced straight-faced.

"Why don't you look happy?" Jackson asked with suspicion.

"The Attorney General wants to make a public example of the leaders, so guess who he's bringing with him."

No. Jackson balled his hands into fists. "The press," he guessed, with sudden misgivings.

"You got it."

Arresting a religious leader on sacred property was contentious enough without the media getting involved. Jackson shook his head. "I can't see Ike agreeing to that."

"The AG's pulling rank on him," Toby answered. "He thinks we'll crush the morale of Ibrahim's followers by filming his humiliation."

"That's just going to piss them off," Jackson declared.

"Our thoughts exactly."

Jackson sighed. "What can I do?"

"Ike wants you to stay put in case something goes wrong. Once the imams are in custody, head toward the highway, keeping clear of the press, and I'll pick you up there. We don't want your face on the six o'clock news."

"What time tomorrow?" Anticipation kept Jackson's pulse elevated. The end could not come soon enough. By tomorrow night he might be home with his daughter, reunited with Lena.

"Mid-afternoon."

"Cool. I'll be ready. Listen, I need you to tell Lena something for me," he requested, recalling recent events.

"What's that?"

"Davis was just arrested for the murder of her sister."

Toby's eyebrows shot up. "No shit. How'd that happen?"

"Some new evidence came to light. I have no idea what. Maybe she can find out. Can you give her a call?"

"Sure," Toby promised.

"Tell her—" Jackson's chest swelled with longing as he recalled her devastation last night, the way she'd blamed him for ruining her plans. He wished he knew what to say to make amends, to ensure that she kept her promise to be with him again. "Tell her I love her," he muttered hoarsely, his face hot with chagrin.

Toby cringed. "You're such a sap, Jack. I'll tell her about Davis, but I am *not* telling her you love her. *Yich.*"

Jackson exhaled heavily. "Fine. Just tell her about Davis."

"Will do. Keep your head in the game a little longer, man. You're almost home free." Toby clapped him on the shoulder, spun him around, and gave him a push back in the direction of Gateway.

Anticipating the sting of a pellet from Toby's airsoft gun, Jackson bolted, only it never came.

Once safely out of range, he tried slowing his pace so he wouldn't tire early but it felt as if his shoes had sprouted wings. He couldn't even hear his footfalls over the sawing cicadas. By this time tomorrow, he'd be reunited with Naomi. And if Magdalena agreed to become part of that picture, his family would finally be complete.

Lena gripped her steering wheel with white knuckled hands as she turned into Artie's parking lot. She would never have guessed she would be returning to the site of her undercover job a mere two days after walking away from it.

But Toby's phone call last night alerting her to Rupert Davis's arrest had led to a phone conversation with the Metropolitan Police. After hours of wrangling with them and enlisting her friend at the DA to help convince them she was on the side of the prosecution, they'd shared the evidence that had prompted Davis's arrest.

Curtis Vandaloo, the troubled teen who'd seen Davis drive off with Alexa in his squad car, had emerged from hiding to reiterate his allegations. But even more astonishing still, he'd been living all that time within the Amish community of Mechanicsville. His relatives had fled there from Pennsylvania out of fear that Davis might track them down.

Lena had known the name Vandaloo was Dutch, but

at nineteen years of age she hadn't considered it might be Pennsylvania Dutch, otherwise known as Amish. Little wonder the PI's she'd hired hadn't been able to find them, especially when the Vandaloos had moved from one Amish community to another and Seth had changed his first name.

Even with her honed investigative skills, Lena would never have guessed that Curtis was now Seth, a man she had come into contact with daily. The odds were impossible; the telltale signs only evident in hindsight. Having recognized Davis the other night, Seth/Curtis had found the moral strength to do what was right and to declare his allegations to the local police, who'd immediately contacted the authorities in D.C.

Lena nosed her Jaguar into her old parking spot and stepped out into the oppressive heat. Across the street, Gateway stood quiet, its occupants cloistered inside to escape the humidity. Ignoring the fact that she could still *feel* Jackson's presence, even with the space— real and emotional—between them, Lena shouldered her purse and walked bravely into the convenience store.

At her entrance, Bill looked up from the hotdogs he was setting on the grill. He sent her an incredulous look. "I'm surprised to see you here," he admitted stiffly.

His words sparked shame. "I'm so sorry, Bill. I never meant to leave without giving any notice." She looked up at him, then, revealing the bruises on her neck that had gone from blue to violet and yellow.

His jaw dropped and his eyes bulged. "Is that the reason—?" He was too appalled to even finish his sentence.

"I was attacked by a man," she affirmed. "Behind the store," she added, bending the truth to suit her purposes. "I didn't want to tell you because I didn't have any proof. Maybe if the camera hadn't been broken…" Plagued by her conscience, she left it at that.

He launched into a stream of apologies.

"Please." She lifted a hand to forestall him. "That's not why I'm here. I need to find Seth, the Amish man," she told him. "It's personal," she added, loath to explain.

Bill's brow furrowed with confusion. But he didn't question her reasons for wanting to find Seth. Jotting directions on the back of a receipt, he urged her to report the incident and not take matters into her own hands.

"It wasn't Seth," she assured him, prompting a look of relief. With a word of gratitude and well-wishes for the future, she headed out the store to her car. As she pulled from the parking lot onto the country road headed away from Gateway, she cast a wistful glance in her rearview mirror.

Be safe, Jackson, she silently willed.

And then she turned her thoughts to Curtis Vandaloo, wondering how he would respond when she told him who she was. Her intent was two-fold: to thank him in person for finally coming forward, and to make sure he didn't fail in his obligation to Alexa a second time.

CHAPTER 18

"What's wrong witchu?" Muhammed hissed as Jackson's elbow jabbed him in the arm.

"Sorry." The men were all seated in a half circle in Ibrahim's office, and he'd been heedlessly stretching in his seat unable to subdue his restlessness. Listening to the delusional imam rant on and on about Judgment Day, while saying nothing of any actual significance was like hearing fingernails being dragged over a chalkboard. Jackson would rather be waterboarded than be tortured this way.

"Most of this bloodshed will take place in the South, far North and far West," Ibrahim read, citing a passage from the Supreme Lessons. "The West will be the fountain of dripping blood and insanity, murder, rape, and a hundred percent total violence."

Jackson wanted to raise his hand and ask, *When you say South, North, and West, do you mean across the country or just in the nation's capital?* But Mr. Rakeem had warned him that a soldier should not ask questions, so he kept his mouth shut.

Besides, in a matter of hours, now, he would be free of Gateway, and Ibrahim and his sidekick, Zakariya, would be sharing their visions in a jail cell.

"Only the Muslim who has taken it upon himself to learn, listen and be completely righteous will survive the Day of Judgment," Ibrahim continued. "Just because you aspire to join the Five Percent, it does not make you righteous. There is only one man in this room who is truly enlightened—your teacher and redeemer." He laid his hand on his chest.

"Yes, Imam," some of the men affirmed, but not Corey, Jackson noted. Corey kept his mouth shut, his face expressionless.

At that exact moment, Jackson was delighted to hear a disturbance in the hallway. Frantic knocking sounded at the door.

"Come in!" Ibrahim called, clearly annoyed by the interruption.

Nadim peered anxiously into the office. "Sorry to disturb you, Imam, but Zakariya sent me to get you. There's police at the door."

"What next?" Throwing his hands into the air, Ibrahim stalked out of the office. The parolees looked at one another then vaulted out of their chairs to chase him down the hall. Jackson was right behind them.

"Stay here," Ibrahim ordered them as he slipped through the glass doors at the front of the building to join his colleague on the marble steps. Conscious of the cameras outside, Jackson looked on over the heads of his peers.

Imam Zakariya was already in earnest conversation with a portly, pompous-looking individual, whom Jackson recognized as Attorney General Wilkes of the U.S. Justice Department, the supreme enforcer of federal law. The SWAT team lined up behind him, bristling with weapons, represented the AG's muscle, but they were only here as window dressing.

With every major television station in the country

tuned into his announcement, Wilkes milked the public relations moment for everything it was worth. He no doubt figured that because the imams were religious leaders, they would submit without a struggle, especially with the SWAT team present.

The Taskforce would've grabbed and cuffed the offenders the second they stepped out of the building.

Not my problem anymore, Jackson reminded himself. He had completed his part of the investigation. Now it was time to get the hell out of dodge without the media catching sight of him.

Backing surreptitiously toward the stairs to the basement, he could hear the AG, with his voice raised in benefit for the press, shouting the half-dozen charges being brought against both leaders. *You are hereby charged with conspiracy to commit domestic violence by stockpiling bombs with the intent to commit mass slaughter.* Christ, this could take all afternoon. At least Jackson had plenty of time to make his getaway.

He was just pulling open the fire door when the AG's litany cut off in mid-sentence. A commotion at the front of building had Jackson peering up the corridor in consternation. When Ibrahim flew into the mosque and slammed the door shut behind him, Jackson let the fire door drop shut again. *Uh-oh.*

"Quickly," Ibrahim hissed at the stunned parolees, "into the prayer hall!"

Arming the alarm, the imam ushered them toward the heavy wooden doors that divided the worship space from the entryway. "Out of sight before the Devil attacks!" he urged. That was when he caught sight of Jackson, standing alone and indecisive at the other end of the building. "What are you waiting for, Abdul?" he called. "Follow me. We must arm ourselves."

Arm? The suspicion that Ibrahim had stashed weapons in the mosque made desertion suddenly impossible. The Taskforce would want to know just how many and what kind of weapons Ibrahim had at his disposal. The fact that the mosque was built like a fortress with all the windows welded shut made the possibility of a stand-off likely.

Well, fuck.

With a shudder of reluctance, Jackson joined the others in the prayer hall. What else could he do? Tackling the imam to the floor in the presence of ten parolees, five of whom had been planning this Friday to swear eternal allegiance to their leader, didn't strike him as the brightest idea. Plus, if this situation escalated into a siege, having an agent on the inside could make all the difference to the good guys, which was why Ike had asked him to stay put, in case something went wrong. Well, it had.

Once they were all in the inner sanctum, Ibrahim shut and barred the oak doors with a thick, carved plank, as functional as it was ornamental. Then he swooped across the floor and mounted the *minbar*, taking two steps at a time. With the men looking anxiously on, he got down on his knees and proceeded to pry loose several floorboards. Reaching into the hole he'd made, he pulled out a flat metal lockbox and keyed it open.

The box proved to contain seven semi-automatic pistols. As Ibrahim loaded, one by one with fresh cartridges, Jackson swept an eye over the silent parolees. Reading dread in the faces of some men, excitement and agitation in others, his concern mounted. He suffered a sinking certainty that he wouldn't get to see Naomi at all tonight, or any time soon, for that matter.

* * *

It was dusk by the time Lena left Curtis's single-story, clapboard farmhouse. Escorting her through a garden abundant with lettuce and green pumpkins, he stood by her car in that awkward, unsophisticated way of his that reminded her of the gawky teen she had met for the first and last time at the pretrial hearing. Thunder rumbled in the distance, promising an imminent rain storm and relief from the heat.

"Thank you," she told him, rolling up on her toes to plant a kiss on his prickly cheek. "I had a wonderful visit. Let's get together again for lunch or dinner during the trial, okay?"

With a self-conscious smile, Curtis nodded his agreement.

"I'll see you in court," she assured him. "Are you going to need a ride to D.C?"

"I've got one."

Lena glanced over at the horse, grazing in the fenced area beside his simplistic home. "Not that one, I hope," she teased.

He gave a rusty chuckle and shook his head. "No, not that one."

"My sister would have liked the man that you've become, Curtis," she felt compelled to tell him.

He scuffed his toe into the dark earth.

"Good night." Easing into her sweltering vehicle, Lena lowered all four windows and blasted the A/C. Waving through the open window, she headed down the long dirt track to the main road. The cooler air wafting into the car smelled of fertile soil and ripe soybeans.

Vignettes of the afternoon crossed the stage of her mind. Curtis, astonished by her visit, had been blown away when she'd identified herself as Alexa's older sister. He would never have recognized her for the plump college coed she was then. After much reassuring on Lena's part that she'd never blamed him for skipping out on Davis's trial, Curtis had invited her to stay for supper. And over a meal of meatloaf and applesauce, he'd admitted, haltingly, that he'd been in awe of Alexa and the way she'd had it all together.

She was kind and beautiful, just like an angel.

Rolling back the cuff of his sleeve, he'd showed her his tattoo, which proved to be Alexa's name in black calligraphy. The first letter had angel's wings coming out of it.

Officer Davis said he'd take her home, Curtis had recollected about the night Alexa had been murdered. But I knew he wouldn't. I knew he was evil because he'd gotten me hooked on drugs then used me to sell them.

You're doing the right thing now, Lena had reassured him.

Turning onto the paved road that wound back to Artie's and Highway 235, Lena raised her windows against the flecks of rain that dropped suddenly from the sky. Drawing a deep breath, she held it a moment before exhaling in a long sigh. Amazingly, after all their reminiscing of Alexa's death, her heart felt lighter than a balloon. It seemed to sail right up out of her chest, through the roof of her car, to the boughs of the trees now waving in the gusting wind.

Paired with the recording of Davis's partial confession, which Lena was certain she could get back from Jackson, Curtis's testimony might very well bring closure to a wound that had been open and bleeding for a decade. Then Alexa's spirit would finally be at peace.

The rain began to fall in earnest as Lena reached the intersection with the highway. Through her water-streaked windshield, she noticed the lights at Artie's were all extinguished. Maybe the store had lost electricity due to the storm.

Across the street, Gateway, too, stood in darkness, except for the parking lot which overflowed with official-looking vehicles. Several police cruisers were there, as well, their blue lights flashing. With rising alarm, Lena recognized several media vans representing prominent television stations. Journalists stood under umbrellas, telecasting live.

It occurred to Lena that Jackson's investigation had come to a head already. Peter wasn't responsible for this media frenzy, was he?

Making up her mind to find out, she waited impatiently for the light to change. Just then, her gaze fell on a familiar Crown Victoria parked right on the highway in front of the dormitory. As the light turned green, and she pulled up behind it, relieved to spot Toby sitting at the wheel.

When she rapped on the passenger door, he unlocked it. She slid onto the seat beside him, shaking off the rain that dampened her clothes and hair. "What's going on?"

Even in the sedan's dark interior, there was no mistaking Toby's consternation at seeing her. "What the hell are you doing here?"

He'd obviously been expecting someone else. "Never mind that." She gestured over her shoulder. "What's happening?" she repeated. "Where's Jackson?"

When he just rubbed his nose and stared at the steering wheel, her alarm mounted.

"The imams' arrest didn't go the way it was supposed to," he finally admitted. "The leader went and locked himself inside the mosque with the parolees. Jackson talked some of them into slipping out a couple of hours ago, along with the staff, but he refuses to leave himself. He figures we need a mole to keep us informed of Ibrahim's next move."

Lena swallowed hard. "I take it this Ibrahim is a terrorist?"

"Oh, yeah." Toby didn't have to ponder his answer this time.

"So, it's a standoff," Lena inferred, concerned for Jackson's safety. "How long do you think the imam and parolees can stay in there?"

"Without electricity, which we cut right away—" he shrugged "—I'd say a couple of days, maybe a week."

A week!

"First they'll get hot without the A/C, then their food'll spoil because they have no packaged stores to rely on since they only eat fresh foods, and they'll get hungry," he predicted darkly.

"I guess you can't just blow the doors off a mosque," she considered out loud.

"Bad PR," he agreed with a sardonic wink.

Sensing Jackson's nearness more than ever, Lena peered anxiously out the window. The only thing she could see of the mosque was the rain-washed minaret reflecting a muted version of the blue strobes below.

But then a jag of lightning lit the upper half of the building in dramatic fashion, accompanied by a deafening clap of thunder that made her jump.

She looked back at Toby. "Why are you parked way over here?"

"The plan was for me to get Jackson the hell out of here as soon as the imams were arrested. Doesn't look like he's going to leave any time soon, now."

It was then she noticed the words on Toby's T-shirt: *I'M WITH STUPID,* and an arrow pointing at her. He'd probably worn it for Jackson to celebrate the completion of this job. Given the gravity of the current situation, the shirt's message fell short of seeming humorous.

"So, he is communicating with you," she deduced with some relief.

Toby lit up the phone gripped in his left hand to display a bit of text. The greenish light cast by his viewing pane, made his expression look unusually harsh.

"What are you not telling me?" she demanded, sensing there was more.

He doused the light, took a deep breath, and scratched a spot on his chin. "The imam has weapons," he said softly. "Seven semi-automatic pistols."

The contents of Lena's stomach pitched. "Oh, my God, this reminds me of the Waco disaster," she breathed, gripping her good-luck bracelets.

Toby whipped his head around to face her. "Don't even say that."

"Sorry. No, it can't end like that." The showdown between the ATF, the FBI, and a religious cult in Waco, Texas, had led to a fifty-day siege and ended in an inferno that left seventy-six people dead, including women and children.

"Look," Toby said, on a more assured note, "Jackson already talked those first parolees into escaping while on a bathroom break. He's working on the others. He thinks he can get them to defy the imam's orders."

And that was supposed to be comforting? He was going to bring the leader's wrath down on him if he kept that up.

Toby sighed. "You shouldn't be here. It isn't safe."

"Well, I'm not leaving," Lena informed him.

He gave a humorless laugh. "Why is that not surprising?"

"It's settled then," she told him firmly. "I'm staying

right here with you until Jackson's free again."

Ibrahim was delivering a powerful sermon. The solid red light on the iPhone he had squirreled away for emergencies bathed him in bloody light. Sweat trickled from beneath his *taqiyah*, but he refused to take it off.

Below him, kneeling on the floor of the dark prayer hall, nine remaining sets of eyes shone up at him, inspiring eloquence on his part. Two cowardly parolees had deserted them earlier, slipping from the prayer hall under the guise of using the restroom in the hall. In the next instant, the alarm had signaled their desertion. From that point on, Ibrahim insisted all the men use his private toilet, just behind the *minbar*. The next man to try to desert him would be shot.

As for the pistols, he would distribute them if the need arose, and only to his most trusted pupils.

"This situation—" he flourished a hand to encompass the standoff at Gateway, "is an allegory, is it not?" He glanced down at the parolees then back into the eye of the camera filming him. "It symbolizes the enslavement of our people by the Devil, who has held us captive for centuries. But do not despair. Instead, be encouraged, my people. For the time is at hand for your delivery." He paused for effect, knowing that his next words would shake the very foundations of the nation.

"My faithful followers, your *Mahdi* is here. Indeed, he has been with you all this time, for I am he." Ibrahim pressed a hand to his heart and smiled sanctimoniously. "And I have come to change you into a new and perfect People. Where the Earth is filled with wickedness, I will fill it with justice, freedom, and equality. I will make the poor-lost found and turn you into rulers of the New World Order. All this I will do for you, but first you must prove your worthiness by freeing me from the Devil's snare.

"Captains and Lieutenants of the Fruit of Islam, your loyalty is being put to the test, just as I foretold it would be. For the New World Order to succeed, you must rally now to my defense. Gather your soldiers and strike hard. This will be the first of many bloody battles heralding the Righteous Struggle. But in the end, the Fruit of Islam will prevail, and the Devil will be crushed like a serpent beneath our heels."

Satisfied that his speech would bring his followers thronging to the area to free him, Ibrahim pressed the button that would upload his message via 3G wireless to his website.

When an error message appeared, he cursed and tried again.

Were the walls of the mosque too thick? Why was his video not uploading?

It dawned on him, with a temporary sense of impotence, that the vipers who'd shut off the electricity had also dismantled his website, preventing him from communicating with his followers that way. No doubt the music site listing Zakariya's top ten picks had also been taken down. But he was not so easily thwarted. Every one of his followers had an iPhone just like his.

Ibrahim accessed his contact list, selected every name on the list, and typed a brief text message. *Watch my video.* He then attached the video to the text and hit send. Within minutes, seventy seven captains and lieutenants in the Fruit of Islam would receive his summons and forward his message to their underlings.

Savoring visions of efforts to which they would go to liberate him, Ibrahim relaxed on the uppermost step of the *minbar* to watch the news in his iPhone.

Tonight, the nation would spin on its axis.

Turning down the volume so the parolees were not privy to opposing views, he viewed the debates taking place on every major news station. The country stood divided over whether or not Gateway's leaders were terrorists, as the government alleged, or whether Ibrahim and Zakariya had been profiled due to race and religion, their civil rights violated.

"Oh, come on," scoffed a white-haired senator, being interviewed on CNN. "These allegations are ludicrous. Have you looked at the upstanding individuals who've graduated from Gateway's reintegration program? Mr. Ali Rakeem is now the principal of an esteemed Muslim boy's school in Columbia Heights. Taimur Amir is the owner of a successful recording studio in Georgetown. Qasif al Bakir is a lawyer working for the Baltimore District Attorney's office. These men are reputable because Gateway taught them that self-worth and hard work pay off. You are not going to tell me these men are members of a radical Muslim group that's plotting to overthrow the government. That's hogwash."

The senator's portrayal of Gateway was flattering but it betrayed the man's absolute ignorance. Amused, Ibrahim immersed himself in the discussion, even as the man's next words shocked the smirk off his face.

"But, Senator, what about the allegations that former parolees have been stockpiling propane in first floor apartments and are intending to use them as bombs?"

Ibrahim frowned. When charging him, the Attorney General had mentioned something about stockpiling bombs. But how could the authorities and the press know of his plans to bring down apartment buildings throughout the city unless the unthinkable had happened. Had one of his followers turned traitor?

"Ridiculous. My sources tell me that distributing propane is one of Gateway's charitable endeavors. That propane was for heating older homes in the city. You know, I hate to allege that our government would plant evidence against American citizens, but I can assure you that the investigative agency making these claims had every opportunity to just that."

"Can you tell us how and when, Senator?"

"How do you think? They put one of their own agents through the program."

Ibrahim blinked. Wait, what? One of his parolees was a government agent?

"When was this, Senator? Is the undercover agent still in the program and could you identify him?"

Ibrahim's heart pounded as he waited for the senator's reply.

"Of course I could, and yes he is. But I'm not going to jeopardize a man's well-being just because I have a different opinion on how American Muslims ought to be treated. I will say this, though. This situation at Gateway defines the reason why we need a new President in the Oval Office."

Fury exploded in Ibrahim's chest. Had he actually been duped by one of his current parolees? Which one?

Turning off his phone, he plunged the prayer hall into darkness. Only the feeblest of moonlight coming through the windows under the domed ceiling illuminated his followers.

Was one of them the traitor? Or had that man been one of the cowards who'd escaped at start of the siege? Picturing Mansoor and Omar, he could not envision either one as a spy. They were both too old and not in good physical condition.

On knees that trembled, Ibrahim slowly rose to consider the men who remained. Was Muhammed the traitor? Not likely; he was as dumb as a rock. Jamal? Ditto there. Hasan? That man could barely speak English. Corey? Too soft. Shahid? Too mean. Abdul? *Ah, yes, Abdul.*

A shiver of certainty wracked his spine.

In retrospect, it seemed so obvious. Abdul had memorized the recitations in one week flat. Ibrahim had assumed his many questions were an indication of his quick mind, but he'd been scrutinizing Gateway and its leaders from the start, hadn't he?

And earlier this week, it was Abdul who'd remained inside the mosque when everyone else went to witness the fire marshal's inspection. No doubt he had seized the opportunity to continue his search that had been cut short the night the alarm had been breached and the mosque broken into.

Ibrahim slipped a hand into his pocket. With a tremor in his fingers, he withdrew the pistol there and released the safety.

There was only one good thing that could come of his discovery. The parolees were less apt to rebel against him when they had a scapegoat to blame for their misery.

CHAPTER 19

Lena stuck as close to Toby as the wicked-looking pistol holstered to his hip. He introduced her first to Ike Calhoun, the Taskforce lead, and then to the Attorney General. When Wilkes called the Taskforce into his plush RV for a conference, he gave her an appreciative once-over and invited her to join them, as well—much to Ike Calhoun's obvious annoyance.

The AG's aid made her a steaming cup of coffee. Thanking him, she told herself just to watch and listen and not stick her nose into matters she didn't understand. But when Ike Calhoun and Wilkes started wrangling over whether or not to storm the mosque, she found she wanted to strangle the latter with her bare hands. Didn't he care about Jackson's safety?

"Time is on our side," the AG insisted, looking relaxed in a cushy captain's chair. "The men in the mosque will soon be out of food, and they have no power. They're going to have to capitulate eventually. All we have to do is to wait them out."

"You're wrong." The Taskforce lead's burning eyes could have blistered leather but that didn't seem to faze the AG. "The longer we wait, the worse this situation is going to get. We can see that the imam's got an iPhone and that he's been using it, but we can't trace the number. How long do you think it's going to take the Fruit of Islam Army to mobilize and ride to his defense?"

Wilkes shrugged. "What are you worried about? The National Guard has barricaded every road in and out of the area."

Calhoun's voice got softer, which made him all the more intimidating in Lena's opinion. "The National Guard isn't equipped to take on twelve thousand men. The more we monkey around, the more time the enemy has to plan their strategy."

Lena gulped her coffee. Fear coagulated like cold grease in her belly.

"What strategy? These men aren't real soldiers, are they? Have they ever been at war?" The AG clearly wasn't worried.

"Trust me, with twelve thousand members, you can bet hundreds of them have had military training. Plus they've planned for contingencies like this. Why do you think the glass in the mosque's windows is bulletproof and the windows are welded shut? This building is their fortress. And as long as Ibrahim can communicate with his followers, he can draw them all to the area in droves. Let's at least knock out the cell tower and suspend his communications."

"Can't do that," Wilkes countered stubbornly. "Too many people around here rely on the cell towers— merchants, law enforcement, and doctors. Imagine how many folk's will die when they can't call 911. I shudder to think of the law suits."

"Oh, for Christ's sake." Ike Calhoun flushed to the roots of his short silver hair. "If we don't take decisive action now, more people are going to get hurt in the destruction and mayhem about to take place. Do this my way and the only person who'll get hurt is Ibrahim. Say the word and my sniper can take him out right now. Done. Finished."

"Good God, we can't kill the imam! What happens when his followers hear that we've executed him? Don't you think that'll incite them even more? You think the country is divided now? We'll have a full-blown revolution on our hands!"

"I disagree. You'll be disbanding revolutionaries that are already—"

Lena's cell phone buzzed unexpectedly, distracting her from Calhoun's terse argument. Pulling it from her purse, she realized she had a message from Peter. *Senator Huxley just stated in an interview with CNN that there's an undercover agent in the program, but he didn't name him.*

"Oh, no." Her cry of alarm prompted Toby to wrest her phone from her limp grasp and scan the message. At the same time, the team lead's radio crackled.

"Sir?"

He answered it with a single syllable. "Speak."

"Our insider's identity has just been compromised by Senator Huxley in an interview with CNN."

Ike's green eyes jumped up and intercepted Toby's worried stare. He turned to the AG. "We need to get our man out, *now*."

"No." Wilkes shook his head so hard his jowls jiggled. "We are not going to storm the mosque and that's final."

Lena's empty coffee cup crumpled without warning in her tense grip. Dear God, Jackson was going to be butchered by the parolees when they realized that he'd betrayed them!

The soft *click click* of a round being advanced into a chamber was often the only warning a Marine got before all hell broke loose. When that sound rattled down from the *minbar* where Ibrahim was starting down the steps, Jackson instinctively knew his number was up.

Pushing stealthily to his feet, he stumbled over the dark forms that strewed the floor as he sought desperately to find a hiding place.

"Ow!"

"Man, watch it!"

In this large, echoing space, there were few places to take cover, a fact he had been aware of since Ibrahim forbade anyone else to leave.

Ducking behind one of the thick, sandstone columns that supported the domed ceiling, Jackson prayed his intuition was wrong and that Ibrahim wasn't after him. But the deafening crack of a pistol accompanied by a burst of light and plaster showering his head confirmed his bleak suspicions.

"Traitor!" Ibrahim thundered in the astonished silence that followed.

Confused by their leader's actions, the rest of the men started scrambling out of his path. *Traitor?* The blood-freezing accusation led Jackson to assume that Schlesser had gone public with his exposé. Maybe he'd warned Lena first, maybe he hadn't. Either way, what could Ike or Toby do for him now? Jackson had placed duty over his obligations to his family, just like Colleen accused him of doing, and now he was going to pay the piper for it.

Short of the SWAT team breaching the building right now, there was no getting out of the situation he was in. He'd done it to himself, and his own personal nightmare was going to play out to the end. Unless he could arm himself and fight back, Ibrahim was going to shoot him and make an example out of him.

"What the hell?" he cried in the voice he used as

Abdul. "Why you shootin' me, Imam? I ain't done nothin' wrong."

"Nothin', he says." Ibrahim's voice took on the sing-song quality of a madman. "I just found out that Abdul is an undercover agent for the government that oppresses and imprisons us," he announced. "He has betrayed you and me and every black man in America with his deceit."

With every word, the imam came closer. Jackson darted out of his hiding place, heading for the next column over. When a bullet hit the wall to his left, he wheeled right toward the *minbar*, hoping to arm himself with one of the six pistols still in the strong box, if the damn thing was even open.

Only, he never even made it up the steps. Ibrahim's pistol barked again, and a burning pain exploded in Jackson's right hip, just like in his dream the other night, only a thousand times more agonizing.

Slipping and collapsing onto the runner, he fought to catch his breath while expecting another shot to peg him in the back and end his life at any moment.

A glance over his shoulder showed Ibrahim approaching, his robes made incandescent by the light reflecting off the clouds and shining through the windows overhead. Parolees gathered in a semicircle at the foot of the *minbar*, eyeing Jackson as if he'd grown horns.

"This man," Ibrahim declared, "is not one of us. It is due to him that you are stuck behind these walls like fugitives."

Through a haze of agony, Jackson spotted Corey shaking his head at him. It didn't take a psychic to read Corey's thoughts. *You lied to me, Abdul?*

"He betrayed our righteous struggle to the Devil who now persecutes us," Ibrahim continued.

With dread, Jackson surmised what was coming

next: that he'd either be severely punished, possibly killed, as an example of what happened to those who resisted Ibrahim's rule or used as a hostage to secure Ibrahim's release. In spite of his agony, he pushed to his feet, clinging to the rails on either side of the steps. "I am not a traitor," he insisted, as blood streamed warmly down his leg. "If I was, I would've left with Omar and Mansoor. Why would I still be here witchu if I was some kinda spy?"

"You told me you worked for Ibrahim," Corey spoke up suddenly, his tone accusing. "That's why you went out sometimes at night, to report to the imam."

"I was with Maggie, okay? I'm in love with her." Jackson's confession, infused with the despair that he might never get to realize his dreams for him and Lena, was met with thoughtful silence on the part of the parolees, especially Corey, whose expression shifted to one of compassion.

"He lies," Ibrahim insisted. "He'll say anything to save himself. He certainly never worked for me. I tell you, *he* is the reason we are cornered like rats. Hasan and Shahid, seize him before he defiles our sanctuary with his tainted blood. Take him into the closet, there, where we keep the prayer rugs. You will find a roll of electrical tape and scissor on the shelf. Bind his hands and feet. Then beat him if you like, but do not kill him. We may need a hostage to barter for our release."

Jackson made a last valiant effort to dash up the *minbar* and arm himself. Hampered by the bullet in his hip, he had nearly made it to the top where he would have still have had to open the box and pull out a gun, when he was tackled from behind and dragged back down to floor level. There, all of the parolees seemed to jump him at once.

Jackson put up a powerful resistance. Jamal sustained a black eye. Nadim was kicked in the stomach and never came back. If he could have gotten back up on his feet, he might have held off all of them. But fighting from a prone position eventually tired him out. And when Shahid clocked him in the side of the head with his foot, his vision blurred and he could no longer see well enough to deflect the blows.

Four men dragged him into the walk-in closet, currently emptied of prayer rugs. Hasan pinned him to the hardwood floor on his stomach while Corey made light with his cell phone and two others bound his hands and feet with electrical tape. Spitting blood, Jackson kept quiet and hoped they wouldn't stick tape over his mouth.

Once they had him tightly bound, they flipped him over. Then Shahid, Hasan, and Jamal egged each other on to kick and punch him while calling him every vile name under the sun.

As the blows came raining down, Jackson fell back on his military training and retreated into the citadel in his mind, where Naomi and Lena greeted him with loving embraces.

When the sound of gunfire penetrated the hull of the RV, Lena saw Toby cut a startled look at his boss, who tabbed the mike on his headset.

Oh, God, Jackson.

"Eagle One, status report." Calhoun was still listening to the report when another shot rent the tense quiet.

Lena gave a moan of terror and dropped her face into her hands. When a third shot rang out, tears of misery filled her eyes. *This can't be happening.*

But the Taskforce lead confirmed her worst fear.

"Our insider's been shot. Sir, we need to breach the building, now."

"It's not going to happen, soldier," Wilkes retorted. "I am sorry about your man, but I've made my position clear."

Ike touched a hand to his earpiece, listening. "He survived the shooting, but now they're beating him," he growled, staring hard at the AG, who looked away from his burning gaze. Bending over him, Calhoun forced the man to look up at him. His voice, as cold and quiet as death, made Lena shiver. "Let me make this perfectly clear to you, sir. When this place becomes a blood-bath, I will hold you personally accountable for Jackson's welfare, plus every injury and loss of life that takes place here."

The tense silence that followed his declaration was shattered by the crackling of his radio.

"Sir!" shouted a voice on the other end. "The National Guard reports that three semi trucks just busted through the roadblock at the intersection of Route 5 and the 301! At the rate of speed at which they're traveling, we've got ten minutes, tops, before they get here. National Guard is in hot pursuit and requesting back up, over."

Lena's heart began jumping in her chest. The cynical curl to Calhoun's upper lip wasn't reassuring.

"Copy," he clipped. "Tell the Marines to launch air support, now. We'll need at least two Cobras. Over." He directed his gaze back at Wilkes. "Looks like the Fruit of Islam mobilized faster than either you or I imagined. Care to reconsider your decision, sir? Or would you rather brace yourself for a dog fight?"

Wilkes's complexion paled and his grip tightened on the arms of his chair. "I stand by my decision," he insisted but with less conviction than before.

Calhoun shook his head. His jaw muscles flexed. He

keyed his mike. "Eagle One and Two, this is Eagle Nest. Be advised, three semi-trucks just breached the roadblock ten miles out and are headed in our direction. Prepare to deflect a hostile assault of unknown strength."

Lena heard a tinny voice on the other end acknowledging the orders.

Ike turned to the AG. "Sir, you need to relocate this RV at the back of the compound between the rear wall and the tree line." He pointed to Toby. "I want you to evacuate every civilian out there who'll leave, and that includes your sidekick, here." A shadow of compassion darkened his gaze as it rested briefly on Lena. "Text Jackson and keep texting him until he answers you."

Toby nodded. "Got it. Let's go, sidekick." Grabbing Lena's hand, he pulled her out of the RV into the quiet parking lot. The pounding rain had subsided into a steady drizzle. Snatching a megaphone from the SWAT van, Toby ushered her toward the dozen or so vehicles and police cars parked across from the mosque's locked doors.

"Attention, people. We have a large, hostile force moving in this direction. If you don't want to get caught in the middle of a firefight, you need to clear the area now. You have five minutes at the most. There's a motel two miles south of here. I suggest you wait there. We'll alert you when the area is clear."

As Toby herded reluctant news crews to their vehicles, Lena whipped out her cell phone, a sudden thought occurring to her. If the parolees had their new iPhones with them, maybe she could find out Jackson's status by texting them all and hoping at least one of them answered.

Glancing up, she saw the AG's RV lumber into the tall grass behind the rear of the mosque. Several fearless news teams caught sight of the RV, too, and followed, ignoring Toby's orders. Lena started after them.

"Hey, where are you going?" Toby caught up to her and caught her by the arm.

She shook him off. "I told you. I'm not leaving Jackson." She pulled out her phone intent on composing a text, but what to say? "Did you hear from him yet?"

"Not yet." Toby frowned at her. "What are you going to accomplish by staying, Lena? You'll just be a distraction."

"No, I'm not. I'm going to text some of the men inside. I might be able to talk them into turning on their leader."

Toby looked thunderstruck. "You have contact with the men on the inside?"

"If they have their new phones with them, then yes."

He searched the bustling parking lot until his gaze fell on a distinguished older gentleman in an FBI flack jacket. "Special Agent Donovan!" He waved the man over. "Lena, this is our hostage negotiator. Donovan, this woman has cell phone numbers for some of the guys inside. Tell her what to do." Under his breath, Lena heard him add, "And get her the hell away from this building."

"You got it. This way, miss." With an implacable grip on her upper arm, the agent drew her toward the very back of the lot where a nondescript sedan was parked. "Let's see if we can talk to the guys inside."

Grateful for his guidance, Lena took a seat beside him and took his cues. If she could keep Jackson alive with a couple of text messages, it'd be a miracle.

Seated in the far corner of the closed closet where Ibrahim wouldn't catch him texting, Corey responded to the message he'd received from Maggie asking him about Abdul.

He's alive. He glanced at the still, dark form at his feet and added, *He betrayed us.* Bitterness welled up in him at the memory of Abdul's lies, though that part about loving Maggie had sounded tragically true. Maybe that's what had kept Corey from joining in when the others attacked Abdul. Hell, the man was already shot. A bullet was bad enough without getting all roughed up.

To Abdul's credit, he'd gotten in some good licks, himself. Nadim was still out there clutching his gut.

Corey's phone buzzed. He read Maggie's response with a furrowed brow. *The only traitor at Gateway is your leader.*

Corey's breath sawed harshly in the small space. Her words sounded just like the voice of reason that he'd been trying to silence in his head these past few weeks. He wondered if any of his brothers were getting Maggie's texts, whether her words disturbed them the way they did him.

Painstakingly, he texted her back. *Things is different now.*

The only thing that's different is that your leader's plans have been exposed. He wanted to bomb Washington D.C. and open fire on white people in the streets. That's genocide, Corey. Do you really want to be a part of that?

Corey stared at the word *genocide* in disbelief. All this time, he'd thought Judgment Day had something to do with spiritual purification, fasting, and maybe atonement of some kind. He'd thought the white devil was a symbol for those who were racists. But now Ibrahim was looking like the biggest racists of all. *No,* he texted back.

There are ten of you and only one of him. It would

be easy for you all to overcome him. Reclaim your future. It's your future, not his.

Awash in a cold sweat, Corey envisioned the future as Ibrahim had depicted it: with each parolee empowered to make a decent living. He pictured himself as part of a powerful network, a Five Percenter. A dream like that only came at a price. Each parolee had to give up his autonomy, to sacrifice himself for what Ibrahim believed was a greater cause—overcoming the status quo by force and establishing black men as rulers, but he didn't know that meant murdering innocent people.

I never got the chance to hear your story, she added. *But always knew you'd be the true hero of my book.*

Her words gripped his heart in a vice.

For the first time, he saw his situation objectively. He didn't want to be a part of anything resembling genocide. If Maggie was right, then the only place any of them were headed from here was straight to jail, unless…unless they did as she suggested.

Fear and uncertainty overwhelmed him. He sobbed silently into his hand.

A hand encircled his ankle, startling his head up. "Corey," Abdul rasped in a pain-laced voice. "Free me, and I'll make certain you don't go to jail."

Still frightened, Corey kicked his foot free. "How you gonna do that?"

"I'm a federal agent," Abdul whispered. "I can protect you. All you have to do is cut me loose and get me a gun."

"I don't know, man. There's six of them and only one of me. They'll kill me if I don't do what Ibrahim says."

"If you don't resist him, every one of you is going to end up dead or back in prison." Abdul shifted, and Corey could see his pale eyes imploring him, even in the darkness. "You're a good man, Corey. I know I can count on you do to the right thing."

Confused and terrified, Corey scrambled out of the closet and put his back to the wall. All around him in the prayer hall, cell phones were lighting up, which meant Maggie was texting the other parolees she had numbers for. Ibrahim, sitting up at the top of the *minbar* didn't seem to notice. He was too preoccupied with receiving his own reports on his iPhone.

Corey swallowed hard. Maybe if others joined him in defying their leader, he would do it, if only to keep from going back to jail.

In the closet, Abdul gave an audible groan.

When the first semi-truck came roaring down the 235, Toby's first thought was that it resembled a Chinese dragon. Painted scarlet with amber running lights, its bold appearance inspired an immediate sense of doom. *What the hell is in it?* Toby wondered, peering around the rear corner of the dormitory.

"Alpha platoon, stand by," murmured the National Guardsman hugging the wall next to Toby. The man was in charge of the soldiers dotting the grassy area between the dormitory and the mosque.

"Eagle One and Two, stand by." Ike's voice sounded in Toby's earpiece.

With a hiss of brakes and the bellow of a downshifting engine, the Chinese dragon abruptly slowed. To Toby's disbelief, it veered sharply across the median, through the oncoming lanes, devoid of traffic, and headed straight toward Gateway.

"Holy shit," Toby braced himself for impact as it bounced through the grassy ditch and, with a roar of acceleration, crashed headlong into the shed where the propane tanks had just been evacuated.

The resulting collision sent the walls and the roof of

the shed flying in all directions. The truck came to a stop. If the propane had still been in it, the impact would have created an inferno so enormous that it would have incinerated the entire truck and obstructed everyone's view of the two remaining semis.

As it was, Toby could see that they'd stopped on the highway, parking in such a way that they blocked all four lanes. Their high beams glared, blinding every set of eyes that could see. Despite the glare, Toby made out what looked like all-terrain-vehicles zipping down ramps at the back of both trucks and dispersing into the darkness.

Christ, they were going to surround the mosque and attack the SWAT team from all sides.

"Heads up," he advised, "I count eight, nine, no, *ten* ATV's fanning out in every direction with several armed combatants in each vehicle. They're circling the campus."

"Everyone spread out and cover all angles," Ike advised.

In the distance, too far away to be helpful, the clatter of Cobra helicopters grew louder as the Marines responded to the request for air support.

When the first burst of automatic gunfire lit the night and strafed the wall where Toby crouched, he realized they were in for a long gunfight.

Up on the rooftop, a member of the SWAT team fired back. Toby heard the *ping-ping* as bullets bounced off an ATV, telling him that the vehicle was armored. *Son of a bitch.*

Like a horde of bees, the ATVs circled ever closer.

"Take a covered position and shoot out the tires!" roared the National Guard captain to his men.

Over shouts of alarm and the barrage of gunfire, Toby heard Ike barking into his headset. "Outrider, what's your goddamn ETA?"

Whatever response Ike might have gotten was drowned out by the detonation of a hand grenade. A member of the Fruit of Islam had hurled it onto the mosque's flat roof where half the sniper team crouched.

The cries of agony that accompanied the grenade's detonation set Toby's teeth on edge. *Oh, hell no.* As the ATV performed a one-eighty to make another pass, Toby hefted his M-21 sniper rifle, pinned the driver's side tire in the crosshairs of his night vision scope and shredded it.

The driver immediately lost control. The ATV flipped, and those who weren't pinned or injured crawled out only to be shot by the National Guardsmen. "Say goodnight," Toby muttered, turning his attention to the next ATV.

At the sound of a loud crash sounding like it had come from the entrance to the campus, Ibrahim leapt to his feet. "Do you hear?" he cried, breaking into Corey's whispered conversation with Muhammed. "That is the sound of my faithful followers, come to liberate their leader. Even now, the Devil quails before the Fruit of Islam." The imam's outburst was greeted with a smattering of applause.

Muhammed and Corey shared a look. They had just been discussing Ibrahim's crazed vision of the New World Order and their reluctance to take part now that they were aware of the gruesome brutality required of them. It sounded like all hell was breaking loose on the other side of the thick walls. Another sudden, loud explosion overhead elicited cries of agony and sent bits of plaster raining down on them.

"Hear the sound of my Righteous Army securing victory," Ibrahim crowed. Hefting the box of pistols he had guarded at the top of the *minbar*, he descended with it. "Come forward, my sons who swore their loyalty to the Five Percent Nation." He waved them closer.

With Davis arrested and Abdul tied up in the closet, only five of his seven chosen pupils remained. "Come and take a pistol," he urged. "As soon as the enemy is weakened, we will escape. You first, Hasan."

Hasan edged closer, and the pistol gleamed like dark pewter as Ibrahim passed it off. Muhammad seized Corey's arm. "What do we do?" he hissed.

"Go ahead and get a gun. I'll give mine to Abdul," Corey answered.

"Muhammed," Ibrahim called, and Muhammed got up and took the pistol given to him.

Gunfire belched on the roof overhead, and Corey glanced up automatically. He had noticed men up there, earlier, watching their every move, perhaps preparing to break in through the windows. He would rather cast his lot with them than be party to the slaughtering of innocent people.

"Yusuf," Ibrahim said, calling him by his conversion name.

Corey stepped forward. When the cool weight of steel filled his palm, his resolve to do what was right gave him courage.

Edging away from the circle of eager men, Corey backed toward the closet where Abdul lay in a puddle of his own blood. Slipping into the dark space, he dropped to his knees to shake him awake. Abdul had slipped into unconsciousness.

"Man, wake up!" Corey whispered, cutting the sticky tape around his wrists and ankles with the scissors. "You said you was gonna help me." Anxiety wicking through his solar plexus brought tears to his eyes. The tape came apart, but even then Abdul remained motionless.

Corey's hopes plummeted. Without Abdul's help, how could he and Muhammed ever overcome the others?

CHAPTER 20

Pain flashed up Jackson's spine from his hip. He opened his eyes with a gasp and recognized Corey bent over him, shaking him awake. "Yes!" Corey's relief was palpable. "Stay awake. You gots to stay awake, man." He thrust a gun into Jackson's hand. "Muhammed's on our side now," he whispered, "and Ibrahim's about to make his move." Corey put a hand on his shoulder. "Good luck," he added before scuttling out of the closet.

The cool titanium in Jackson's hand sharpened his senses, helping him to rise above the radiating pain. Gritting his teeth, he rolled toward the cracked closet door and searched the shadowy prayer hall to assess what was going on. Ibrahim now stood at the barred door, surrounded by the parolees. They seemed to be waiting for a signal of some kind.

Jackson painstakingly coaxed his cell phone from his pocket. The very walls of the mosque shook with incessant thunder. It sounded like a war was taking place outside, only what the hell was making those lawn-mower noises?

Christ, his hip hurt. Ignoring the pain, he texted Ike

and Toby simultaneously with fingers that shook. *Hit but fairly mobile. Have pistol and two allies. Ibrahim poised to exit.*

As he waited for a reply, he took inventory of his wound. His blood had apparently clotted as it had ceased to leak from the hole in his shorts. Good thing, too, for he had no way of binding the wound, and that would have only made it obvious he still had his head in the game.

Ike's reply lit up the tiny screen. *Sit tight. Air support en route.*

Relief lessened Jackson's pain. Maybe he wouldn't have to address Ibrahim alone.

But then an explosion shook the walls and brought plaster raining down on his head. Christ, it sounded like his teammates were balls to the wall defending the mosque from Ibrahim's army. Closing his eyes, he envisioned what he was hearing. Those small engines were apparently attached to light, fast-moving vehicles that swept around the building, swapping fire with those defending it. It sounded like the good guys were hard pressed in keeping the Fruit of Islam at a distance.

Jackson couldn't wait for air support to tip the scales of the battle, not if Ibrahim slipped away while his Army had the upper hand. In fact, now was the perfect time to take him out.

Steadying his pistol with his other hand, he took aim at Ibrahim's head through the cracked door. The imam stood with his iPhone in one hand, his pistol in the other, an easy target. Still, it'd been a long time since Jackson had killed anyone, since the damn war, before Colleen died.

Ibrahim's phone lit up suddenly. Energized by the message he received, the imam shifted toward his followers, so that he no longer stood in Jackson's direct line of sight. "Come, my sons," he called waving the anxious, milling men closer to the door.

"Move," Jackson breathed, willing Jamal to step aside so he could fire his shot. He could see that Jamal was also armed, as were Ibrahim's other chosen few. Question was, would they all turn their weapons on Jackson when Ibrahim went down? He swallowed hard at the thought. Would Muhammed, who also had a gun, be any help?

"Shahid, Hasan," he heard Ibrahim call, "bring me the traitor. You will have to cut free his feet so he can walk."

"We got him," Corey volunteered, speaking on just the other side of the door. In the next instant, he and Muhammed edged into the closet, and the opportunity to shoot Ibrahim was gone. Corey dropped to his knees beside him. "How you gonna do this?" he whispered anxiously.

Jackson had to rethink his plans. "Just trust me," he gritted, tucking the pistol under his T-shirt, beneath the elastic waistband of his shorts. "When we get to the part where I tell you to get down, just do it. Muhammed, I need you to shoot anyone who takes a pop at me."

Muhammed nodded, his eyes as big and bright as marbles. "A'aight."

"Remember, you promised we wouldn't go to jail," Corey reminded Jackson frantically.

"I don't want to die," Muhammed blurted in falsetto.

"I won't let either of you die or serve time for this," Jackson promised, hoping he wasn't telling a lie. "Now hurry up and drag me out of here. Go ahead and treat me rough; it'll be more convincing that way. Let's go."

Keeping his arms behind his back as if they were

still bound, Jackson braced himself for the agony that ripped through him as they pulled him to his feet. Then he let himself be alternately dragged and shoved toward Ibrahim, who clutched his pistol and extended it straight-armed at Jackson's forehead.

I could disarm him now, Jackson considered, but with the others standing so close in their haste to get out the door, the odds of a successful nab and grab were slim.

"Unbar the door, Shahid," Ibrahim directed. "The rest of you will surround me like body guards. Remember that I am your *mahdi,* and it is an honor to die for me."

As Shahid drew the door open, the parolees surrounded their leader like a phalanx, with Jackson positioned directly in front of the target, acting as a human shield. Moving all together, they stepped into the corridor, where the sounds of battle echoed off the tiled floor and fantastical shadows leapt on the wall. Jackson was pleased to hear the unmistakable thunder of air support drawing closer. With their tracking capabilities, aerial gunners could home in on the fleet attack vehicles and take them out, giving the Feds an immediate advantage.

"We wait here," Ibrahim shouted, his voice strident with immediacy, his pistol gouging Jackson's spine. "When my army blows the doors open, we will hurry outside and climb into the vehicles coming to collect us. Cover your ears," he warned.

Jackson pretended to sway. Out of the corner of his eye, he saw Corey shoot him an anxious glance as he and Muhammed jerked him roughly upright. It couldn't have been more obvious that Corey was wondering how the hell Abdul was going to save them.

Funny, he was wondering that same thing.

* * *

When three armored ATVs whipped through the parking lot from around the back of the building, Lena gave a cry of alarm. For the past half hour she had watched the enemy circle the mosque in ever tightening rings. With spurious grenade attacks and well-aimed gunfire, they had managed to break through the National Guard's perimeter, getting close enough to the mosque to harry those defending it.

"Get down!" the hostage negotiator warned her, as he fired out the window of their parked car.

Lena halfheartedly obeyed him. Peeking over the dashboard, she watched as his bullets missed the tires and bounced ineffectively off the bullet-proof hull. Despite gunfire lighting up the night sky like fireworks, it wasn't herself she was worried about. She had heard nothing from Corey for the past half hour but silence. Jackson could be dead for all she knew. And despite the best efforts of the SWAT team, National Guard contingent, and local police, the invading force was clearly gaining the upper hand. Only the helicopters thundering closer and Douglas's assurance that a second wave of National Guardsmen was due to arrive at any moment kept her fears from spiraling.

But then a deafening crash startled a scream from her throat.

"Shit!" exclaimed Special Agent Douglas, throwing his chest over her torso and shoving her cheek against the vinyl seat.

"What happened?" she cried.

Douglas peeked outside. "They just blew the doors off the mosque. Oh, Christ, the leader's coming out."

"Let me see." Struggling free of his protective encasement, Lena peered outside. A cloud of dust flickered from blue to red thanks to the lights of the emergency vehicles. For a moment, the firefight died down. Then, out of the gaping hole emerged the familiar faces of the parolees she'd befriended— Muhammed, Corey, Jamal, Hasan, Shahid, and Nadim. When the man in front straightened, and Lena recognized Jackson, she could have sworn a host of angels burst into song. His thigh glistened with what was obviously matted blood, and he stumbled before a bearded man wearing a flowing robe, but he was still alive, and that was all Lena cared about—until she realized the imam held a pistol to his back and was using Jackson to protect his own person.

Fear twisted through her anew as the leader urged his small troop toward the idling ATVs. Oh God, if Jackson was stuffed into one of those vehicles, would she ever see him again?

Weaving unsteadily on his feet, he started to collapse.

"No!" Lena screamed.

But then, in a move as fluid as it was unexpected, he knocked the pistol from Ibrahim's grasp as he spun around and came up behind his captor, twisting his arm behind his back and pressing a gun that had come out of nowhere to his head. "Everyone down on the ground!" she overheard him shout. As Hasan and Shahid swung around with their own pistols, Muhammed, who had fallen to a crouch, shot Shahid in the shoulder and Hasan in the thigh, and both men dropped their weapons in shocked agony.

The *whop-whop-whop* of approaching helicopters grew louder, drowning out Jackson's words as Corey and Muhammed fell prostrate to the ground, prompting those still standing to do the same. They all ignored Ibrahim who vociferated loudly and gesticulated at the ATV drivers, no doubted ordering them to come to his defense.

In the next instant the very ground seemed to shake as two ominous silhouettes swooped down from the clouds overhead. Instead of obliging Ibrahim, the ATV's scattered, and the helicopters banked sharply, in hot pursuit. The sound of gunfire abruptly abated.

"Finally," Special Agent Douglas muttered, smiling grimly at Ibrahim's obvious dismay. "It'll be over soon," he predicted.

Lena took her eyes off Jackson just long enough to assess that the SWAT team on the ground was coming out of hiding with their weapons trained on the parolees. From what she could tell, it was already over. With only one thought in mind, she shoved her way out of Douglas's vehicle.

"Hey, come back here!" the negotiator shouted.

By then Lena was halfway across the parking lot, just behind Ike Calhoun and the dozen black figures now wrestling Ibrahim to the ground, pouncing on the parolees, and snatching up their weapons.

"Jackson!" In her haste to get to him, Lena hurtled the crouching figures in her way.

By the time she elbowed her way to the center of the crowd, Calhoun was kneeing Ibrahim in the spine and muttering dark promises into his ear as he cuffed him. Jackson clutched the railing, which appeared to be the only object keeping him upright. Throwing steadying arms around him, Lena gazed up into his beautifully familiar face.

"I've got you," she vowed. "Hang in there, baby."

His pain-glazed eyes abruptly cleared as he stared down at her, clearly horrified. "What the hell are you doing here?"

But the danger was clearly diminishing. The only things exploding now were the ATV's, which were falling prey, one by one, to the gunners on the helicopters. Ibrahim's army was fragmenting and disbanding. She could hear one of the semis parked on the highway starting to pull away. They wouldn't get far with the second wave of National Guardsmen bearing down on the scene.

"I need a paramedic here!" she shouted. Spying a line of ambulances hovering at the periphery of the campus, she waved her arms frantically to get their attention.

At last, they deemed it safe enough to enter the ravaged parking lot, so they could tend the wounded.

"You, bring a stretcher!" Lena ordered the first paramedic to open his door.

"I'm all right, Lena," Jackson assured her, but he leaned on her heavily, and his speech was slurred.

"Like hell you're all right," Calhoun growled, standing up to join Lena in barking at the first responders. "Treat this man for a gunshot wound, pronto."

Responding to the authority in Calhoun's voice, the paramedic and his assistant hurried over with a gurney.

Groaning in a way that tore at Lena's heartstrings, Jackson lay down at their urging. Blood glistened wetly on his thigh. When he closed his eyes, his face was etched in agony. Lena caught it in her hands and leaned over him. "Don't you go and die on me, Jackson," she warned in a voice that quavered uncontrollably. "Now that you made me fall in love with you, you had better pull through, you hear me?"

A smile chased the suffering from his face and made his dimple flicker. "I'm not going anywhere, sweetheart," he assured her, with an undercurrent that warmed her heart. He even managed to slit his eyes. "And for the record, I'm in love with you too."

With a sound that was half-laugh, half-sob, Lena pressed her lips to his cold ones. By degrees, she became aware of the T.V. crews converging on the scene. Concerned that they would immortalize him as the agent who'd gone undercover to deter the fanatical leader, she sought to wheel him away.

Only, it became evident that the media was focused for the moment on Attorney General Wilkes, who'd emerged from his palace on wheels to take in the battle's aftermath. With a dazed look on his face, he climbed the steps of the mosque and stood amidst the rubble like he couldn't believe what he was seeing. Behind him, the cuffed, cursing imam was being read his Miranda rights.

"Sir, can you give us a comment?" pressed a bold member of the press, pushing to the forefront of the chaotic scene.

Lena glanced at Wilkes to see what he could possibly say in his own defense. In her opinion, it would have saved both lives and valuable property if he had just used force to arrest Ibrahim like Ike Calhoun had suggested. Jackson might not have been injured in the fall out.

"Well, you know, we're all shaken by what's transpired here in the last twelve hours," the AG stammered, for once at a loss for words.

Jackson squeezed her hand, recapturing her attention. "Look, it's Toby," he whispered.

Following the direction of his gaze, Lena saw Toby mount the steps while sticking a fake moustache to his upper lip. Sending her and Jackson a wink, he tugged the brim of his black cap over his eyes, sidled closer to the AG and started unbuttoning his flack jacket. *He wouldn't*, Lena thought, as Wilkes launched reluctantly into a press conference.

Toby still wore the same T-shirt she had noticed him wearing the previous evening. As the AG defended his reasons for not storming the mosque at the outset, he positioned himself on the man's left side so that the arrow on his T-shirt under *I'M WITH STUPID* pointed directly at the supreme head of the Department of Justice. By all appearances, Toby was listening attentively.

Lena shook her head and marveled at his gall. Every news station in the country was airing the AG's comments live. Toby was just asking to get sacked.

Quickly, before the press realized the hero of the hour was lying immediately behind them on a stretcher, Lena gestured to the paramedic to evacuate Jackson from the scene. The love of her life deserved to be honored as a hero, but reprisal by the crazy imam's followers was definitely something he could live without.

Resisting the tug of drug-induced lethargy, Jackson forced his sticky eyelids open, only to flinch at the bright sunlight shining through the window.

Disoriented, he took a moment to gather his bearings. He found himself propped up in a hospital bed, an IV in his left arm and a blanket up to his chest. He couldn't feel even a pinch of pain. The lime-green walls were enhanced by an enormous bouquet of wild flowers set in a vase on the bureau to his left. Yet the most uplifting vision of all was that of Lena curled up in the recliner under a small hospital blanket, fast asleep.

With his heart stuck in his throat, Jackson feasted his eyes on her. For several hours there, back in the mosque, he'd honestly thought he'd never live to see Lena again, or Naomi, for that matter. What Colleen had warned him about—his penchant for putting service to country over his obligation to those he loved—had finally bitten him in the ass, literally. It had seemed like fate. If he'd died, his punishment would have been never getting to tell Lena that he loved her.

To think that she'd been right outside, on the scene, the entire time. He shuddered to imagine it. Nor would he have believed, in his urgency to tell her what she meant to him, that she would blurt out the words first. *Now that you made me fall in love with you, you had better pull through, you hear me?*

The echo of her belligerent confession made him smile. It was just like Lena to beat him to the finish line. He was going to have to get used to being on the losing end, he supposed.

Regarding her dark curls and the childlike way that she clutched the blanket to her chest, he couldn't have cared less. He had learned that her tough, competitive spirit disguised a heart as vulnerable and breakable as glass. And that truth made him love her all the more.

If he could spend the rest of his life on the receiving end of her sassy tongue and her passionate devotion, he'd be the luckiest man in the world—a man who'd learned the hard way what counted most in his life.

Sucking in a deep breath, he realized he'd forgotten to breathe. At the sound of his gasp, she lurched awake, threw off the blanket, and rocketed out of the chair like a cat off a hot, tin roof. "Jackson! What's wrong. Are you hurting?"

He realized he had tears in his eyes. "No."

She clearly didn't believe him. "I'll go get the nurse."

"Whoa, slow down." He caught her wrist and tugged her back. "I'm fine, sweetheart." He twined his fingers through hers, keeping her locked by his side. "Don't go anywhere. I was enjoying looking at you."

The blush that streaked across her cheekbones warmed the cockles of his heart.

"How are you feeling?" she asked him with a

worried, searching look.

"Excellent. I must be on some good pain meds." He dared a peek under the blanket and groaned. It wasn't so much the sight of his bandaged hip as the catheter tube coming out from under his hospital gown that dismayed him.

"They had to dig the bullet out." She grimaced to convey her empathy. "You were lucky that it didn't hit any major arteries, but it damaged some ligaments. You'll need some time to heal."

"I feel as good as new," he assured her. "How about you?" His gaze slid to the wrinkled, formfitting blouse she wore. For a woman who'd been up all night witnessing terrorism at its finest and standing by her man while he underwent emergency surgery, she looked pretty damn sexy.

"Great," she assured him, but her smile struck him as forced.

"I think we both could both use a vacation," he declared, suddenly inspired. He could see it now: Lena in a floral bikini walking through a warm rush of turquoise water. His body tingled in anticipation, making him feel good enough to jump up and run a mile.

Lena's sherry colored eyes filled with unmistakable longing. "That sounds so good," she agreed. "To where?"

"Grand Cayman Island," he answered with confidence. "That's where I grew up. I'd like to take you there."

To his surprise, she seemed at a loss for words.

She was just opening her mouth to supply an answer when a young voice squealed in the hallway and the door flew open. Naomi rushed into the room with wide, worried eyes, followed by a harried-looking Silvia and then Toby, who'd swapped out yesterday's

T-shirt for a new one.

"Dad!" Naomi flung herself over the bedrail, heedless of Jackson's healing wound, to hang on his neck.

He flinched automatically but felt no pain as he gathered her more securely against him and returned her fierce hug. "There's my princess. I feel better already." And that was no exaggeration. The feel of her warm skin against his and the smell of her fragrant hair made every agony he'd endured worthwhile.

She pulled away just far enough to run an assessing eye over him. "Mr. Burke says you were shot in the butt," she announced.

"Actually, I was shot in the hip, but I'm going to be fine," he assured her, shooting his colleague a warning glare. "Good morning, Silvia," he added, countering her look of concern with a reassuring smile. "It's nice to have you both here."

"We brought you a card," Silvia said, moving to place it by the flowers. "Oh, aren't these lovely? Did you see who they're from?" She passed the small envelope to Jackson, who had to let go of Lena's hand to read the note inside.

Naomi strained to read it, too.

"They're from Ike's wife," he said, scanning the message. "She says he had to return to D.C. for a debriefing but he sends his *love*."

Toby snorted. Setting the card aside, Jackson looked over at him.

Lena was eyeing him, too. "Haven't you been fired yet for that stunt you pulled last night?" she inquired.

Toby folded his arms over his chest. "If you're talking about that clown with the T-shirt who was standing next to the AG, no one has managed to identify him." Toby's face could've been carved from stone. "Nope, the only guy who's been fired is Wilkes himself. The President declared the showdown a fiasco and promptly replaced him."

Jackson was stunned. "Seriously? With whom?"

"One of the justices on the Supreme Court. Richardson, I think."

As Toby dropped his arms, Jackson took note of the message across his chest. SHIT HAPPENS. "What's with the pessimistic attitude?" he inquired.

Toby's lips thinned. Reaching for his back pocket, he pulled out a rolled publication, prompting Lena to gasp in horror. Jackson could see why. It was the tabloid she wrote for, *Crime and Liberty,* and today's cover was a full color photo of Jackson and Toby leaving the mosque together. "Your boss ran his exposé this morning," Toby added unnecessarily.

"That skunk!" Bristling with outrage, she went to reach for her phone. "He promised me twenty-four hours' notice."

"Which he didn't give you because he changed his tune." Removing his hand from the bottom of the article, Toby revealed the title *Undercover Hero.* "I guess he realized Ibrahim really was a terrorist, so he hailed Jackson as the hero who saved America."

Jackson snorted and Lena sent him an anxious look. "Aren't you worried about reprisal?" she asked him.

He shook his head. "Ike is big on security. He's not going to let anything happen to me or my family."

Lena held her hand out for the tabloid and Toby passed it to her. "I can't work for Peter after this," she declared, shaking her head.

"All the more reason to take a long vacation," Jackson prompted.

To his disappointment, Lena flipped through the article, keeping quiet.

"I have more bad news," Toby inserted, recapturing their attention. "I saw it in an interdepartmental alert in my email. It's about Rupert Davis."

Jackson flicked Lena a look. She didn't seem too startled. "What about him?" he asked Toby.

"He escaped from custody on the way to Arlington Corrections Facility yesterday. One of his old buddies, incidentally a Five Percenter, unlocked his cuffs. Davis overcame both the security officer and the driver, crashed the transport vehicle, and took off. No one has seen or heard from him since."

Still Lena said nothing. She had to be shocked by Toby's announcement.

Jackson put his free arm around her. "The authorities will find him," he reassured her, smoothing a hand up her rigid back. "Don't worry. I'm not going to let him get anywhere near you."

The banked desperation in her eyes when she looked down at him made his scalp tighten. "Actually," she said in a hesitant voice, "you're going to have to."

He searched her gaze. "What the hell does that mean?"

The edge in his voice made Naomi ease away to look back and forth between them.

"I'll tell you later." Lena glanced pointedly at his daughter.

"Tell me now," Jackson growled. "Naomi's grown up enough to hear."

"Fine." Lena drew a deep breath. "Davis already called me at the crack of dawn this morning."

The unexpected news shattered his contentment like an ice pick breaking up ice.

"I'd given him the number to my throwaway phone the night he attacked me. He says he wants me to meet him on 15th Street South East tomorrow afternoon. In exchange for five thousand dollars, he'll tell me the rest of his story."

Jackson's anxiety abated somewhat. "Okay, so we'll alert the authorities, and they can recapture him."

"Not until I get the rest of his story," she said in a soft, stubborn voice.

Jackson just looked at her. Was she fucking crazy?

"Curtis Vandaloo's testimony might not be enough to ensure Davis's conviction," she added quickly. "I have to get the rest of his confession. It's the only way he'll get life in prison."

No wonder she'd fallen silent at his offer to take a vacation. She didn't know what the future held.

Defeated, Jackson let his head fall back onto the foam pillow. He briefly closed his eyes.

Just when he'd thought every issue in his life had been resolved and he'd been blessed by a second chance to put his family above all else, this critical event materialized like a dark cloud to rain on his parade.

"Fine," he conceded, breaking the tense silence as everyone in the room held a collective breath.

Opening his eyes again, he sent Lena a longsuffering look. "But you're not going into that building without a wire tap, a weapon, five police officers within shouting distance, and me keeping an eye on all of the above."

Lena blinked down at him, her brow furrowing. "How are you going to do that? You're supposed to stay in bed for a week."

"My presence tomorrow is non-negotiable," he insisted.

Her look of worry shifted into a grimace of gratitude. "Thank you," she breathed. Bending over him, she rewarded him with a warm, lingering kiss.

Naomi went perfectly still against his left side, then threw back her head with a shriek of unmistakable delight. "I knew it!" she crowed.

* * *

Ignoring the foreboding that pinched the muscles at the base of her neck, Lena headed briskly toward her appointed rendezvous with Davis, leaving Jackson frustrated and irritable in the passenger seat of her car.

The staccato of her high heels kept time with her anxious pulse. She reminded herself there was nothing to be afraid of. Knowing ahead of time where Davis had planned to meet her, the police had rigged the place with cameras and hidden officers inside the building. They were as eager to ensure Davis's conviction as she was, or they would have just nabbed Davis when he showed up. Instead, they were allowing her to speak with him first, in the hopes of eliciting the rest of his confession.

An undercover cop, disguised as a street bum, trailed Lena within fifty feet. It was he who'd supplied her with the briefcase full of money she carried. She could see no one else on the street but a young woman pushing a shopping cart and an old man sitting on the porch of a derelict row home. Where was everyone at ten on a Saturday morning?

When the abandoned meat processing plant came into view, Lena's confidence faltered. The brick monstrosity was a relic from the 1940's. With its barred windows and boarded up doors, it resembled a prison.

Davis had instructed her to enter the door closest to the loading docks. It was here that delivery trucks used to offload huge hocks of meat to be sliced up and distributed to grocers.

The bolt on the door had been sawed in half. With a deep breath, she pushed her way inside. Behind her, the undercover cop lurched to a stop and slid down the wall as if passing out.

The odor of decay hit her in the face as she waded

into the gloomy chamber. Light leaked through the high, dusty windows showing the meat hooks that still dangled from metal tracks. Davis had told her he would be in an office on the second story. Seeing no sign of the officers concealed within the building, she climbed the central staircase on knees that shook.

"Up here." Davis's voice called, echoing in the near-empty office above her and making her long for her micro-pistol. Paying no heed to Jackson's objections, the police had assured her she wouldn't need it. She gained the second level and edged into the room.

Davis sat like a pedagogue at the old desk, his hands resting on the desktop like he owned the place. The sight of him in a grimy T-shirt, his eyes glazed like he'd done drugs recently, knotted her stomach. There was no sign of any hidden cameras, but then she didn't know what to look for.

"Shut the door," he said, watching her carefully.

The last thing she wanted to do was to close a door between her and her back up. She pushed it tentatively shut.

His gaze rested on the briefcase. "You got the money?"

"I only brought half," she admitted.

He rose so suddenly from his seat that the chair toppled over backward. "Half?" he raged. "What the fuck, bitch?"

His violent reaction made her quail, but Lena spoke up quickly so the cops wouldn't interrupt before she had a chance to elicit his confession. "If you want the rest you'll have to finish your story," she insisted.

"You think I'd try to cheat you?" he scoffed.

You think? "Your story is essential to my book, Sulayman. Tell me the rest, and I'll see that you get your money. You were telling me about the school girl you picked up. How old do you figure she was? What did she look like?" Lena bit her tongue. Asking too many questions would arouse his suspicions.

His eyes narrowed with suspicion. "Why're you so interested?"

She was my sister!

It took all of Lena's willpower not to back away as he circled the desk. This was her last chance to put Davis away forever. For the sake of all of his victims, not just Alexa, she had to do this. "Because I admire you for what you've gotten away with," she lied. Luckily, her voice, husky with fear, sounded sultry. "You're a bad boy, Sulayman." As he stepped close enough to breathe on her, she laid a hand on his chest to ward him off.

"That's right, I'm bad," he growled in agreement. "That's why I brought you here, bitch. 'Cause I know you like it rough." Eyes glinting with excitement, he seized her upper arms.

"Tell me first," she begged, sensing that the police would intervene at any minute. "How old was that girl? Just how bad are you?"

He shrugged. "I don't know—fifteen, sixteen."

He yanked her to him, and every muscle in Lena's body recoiled at the feel of his arousal. "You said she proved not to be worth it. What happened?" she persisted.

"You want to know what happened?" The rough edge of his voice conveyed his impatience with her questioning. "I slapped her hard, like this, and broke her fucking neck."

The stinging blow that whipped Lena's head to one side brought tears to her eyes. The briefcase she still clutched fell with a thump to her feet. A thump in the hallway echoed it, making Davis freeze. "What was that?"

Without warning, the door exploded inward. The hinges popped loose, and it crashed to the floor, throwing dust into the air.

Broad shoulders filled the doorway. "Police! Step away from the woman and get down on the floor!"

Lena moved quickly toward the cops, but with a yank on her hair, Davis caught her back. Quick as a snake, he squeezed her throat, just like at Artie's.

"Best back away or I'll shoot her dead!" Out of nowhere, he produced a gun. The bite of a barrel assured her he wasn't bluffing.

Shocked, Lena sought to free herself. With starbursts swimming before her eyes, she heard the cops reiterate their demands, heard Davis threaten to kill her if they didn't back off.

This is not the way it's supposed to end. She pictured Jackson's reaction at the news that the sting had gone awry. She envisioned her parents' anguish. *I can't let this happen.* Yet, there was nothing she could do.

Davis backed up, groping for the wall behind him. When he jerked her out of the building into brilliant sunshine, she realized he had pulled her outside onto an old fire escape. Slamming shut the metal partition, he flung Lena aside.

She barely caught herself from spilling over the rickety, metal railing. Out the corner of her eye, she saw Davis swing his legs over, preparing to jump. The stairs were long gone.

Two gunshots rang out. In the next instant, Davis landed at her feet, causing the whole apparatus to shudder. The stunned look on his face and the crimson circle spreading on his shoulder assured her that he'd been shot. Seeking the shooter, Lena recognized both the cop dressed like a bum and Jackson—not resting in her car like she'd left him, but propped against a telephone phone pole, clutching his pistol. It was hard to say whose bullet had stopped Davis, but Lena's money was on her man.

As she met his harried gaze, tears of relief and gratitude flooded her eyes.

Jackson shook his head in exasperation. "Can we get on with our lives now?" he shouted up at her.

Her heart replete with love, Lena gave a watery laugh. As the door separating her from the officers burst open, she shook off the concerns of the uniformed cops and slipped past them. Hurrying through the old building and out the nearest exit, she flew across the patchy grass to arrive at Jackson's side just as he was keeling over. The wail of sirens grew louder.

"Here, lie down." She lowered him gently onto the dirt and weeds and collapsed beside him, trembling uncontrollably.

"You okay?" he asked with a worried once-over.

"You're the one who should be in the hospital right now," she retorted. He had walked out that morning, against medical advice, without so much as a crutch to help him get around.

"It's not my hip," he assured her. He put his hand over his chest. "It's the shock of almost losing you. I can't go through this again, Lena," he confessed.

She rolled toward him, laying a hand on the side of his face. "I promise, everything will be roses from here on out."

Chuckling in disbelief, he caught her face in his hand and drew her lips to his for a heartfelt kiss. "God, I love you," he confessed.

"I love you, too, Jackson."

An ambulance screeched to a halt at their feet. Paramedics rushed up to them, but Jackson waved them away. "About that vacation," he began.

EPILOGUE

With her eyes, Lena followed the dark, graceful figure leading Naomi under the palm trees. Fontana Maddox made a habit of walking down to the beach every evening to watch the glorious sunset. Lena marveled at how much Jackson resembled his mother, if only in physical form.

"Why didn't you go with them?" Jackson asked, stepping out onto the patio to join her, cane in hand. He'd healed well over the past month. Physical therapy would begin after their vacation, and soon he wouldn't need the cane at all.

A warm breeze, smelling of pineapple and coconut oil tussled Lena's curls as she turned to smile at him. The frangipani flowers surrounding the patio fluttered in the fading light. Wrapping her arms around him, she savored how solid and real he felt in her embrace. "Because this is our last evening here, and I wanted to spend it with you," she explained.

Every day of their week-long vacation, Jackson had made it down to the water to enjoy the beach with them, but slogging through the soft sand twice in a day was still too much for his healing ligaments.

"I'm sorry." He sent her a remorseful look. "I should have whisked you away on a vacation where it was just the two of us."

She rolled her eyes at him. "That's not what I meant. I've loved every minute of getting to meet your mother and seeing where you grew up. And I've loved having Naomi with us. But a little romance at sunset, just the two of us, is just what the doctor ordered." She fastened her gaze deliberately on his mouth.

"I see," he murmured, rewarding her with the kind of kiss that never failed to promise paradise.

Desire heated the already sultry evening air as their tongues tangled and the kiss deepened. For Lena, the week had passed in a blur of sensual indulgence and emotional fulfillment. She had never been so happy in her life. The only experiences that eclipsed her happiness by day were the nights spent in Jackson's arms. Fontana had conveniently placed them in the same guestroom, and Jackson had no difficulty whatsoever maneuvering in bed.

"Your mother is nothing like your father, is she?" Lena had met Martin Maddox the previous week. Proper and reserved, he'd made her feel like a bug under a microscope. "How on earth did those two meet, anyway?"

Jackson gestured to the hanging bench suspended from an arbor. "You'll have to sit for that story."

"Okay." She led the way to the bench, holding it steady as he eased down beside her.

"I think it was a case of opposites attracting," he began, using his good leg to swing them back and forth. "My father had just finished law school and was down here with his buddies, celebrating the passing of their bar exams. My mother, who'd worked at the hotel where he was staying, caught his eye. I guess because he was on vacation, he wasn't as straight-laced as he usually is. In her words, they enjoyed a whirlwind romance, if you can imagine that. When he left a week later, he gave her his address. A month after that, my mother realized she was pregnant."

"Oh, dear." Lena hung on every word.

"She wrote to my father, hoping for child support," Jackson continued, "but instead of sending her money, he flew down and insisted she marry him."

"Well, that was honorable."

"My father is nothing if not honorable," he replied.

"What happened then?"

"My mother returned to the States with him and they tried their best to share a life together, but…" He shrugged. "Like you said, they're nothing alike."

Lena looked away and sighed. "That's so sad."

But Jackson wasn't finished. "By the time I was two, she realized that much for herself and brought me back to the island to raise me here. My father, being the man he is, made certain she had all the creature comforts she needed." He waved a hand to encompass the sprawling, white-washed home behind them with its red-tiled roof.

Lena's opinion of Martin Maddox rose a notch higher.

"When I was twelve, my mother decided I should get to know my father better, so she sent me off to live with him."

The roughness in Jackson's voice prompted Lena to wrap her arms around him. "That must have been hard for you," she sympathized, "leaving your mother behind and all your friends."

"It was hard at first," he acknowledged, "but I'm more like my father than you realize."

"If you say so," she said dubiously.

"We eventually adjusted. He sent me to a good

private school, encouraged me to apply to VMI. I eventually became a Marine Corps Officer, fell in love, got married, and the rest is history."

"And they never divorced?" Lena asked, still thinking of his parents.

"Never."

She let herself dwell on the end of his story. "Were you and Colleen as happy the way we are?" Given what Naomi had admitted, she had her doubts, but this was the first time she'd dared to ask.

"Baby, you don't ever need to compare yourself to her."

"I know. I'm just curious."

Jackson sighed. Even in the gathering dusk, there was no mistaking the grief that cloaked him, still. "Colleen was a warm and carefree spirit, like Naomi is. She used to accuse me of being cold. And it was hard for her to tolerate negativity. Everything about my life seemed negative to her—the war, me being gone all the time. It sucked her down. To stay afloat, she drank. And, in the end, it killed her."

"Oh, Jackson, I would never call you cold," Lena assured him.

He smiled down at her. "You have a distinctly thawing effect on me," he drawled.

"And you should know by now that I can handle negativity."

He twisted his upper body so that they were sitting face to face. In the purplish light his eyes resembled amethysts as he lifted a hand to cup her face. "You're the strongest woman I know. It's just one of the hundreds of traits about you that enthralls me. In fact…" He thought for a minute then slipped a hand inside his pants pocket. "I've been waiting for the perfect moment to do this, and if I wait any longer, I just know you're going to beat me to it."

Lena eyed the diamond solitaire glinting between his thumb and forefinger in disbelief. "Jackson!" she exclaimed.

"Will you marry me, Lena?" he asked her intently.

Stunned, she said the first thing to pop into her head. "We've only known each other for a couple of months. And two weeks of that time, I thought your name was Abdul."

"So that's a *no*?" Sounding not the least bit put out, he gave a shrug and started to put the ring away.

"Wait! Can't I at least look at it?" Her heart was pounding with elation. Jackson had managed to catch her utterly by surprise.

"It's too dark for you to really see it," he insisted, but there was laughter in his voice.

"Please!" Now that she found herself considering marriage, she couldn't see what was holding them back. Certainly, she was in the midst of making a career change, but having decided to write the book about prison conversion, after all, her new job allowed for flexibility. Jackson was moving to a new gated community into a house big enough to accommodate all of them. The Five Percent Nation faced aggressive dismantling across the nation, making the specter of reprisal far less fearful than it might have been, even if Ike Calhoun had not taken measures to ensure his team members' safety. Lena gave Jackson's arm a shake. "I just wasn't ready. Ask me again, now that I'm prepared."

"How about I put it on you and then I ask?" He reached for her left hand. "I'd get down on one knee, but then I might never get back up again."

"Don't you dare even try," she warned him, as the glimmering ring slid coolly up her fourth finger. "Oh, I love it," she breathed.

The sweet air, the unexpected surprise, the integrity

of the gorgeous man asking to link his life and hers forever—she'd never felt more joyfully intoxicated. "Yes, I'll marry you," she cried, throwing her arms around him.

He chuckled in her ear. "I know one young lady who'll be pleased with the news."

Lena gasped and pulled back. "Let's get married here!" she suggested, harking back to a playful suggestion made by Naomi earlier that week.

Jackson frowned. "I don't know. My parents got married here. Wouldn't it be bad luck to follow in their footsteps?"

"Don't be absurd. If we marry at home, it'll be a nightmare. You've seen the movie *My Big, Fat Greek Wedding*, right? Trust me, my parents will settle for nothing less." She clutched his arm, paralyzed by the pictures in her head. "Oh, Jackson, we have to elope."

"Naomi can't miss another week of school," he pointed out. "Besides, I kind of like the idea of a big, fat Greek wedding."

Lena groaned. Her mother would demand a three-hour Greek Orthodox church service followed by a lavish reception with at least five courses that would cost her parents so much money, they'd end up taking out a second mortgage on their home to pay for it. It would be so much easier just to show up at their doorstep already married.

On the other hand, how could she deprive her parents the joy of marrying off their only living daughter? If Alexa were alive, she'd have gladly indulged their parents, but she wasn't. At least Davis was rotting in jail now to atone for that sad fact. "I suppose you're right," she conceded with a sigh.

Jackson grinned at her doleful expression. "Don't worry, sweetheart. You'll survive the nuptials. And then I'll sweep you away on another enchanting vacation like this one."

The thought immediately consoled her. "Where to this time?"

"How does the French Riviera sound?"

He'd won this round hands down. "You're such a good man, Jackson."

Turn the page for an

excerpt from

THE ENFORCER
The Taskforce Series
Book Three

Marliss Melton

He didn't give her time to backpedal. "Do you know what I see when you smile?"

"What?"

He stepped closer, holding her gaze captive. "I see who you really are." Amazingly, he didn't have to work hard to find the words to sweet-talk her. They rolled effortlessly off his tongue, probably since he was being completely honest, for a change.

In the stunned silence that followed, he could hear a cricket chirping in the grass beneath their feet. A bird twittered in the trees behind them.

"Sorry." He grimaced and shoved his fingers into the pockets of his jacket. "I don't know where that came from. I'm not trying to be insubordinate or anything, but you work so hard to hold everyone else together. What about you? What about your happiness?"

Bravo. Suddenly, it was like he was standing off to one side watching his own performance, along with Dylan's reaction.

Damn, you're good, Toby. Judging by the look on her face, his remark had struck gold. *You manipulative son of a bitch.*

Dylan couldn't find her voice. Protocol demanded she rebuke Tobias for his impertinence. How dare he speak to her on such a personal level? But his words had stripped off her façade as militia leader, and, for the life of her, she couldn't seem to slap it back on.

"Don't get me wrong." He bent toward her, pitching his voice lower. The velvety timbre soothed the pinpricks of agitation needling her skin. "I think what you've done for the soldiers here is a good thing. You've given them a sense of purpose, someone to lean on. But who's taking care of you?"

Where was he going with this? "Why would I need taking care of?"

"Come on, now," he chided her with a wry and sympathetic smile. "I know from Morrison that you used to retrieve the fallen. Let me tell you what. You wouldn't be human if the things you've seen didn't get to you sometimes."

A lump swelled in Dylan's throat, lodging her cool retort as a vision of her boys lying broken in their coffins panned across her mind.

Tobias's hands came out of his pockets. Stepping closer, he lifted them slowly, cautiously to her face. The breath evaporated from her lungs as his warm and lightly callused hands cupped her cheeks.

"It's okay to lean on people." His dark gaze, nearly the same color as the cobalt sky, searched her face before sliding toward her mouth. "If you want to lean on me from time to time, that's okay, too." In the next instant, he lowered his head, startling her with a swift, sweet kiss that left her lips tingling.

Taking in her stunned response, he slowly dipped his head again, giving her time to pull away before his lips settled snugly over hers, thawing her from her frozen state with a deft, warm, unthreatening kiss.

Like melting wax, Dylan's lips softened then parted, allowing his tongue to glide against hers, filling her with an intimate knowledge of his taste, his texture. He intrigued. He intoxicated. Parting her lips wider, Dylan sought more, rolling up on her toes in a tribute to the woman buried deep inside.

Fill me. She coiled her arms around his neck and kissed him until her head swam. *Fill me with your light and warmth and laughter.*

And he did, kissing her with such gentle skill that it stripped away her captain's guise and left her nothing but a woman utterly at the mercy of her own desire.

So this was how it felt to be alive. She'd forgotten. The bloodbath that had ended her career had robbed her of the memory. But it rose in her anew, like a resurrected Lazarus. She reached for the quenching beauty with all her heart, wanting to hold it close.

Her pebbled nipples grazed the sturdy fabric of his jacket. Desire traveled in a slow burn along her neural pathways. She ached to touch his skin, but his jacket and clothing formed a frustrating barrier.

Slowly, lingeringly, Tobias lifted his head and ended the magic. Fresh air cleared Dylan's head. The reality of their embrace speared her consciousness, and she guiltily jumped back.

"My fault." He was quick to take the blame but sounded not at all repentant.

Dylan wedged her tingling hands under her crossed arms, whirled away, and stalked blindly along the path skirting the tree line.

What just happened?

Her mind scrambled to make sense of that kiss. Sergeant Burke had crossed the line, but so had she. Worse than that, she'd sucked him in like a black hole. God, how humiliating!

Glancing back, she ascertained that he was following. Yes, and much closer than she'd thought, not having heard his footsteps. Adrenaline spiked her pulse. She'd almost forgotten that he used to be Special Forces. He must have been a stealthy fighter, a masterful tactician.

"You don't have to worry that I'll say anything."

His softly spoken promise was meant to reassure her, but to Dylan it sounded smug. She spun around to face him. "I am your commanding officer," she bit out, swiping her own hair out of her eyes. "What just happened between us was a complete breach of protocol. It *cannot* happen again."

Her firm reproach would have made any of her other soldiers back away.

Tobias looked down at his boots. A devilish glitter twinkled in his eyes when he looked up again. "Well," he drawled, clearly measuring his words, "if we were *actually* in the service, ma'am, I'd have to agree with you. But we're not. No matter how much you pretend for the sake of the others, you're as much a civilian as I am."

His logic undermined her authority completely. At the same time, a weight seemed to lift off her shoulders. She *was* a civilian. For a second time in just minutes, he'd left her with nothing to say.

"I don't see anything wrong with us getting to know each other better." He sent her an appreciative and appraising look.

Squelching the pleasure evoked by his words and his obvious interest in her, Dylan clung to her righteous anger. "Our discussion is over, Sergeant Burke. Kindly go back and help the others," she commanded.

He tipped her a disappointed-looking nod and turned away, but his stride remained confident.

Watching him walk away, Dylan's knees shook. She would never accept his offer to lean on him. To do so would make her appear weak to the others. Yet there was a certain truth to what he'd said. She *was* human, and the gruesome atrocities she'd seen did get to her sometimes.

When he disappeared from view, she turned and walked blindly toward the light pouring out of the kitchen.

Alive. A fragment of her earlier exhilaration clung to her, still, lightening her step as she approached the rear entrance.

THE ENFORCER

available in print and ebook

THE
TASKFORCE SERIES

The Protector
The Guardian
The Enforcer

Marliss Melton is the author of ten gripping romantic suspense novels, including a seven-book Navy SEALs series and continuing with The Taskforce Series. She relies on her experience as a military spouse and on her many contacts in the Spec Ops and Intelligence communities to pen heartfelt stories about America's elite warriors and fearless agency heroes.

Daughter of a U.S. foreign officer, Melton grew up in various countries overseas. She has taught English, Spanish, ESL, and Linguistics at the College of William and Mary, her alma mater. She lives near Virginia Beach with her husband, tween daughter, and four young adult children.

You can find Marliss on Facebook, Twitter and Pinterest. Visit www.MarlissMelton.com for more information.